A CHANGE
of HEART

ALSO BY BARBARA LONGLEY

FAR FROM PERFECT
THE DIFFERENCE A DAY MAKES

A CHANGE of HEART

A LOVE FROM THE HEARTLAND NOVEL

Barbara Longley

Montlake
Romance

Text copyright © 2013 Barbara Longley
All rights reserved.

Published by Montlake Romance, Seattle

www.apub.com

ISBN-13: 9781477849040
ISBN-10: 1477849041
Library of Congress Control Number: 2013911838

Printed in the United States of America

This book is dedicated to all the women who don uniforms and blaze trails. You pave the way for the rest of us. Thank you.

CHAPTER ONE

SILT. NO, MAKE THAT SLUDGE. Cory's blood had turned to thick, muddy sludge in her veins, and all the internal heaviness left her immobilized. Cracking an eyelid, she peered around the room. Nothing had changed in twenty-three years—not the worn blue bedspread with the white fluffy clouds or the mismatched dresser and desk. Not even the saggy twin mattress and box spring on the bare metal frame. Nothing. Her days in the double-wide on the south side of Evansville, Indiana, were supposed to be behind her. Yet here she was right back where she started, living on the fringes of the seedy side of town.

No career. No future. Trailer trash.

A single tear slipped down her cheek. She'd fought so hard to become something else, something better—like her dad, the decorated war hero she barely remembered. Eight years of her life devoted to a military career—brutally stolen. Gone, with nothing to show for it but this suffocating, sludgy misery pressing her down into a lumpy old bed. Another tear followed the first, and she pulled the bedspread over her head.

"Cory, baby." Her mother knocked on her door. "Brenda Holt is here to see you."

"Tell her I'm not feeling well." She couldn't face anyone. Not now. Maybe in a week or two the heaviness would lift, and she'd be able to figure out the rest of her life…or at least the rest of the afternoon. "Tell her I'll give her a call…sometime soon. Real soon."

The door creaked open. "You haven't been out of this room for more than half an hour at a time since you've been home." Her mom's voice scraped along her frayed nerves. "I'm not leavin' this spot until you agree to come out and say hello. Brenda made the effort to visit. Now you're gonna make the effort to haul your butt outta that bed. You hear?"

She knew that tone. When Claire Marcel made up her mind, nothing could sway her. She'd stand in that doorway all day if she had to. Cory groaned. Hopefully a fifteen-minute conversation would satisfy her mother. Then Cory could crawl back into her black hole and sleep away another day. "Fine." She threw the covers off and sat up. "Give me a few minutes."

"Good. We'll be in the livin' room."

The door shut, and she dragged herself out of bed to the army-issue duffel bag on the floor. She found an almost clean pair of sweats and pulled them on over the oversize T-shirt she'd slept in. Her hair hung in a lifeless mess to her shoulders. Not bothering to pull a brush through it, she snatched a rubber band off her dresser and pulled it back into a ponytail. Maybe she could manage a shower today. Or not. Who cared whether she bathed, brushed her teeth or washed her hair? What difference did it make to the four walls of her childhood bedroom?

She forced herself down the hall to the living room. Her mother and Brenda sat on the couch huddled over her mother's scrapbook of the media frenzy surrounding Cory's court case. The humiliating history of her total annihilation lay open on their laps. Her stomach hit the floor. *Dammit.* How could her mom show that to anyone? Why would she want to? Bile burned the back of her throat. She turned around and headed back to her room.

"There you are," her mother called. "I was just tellin' Brenda how proud I am of you."

"Proud of me?" She leaned her head back and shut her eyes. "For what? Letting my guard down—for being careless?" It's not like she hadn't known better. *Stupid, stupid, stupid mistake.*

"'Course not." Her mom's tone carried a hint of exasperation. "I'm proud of you for standin' up for yourself."

"Hey, Cory." Brenda took the dreaded scrapbook from her mother's hands and set it aside. "It's been forever since we've seen each other. Let's go for a walk."

"Outside?" Her heart raced, and dread spread like an oil spill in her chest.

"Unless you want to walk up and down the hall here." Brenda's expression filled with sympathy, and something else— concern? "Let's go to the playground like we used to when we were kids."

"What's it like out there?" Cory frowned, assessing the risk.

Brenda raised a single, arched eyebrow. "Is that a rhetorical question?"

"No. It's more like a weather question." She averted her gaze and swallowed hard. Brenda must think she'd gone mental. She had. In fact, she'd been treading water in the deep end of the crazy pool for a while now, and it was getting harder and harder to keep her head above the surface.

"It's like a typical late April day in southern Indiana. The sun's out. It's going to get very warm, and you're way overdressed."

"I'll be fine." Baggy sweats had become her style of choice lately. Not only could she wear them in bed, but out of bed as well. Plus, they didn't attract attention. A shudder ran through her at the thought of *that* kind of attention. *Don't need it; don't want it.*

She slipped her feet into an old pair of flip-flops by the door and followed her childhood friend outside. Hypervigilance and the prickly sense of being watched consumed her. Scanning the area, she walked beside Brenda toward the old playground where they'd spent countless hours as youngsters.

The slide had taken on a pronounced tilt to the right, and the heavy steel frame of the swing set had more rust than she remembered. Someone had tossed one of the swings over the top several times until it coiled with the seat a few inches from the crossbar. The rickety wooden fence separating their trailer park from the trucking company next door was covered in graffiti, and the grass hadn't been mowed in weeks. Not much had changed here either.

The day promised to be warmer than average with a generous dollop of humidity thrown in to make everybody miserable. She must look odd in her long-sleeved sweatshirt and heavy sweatpants. Brenda, on the other hand, looked cool, fresh and as gorgeous as ever. Her thick blonde hair had been done up in a french braid, accentuating her high cheekbones and big blue eyes. She wore a stylish outfit designed to show off her curvy figure.

What a pathetic contrast she must make to so much put-together attractiveness. If she didn't get her appetite back soon, Cory wouldn't have any curves left at all. That suited her just fine. *Who needs them?* Easing herself down, she took a seat on one of the three remaining swings and did another perimeter scan.

"Claire means well," Brenda said. "Your mom is proud of you. We all are, and it's not because your image has been plastered all over the media for the past year either. It's because you managed to do something few women in the military have been able to." Brenda glanced at her. "You're kind of the poster child for—"

"Can we talk about something else?" Cory's empty stomach churned, and she studied the stunted grass growing around the bare patch of dirt under her feet. "What are you doing these days? Last time I visited, you were in school."

Brenda sent her swing into motion. "I graduated from cosmetology college quite a while ago, and I work in a really nice salon in town now. I'm doing OK for myself." She planted her feet to stop the swing. "Did you hear Wesley's home? He retired."

"No, I hadn't heard." Her eyes widened. "We were just little kids when your brother joined the marines. I still remember the day he left for boot camp." She shook her head. "Wow. Has it been twenty years already?"

"Yeah. Which leads me to my next question. What are you going to do now that your case is behind you?"

"It's not *behind me*." Hot, angry tears filled her eyes once again at the ultimate betrayal of her loyalty and trust. "The Yale Law School's Veterans Legal Services Clinic is working on getting disability benefits for me."

"Is that what you want? Disability checks for the rest of your life, while you hide out in your mom's mobile home? That doesn't sound like the Corinna Lynn Marcel I've known since we were four."

"That girl is gone." Rage exploded into a flash-and-burn conflagration in her chest. Once she'd been happy, optimistic about her future and open to the possibility of meeting someone special. She'd even thought she'd marry and have a few kids someday. That dream was dead. Her breathing came in short, ineffectual gasps, and her heart lodged itself in her throat. Brenda reached out and touched her forearm. Cory jerked away. Touch, a basic human need, was no longer tolerable.

"Hey, it's just me." Brenda set her hands back in her own lap. "Wesley is working at a custom furniture company in Perfect, a small town about forty-five minutes east of Evansville. The owner is a veteran who survived a suicide bombing in Iraq."

"Oh." Her mind was only half engaged. The other half floated from a distance, watching the conversation with disorienting detachment.

"Langford & Lovejoy Heritage Furniture only hires veterans. Wes told me they're looking for someone to take over maintaining their social media, website and stuff like that."

The pervasive sense of detachment spread. Time to go back to bed.

"He told the owner about you."

"What?" Cory blinked back to full attention. "Why?"

"Because you have skills. You *were* an IT specialist, and you've always been a whiz kid with anything having to do with computers and electronics. You're perfect for the job."

Shit. "I'm not perfect for anything." Not fit to serve and less fit to live, no way could she face a group of strangers inside an enclosed space. "I can barely get out of bed. I don't think—"

"You can't give up now, and spending the rest of your life in this trailer park is not an option." Brenda shot up from the swing and came to stand in front of her. She grasped both chains of Cory's swing and gave them a shake. "I won't let you do this to yourself. I can't stand by and do nothing while you slide down the drain a little bit more each day." She glared. "In fact, I gotta tell you, I'm really pissed that you've been home for three weeks and you didn't even bother to give me a call."

"I'm sorry." She blew out a breath. "I'm sorry, I…I can't—"

"Nope. Stop." Brenda shook her head. "This is what's going to happen. You're going to go take a shower and brush your teeth. Please." She waved a hand in front of her nose. "Shave your legs and pits while you're at it."

"Well, that was brutal."

"You need brutal." Brenda stared a hole through her. "I brought my equipment with me. Once you're cleaned up, I'm going to cut your hair and put in some highlights. Then we're going shopping for something to wear besides those raggedy old sweats and baggy army-issue cammies." She canted her head to study her. "And makeup. You need makeup."

"I don't think I can do the shopping thing." Her mouth dried up like a sponge left out in the sun. "And I'm positive I'm not doing the makeup thing."

"You're going to do both if I have to drag you kicking and screaming. I'll be right there beside you, and if anybody messes with you, I'll lay 'em out flat."

A choked laugh broke free, and memories poured through her of the way she and Brenda had always watched each other's backs. Their friendship had been like a flower growing through a slab of concrete—tough and resilient, thriving against all odds in a barren landscape. They'd fought the trailer trash stigma together all through school, shared their secrets and dreams and been as close as twins. "I don't have any money, Bren. I haven't seen a regular paycheck since the army cut me loose."

"I know. I'm floating you a loan, which I will not allow you to refuse. We're just talking Target here, not Neiman Marcus. Jeans, a few pairs of shorts, blouses, T-shirts, shoes and a few new necessities. It'll help you feel good about yourself again. I promise."

"You're still the same pushy bitch you always were," Cory muttered affectionately.

"That's right, and I'm going to help you reclaim your own inner bitch. Somehow you managed to get through your court case, testify before congressmen and senators, and have your picture and story plastered all over the media. You're tough, my friend. Don't crumble now."

"Too late. I crumbled months ago." Her jaw clenched. "I don't know if I can do shopping, makeup or a regular job. All of that stuff you mentioned I did? It was fueled by rage. Rage was my sole reason for getting out of bed each day. It's done. I'm out of momentum and reason." She crossed her eyes and twirled her finger by her temple. "In more ways than one."

"Then it's time to find a new reason to get out of bed." Brenda's face took on a resolute, dogged expression. "You have a job interview tomorrow afternoon, and I'm here to make sure you look your best."

"What? *No!*" Her blood turned to ice water, chilling her to the sludge-filled center of her bones.

"Yep. Let's go. Hup, hup." Brenda pulled her up and pointed her toward home. "Right, left, right, left. March. You stink, and your hair is a greasy, stringy mess."

"I like my hair this way."

"No, you don't." Brenda gave her a gentle nudge. "Ready or not, here comes your new life."

"I'm not ready." Panic sent her heart racing, tightening her chest and robbing her of breath. "I'm not *ready*, dammit."

"I can't believe you did it again," Ted shouted, plowing both hands through his hair. "You swore I would be part of the hiring process. You swore." He glared at Noah.

They had twelve employees now, split between two shifts. With the exception of Paige, all their staff belonged to the same exclusive club, sharing the bond of brotherhood their veteran status gave them. Ted didn't belong. He was an outsider in his own business, a company that had been *his* idea from the start.

No one seemed to care that he was the Lovejoy part of Langford & Lovejoy Heritage Furniture. Despite Ted being half owner *and* the human resources director to boot, Noah continued to make staffing decisions without conferring with him first. That cut him deep, and in this case, completely severed his last tether.

"This was an emergency call on my part." Noah widened his stance and crossed his arms in front of his chest—his commander stance. "Besides, I never swore. I said I'd *try* to follow the hiring procedures, and for the most part I have. Cory is an exception. We talked about it, and you agreed we need someone to take over the web maintenance, social media, and order processing. I'm adding shipping to that roster, which will ease up your load considerably. You can spend more time in production, which is what you said you wanted."

"That's beside the point. Did you post the job? Take applications? How about an interview with me included?" Restless and edgy, Ted couldn't shake the feeling that it might be time for a change. Langford & Lovejoy flourished, while his discontent grew by leaps and bounds.

"Hey, kid. What's got your boxers in a bunch?" Ryan strolled into the conference room for their usual Monday morning meeting. "We could hear you shouting from the first floor."

"Maybe it's the fact that you and everybody else around here still see me as a *kid*. It's damn insulting," he shouted again. "I have a master's in business administration, and *I* sign *your* paycheck."

Paige waddled in behind her husband, rubbing her distended belly. "Watch your language. I don't want the baby to pick that stuff up."

And there it was, the other exclusive club he couldn't gain entrance to—the happily married and reproducing group. Ryan and Paige had just finished building their house on the west side of town and were expecting their first child. Noah and Ceejay were also expecting. This was number four for them. Ted rolled his eyes. "I doubt that pea in the pod is paying any attention to what goes on here."

"They do." She laid her folder on the table and settled into her chair. "Babies can hear things."

"Whatever." He took his customary place with his back to the door—something he always did out of deference to Noah and Ryan, who both coped with PTSD. They had to have their backs to the wall, and Ted didn't care where his back faced. "Noah hired someone without consulting with me first. We've been having the same argument for five years now, and my bungee cord is just about out of stretch."

He'd worked his ass off to get through school, worked around the clock to grow their business into a thriving success. What did he have to show for all that sacrifice? He'd become a twenty-four-year-old workaholic with a healthy savings account and pockets full of nothing but loneliness. No one respected or included him. He hadn't even taken a vacation in all that time, and he was worn to a stressed-out frazzle. Did anyone bother to notice? Nope. "I don't care if this Cory guy is a freaking genius. You had no business hiring him without my say-so," he snapped.

Noah's jaw twitched. "Cory is—"

"I'm sorry. Maybe I should leave," a soft feminine voice said from behind him.

"Don't listen to him, Cory." Paige leaned back and smiled a welcome. "Come in and have a seat."

Huh? Ted whipped around, his eyes widening at the sight of the waif standing uncertainly in the doorway. Feathery layers of dark brown hair with lighter golden-brown highlights framed her wide-set, luminous dark brown eyes. She wore jeans and a peasant blouse that failed to hide how thin she was. He brought his gaze back to those alluring eyes of hers and stumbled right in. They held a sadness so profound it would take a deep-sea submersible to get to the source.

A throat cleared, decidedly male. How had he missed Wesley Holt and his three-legged dog hovering in the hallway behind their newest "emergency"? Wesley scowled at him. Ted scowled back, unintimidated by the big marine. What was Wesley to Cory anyway? His protective stance suggested close familiarity.

Noah cleared his throat and shot him a look that said he'd better make nice or else. "Ted, meet Cory Marcel. Cory, this is Ted Lovejoy. This is my sister, Paige, and her husband, Ryan Malloy. Cory is an IT specialist, and a whiz with computers."

Ted shot up from his chair, almost knocking it over in his haste. It couldn't have been pleasant for her to hear his rant. "Welcome to L&L. It's good to have you aboard." Their eyes met and held. Her brow creased, and she looked away, but not before he caught a glimpse of the alarm clouding her features. *I'm alarming? Great.* Lately he'd been unraveling like the edges of an old burlap feed bag, and he couldn't deny being more than a tad alarmed himself.

Shifting his attention back to their newest employee, he wondered what it was about her situation that had prompted Noah to disregard their protocol. He also wondered what it would take to coax a smile out of her. What would a full-on smile do to her delicate features? No doubt it would do a number on his heart. An inexplicable urge to be the one hovering protectively near her shot through him, sending him into a tailspin. *What? No.*

Did he even want to get involved with a troubled waif? No. He had enough problems of his own. Besides, she'd soon become a member of the exclusive we're-veterans-and-you're-not club at L&L. "We can take it from here, Wes. Thanks for showing her to the conference room."

Wesley reached out as if he meant to place his hand on Cory's shoulder, and quickly pulled it back. "You gonna be OK, Squirrel?"

"Yeah, Bunny. I'll be fine." She glanced over her shoulder at him. Wesley nodded his head once and turned on his heel to leave, his dog trotting behind him.

Squirrel and Bunny? Lord help me, the two are a petting zoo. Only someone very close would call a guy like Wesley Holt "Bunny". "You and Wes are…" He clamped his jaw shut. None of his business.

"Wesley and I grew up in the same tr—er…*neighborhood.*" She slipped into the room and took the chair next to Paige. "His youngest sister and I are good friends."

Ted nodded, sat back down and stared. Were she and Wesley a couple, or just childhood friends? Why should he care? He had no clue. He tried redirecting his attention, but his gaze kept drifting back to her, drawn by the mystery, no doubt. That's all. She was pretty enough, but too thin for his tastes.

Noah cleared his throat, and he caught the odd look focused his way. Ryan wore a crooked smirk. Ted glared. "What?"

"Nothing, kid." Ryan chuckled. "Nothing at all."

Paige passed them each a sheet of paper. "This is the list I made of Cory's responsibilities." She turned to face their newest employee. "I'll be training you on the website and social media end of things. Ted will go over ordering and shipping." She grinned. "I can't tell you how happy I am to have another woman in the building."

"Thank you." Cory skimmed the list. "Where will I be working?"

"You and I share the office at the end of the hall by the back stairs," Paige told her. "The guys built a desk for you, and there's a brand-new Mac still in the box. You can get that all set up once we're done here."

"Does the…" Color rose to Cory's cheeks, and her expression closed up tight. "Is there a lock on the door?"

Paige leaned forward and rested her forearms on the table. "You're safe here, Cory. The men who work for us are more likely to be overly protective than anything else, and most of them are happily married. As the only woman on this all-male staff for the past three years, I can personally vouch for every one of our guys."

Mystified by the exchange, Ted frowned. "If that's what you need, I'll put a deadbolt on the door right after we're done here."

"Thank you," she whispered, her gaze meeting his for a fraction of second. "I'd appreciate that."

"I know you and Wes go way back, and you trust him, right?" Noah added.

Cory nodded. "I've known him for most of my life."

"He lives in the apartment on the third floor. If you ever feel uncomfortable, he's already sworn to stick by your side whenever you need him. Wes adopted his dog, Rex, through a program that matches veterans with retired military working dogs. If you want, he also said you can have Rex with you during the day."

Cory's lips pressed together, and she gave a slight nod,

keeping her eyes on the list. What the hell had happened to this woman? Had she been captured by the enemy? Tortured? She reminded him of one of the stray dogs his family had adopted when he was a kid. The mutt always seemed spooked, crouching low and tucking tail whenever anyone reached out to scratch him behind the ears. It had taken months for that dog to trust them. Why had Cory's eyes filled with alarm when they met his? More important, what would it take to gain her trust? Whoa, he was already getting sucked in.

"We have ads coming out this August in *Architectural Digest* and a couple other upscale magazines," Paige said. "We want to be prepared for a spike in business." She beamed. "That's one of the reasons we wanted someone to take over the web and order processing. Both have gotten so big, managing them has become a full-time position."

"What's your operating system? Who's your web host?" Cory leaned forward, a spark of interest dissipating the haunted look she wore.

Ted settled back, listening and watching as she and Paige went on about their systems and what Cory's job entailed. He glanced at Noah and Ryan. Both were staring at him with smug expressions. "And again, what?" He scowled.

"Nothing." Noah rose from his place and picked up his coffee mug. "Do we have any other new business to discuss, Paige?"

"No, not really. You guys can go. I'll give Cory the tour."

"I'm heading to the hardware store to pick up that deadbolt. I'll put it on when I get back." Ted rose. "You can fill out the paperwork to get on our payroll then, and we can start training on the ordering system." He glanced at her. "Once you have that down, and you're comfortable, we can add the shipping stuff. There's no hurry."

"We're taking you out to lunch today," Ryan told her. "It's a tradition with new hires."

"Thank you," she muttered, more color flooding her cheeks.

Ted wondered what his aunt Jenny would make of her. "I'll introduce you to my aunt. She owns the Perfect Diner down the street. They're open for breakfast and lunch." She nodded without taking her eyes from the table, and he kind of wished she'd look at him again. He wouldn't mind another look at her pretty brown eyes. He followed Noah and Ryan down the hall toward the back stairs. "Noah, can I have a word?"

"Why? You feeling the need to shout some more?"

He thought about it. Curiosity about Cory trumped his irritation. "Nope. I'm done for today."

"All right. There are a few things I need to pick up for home. I'll come with you to the hardware store."

"I recognized that dumb-ass stricken look on your face back there." Ryan slapped Ted's shoulder on his way past them down the stairs. "You're in for it, kid."

"He is, isn't he?" Noah barked out a laugh.

"I don't know what the hell you two are talking about. I was surprised, is all. I thought Cory was a guy's name."

"Her name is Corinna Marcel." Noah preceded him out the back door toward the 1968 Mustang convertible. "By the way, I get to drive your car today since you yelled at me for nothing." He held out his hand for the keys.

"Fine. You can drive, but the yelling wasn't for nothing." Probably just as well, since he couldn't concentrate. Thoughts of their newest employee circled around in his brain. *Corinna.* He liked her name and practiced saying it to himself. It suited her much more than the shortened version. *Corinna.*

Ted handed Noah his car keys and settled himself in the

passenger seat. The Mustang's engine purred to life, and they headed down the alley before he said anything. "What's her story? Why was hiring her such an emergency that you couldn't involve me?"

"I'm surprised her name isn't familiar to you." Noah glanced at him before turning onto the road. "She's been all over the news for the past year."

Ted shrugged. "Finishing my master's and working full-time, I haven't had a lot of time to pay attention to current events. Just tell me."

"Cory was sexually assaulted and badly beaten while deployed in the Kandahar Province of Afghanistan."

"Shit." All the breath left his lungs. "Was she captured? How'd she get free?"

"Uh, no. She was assaulted by her CO, a noncommissioned staff sergeant." Noah's jaw tightened. "I never tolerated any kind of harassment in my platoon, and my troops knew there'd be hell to pay if they stepped over that line. It was far too common elsewhere, though. Most cases of sexual assault in the military go unreported, because the women are threatened with demotion or at least no more promotions. Then there's the army's response."

"The army's response?"

Noah nodded, a single eyebrow raised. "They've been known to slap a personality disorder diagnosis on any woman who reports sexual assault and pushes the issue. They're found 'unfit to serve' and kicked to the curb."

"I think I did hear something about that in the news recently, or I read about it on the Internet."

"Knowing all of that, Cory came forward anyway and fought to put her assailant behind bars. Her name and story created quite a media frenzy and blew the lid off the issue of rape in the

military. Wesley came to me because Cory's mo[r]
est sister were worried about her. Once the cou[
she slipped into a pretty serious depression."

"Man, she has guts. I can't imagine what
for her to face her assailant *and* the army." An
muscles between his shoulders. He wanted a sh
who'd done this to her. "Did she win her case?]
bars, because if he isn't—"

"He is. She won, but…it's not over. Not e[r]
fighting to have the borderline personality dia
from her record. She's been diagnosed with P
pendent psychologist, and the Veterans Lega
at Yale Law School is working on getting her
ened out."

Ted shook his head. "Raped by one of her o
army rubs salt in the wound by finding *her* un
She's been through the meat grinder more than
fered the worst kind of trauma, and that had to l
wonder she wanted a lock on the door.

"Cory hasn't had an income since the army
was about a year ago," Noah told him. "I had
spot. You remember how it was with Ryan. He v
afraid that if I didn't step up for Cory…" He sh

"Yeah. I get it, and I'm glad you did." Ted
"But you could've filled me in at any time, like
you, or—"

"You're right. My bad."

Ted let out a long breath. "Damn."

"Damn is right." Noah pulled into the p[
local hardware store. "She's going to move
house, which reminds me." He shut off the e[r]

having an ultrasound this afternoon, and I want to be there. I was hoping you'd give Cory a ride home after work."

"Sure." His heart raced at the thought. Why was that? He shook it off, focusing on more immediate needs. "I'll take her grocery shopping first, help her get stocked up. It's going to be awhile before she gets her first full paycheck."

"Tread lightly. She has a lot of pride. It can't be a personal loan. Give her an advance on her pay, or she won't accept it."

"Good idea." With his mind on other things, like what he could do to gain Cory's trust and help her to feel safe at L&L, he wandered through the hardware store aisles by rote, picking up a deadbolt lock and everything he needed for installation. He waited by the cash register, a semideveloped plan in mind. "I have another errand to run after I drop you off." Ted fell into step beside Noah as they left the building. "I'll be back in an hour or so."

"Where to?"

A smile broke free as certainty settled his mind. "The sporting goods warehouse store outside of Evansville."

"Really?" Noah's brow creased. "You gonna take up fishing?"

"Ha. Like I have the time." He met Noah's curious stare. "Don't worry. It's just an idea I have to help Cory feel more comfortable in her new surroundings."

"Do *not* buy her a gun, Ted. In her present state, that's not a good plan."

He laughed. "Nope. No firearms. I'm not that stupid."

"Maybe I should tag along..."

"Not this time." He held out his hand. "Give me the keys."

CHAPTER TWO

CORY TRIED TO CONCENTRATE ON setting up her new workstation and Mac desktop, but with Ted Lovejoy installing a deadbolt on the office door, keeping her mind on what she was doing was impossible. He confused her. One minute he'd been ranting about not wanting her here, and the next he offered to put a lock on the door so she'd feel safe. Which she didn't. Good thing Paige was with her, otherwise she'd be forced to leave until he finished the job.

She sneaked another peek at his clean-cut country-boy good looks. All that thick, curly blond hair, his serious gray eyes and well-formed physique…If this had been a couple of years ago, she would've flirted with him. But it wasn't a few years ago. It was now, and things had changed. She'd changed.

That leather tool belt strapped low around his narrow hips, his biceps all manly looking, and all that muscle shifting going on as he worked sure didn't help matters. Too bad he wasn't homely. No. It wouldn't make any difference. Homely men were just as dangerous as the good-looking ones.

How the hell could she spend every day of the week working for a man she found sexy? She didn't want to feel attraction, and this betrayal by her own body was more than she could handle. She squirmed, uncomfortable in her own skin, and fought the urge to flee. Dragging her eyes away from him, Cory booted up the Mac and focused on the task before her—installing the software needed to begin her job in earnest.

Ted glanced at her. "I need to make a copy of your Social Security card. Did you bring it with you today?"

"Yes." His voice set off a flurry of anxiety inside her chest. *Get a grip, dammit.* She studied Paige, gauging her reaction to the situation. Paige knew Ted well, and Cory tried to emulate the other woman's obvious calm. "Thank you so much for putting the lock on the door. I know it must seem…"

"Don't give it a second thought. It's no big deal." Ted stepped back to survey his work. "Let's give this a try." He shut the door and slid the lock into place.

Click.

A tight space with a man on the wrong side of the locked door, shut in with him blocking the only way out. Not good. Not good at all. Cory's heart pounded so hard, she was surprised neither of them said something about the noise. A fine sheen of sweat beaded her forehead, and she couldn't get enough air into her lungs. She shot up from the chair and backed herself up against the wall, her muscles tightly coiled and combat ready.

Ted and Paige stared at her as if she'd turned into some kind of wild animal trapped in a corner. Not too far from the truth. "I have a charley horse." She leaned over and massaged her calf, glancing up when neither of them said a word.

Ted's expression had shifted into confusion and concern. He unlocked the door and opened it. "I'll go get the paperwork."

Relief flooded her. She sucked in a huge breath, then another, letting it out slowly. Giving her calf one more rub just because, she finally slipped back into her chair.

"Ted is harmless," Paige said, returning to her work. "He's the sweetest guy in the world."

"I'm sure he is." The chaos he set off inside her said otherwise, but she couldn't explain. She cast around for a change of topic. "When are you due?"

"Middle of September." Paige's features softened. "We're having a little boy."

Yeah, this felt safer. Her pulse began its slow descent. "Do you and Ryan live in town?"

"No, but we used to. Ryan and I had the third-floor apartment before Wesley moved in. We built a new house on an old farmstead bordering the river. It's about twenty minutes west of town. We just moved in a few weeks ago."

"Oh." Cory nodded, trying to fathom what it must be like to be able to buy acres of land on the Ohio River. She'd grown up dirt-poor, and as a child, she couldn't even have imagined what it might be like to buy brand-new clothes for school each year. Instead, she and her mother both wore secondhand wardrobes from the thrift stores in town. "It sounds really nice."

"It will be once we have everything in order. Right now we're working on getting the nursery ready." She let out a happy sigh. "You'll have to come over sometime."

"I'd love to." Paige had made her feel so welcome. She had an open friendliness that drew Cory in, and she hoped to get to know her coworker better.

"We'll plan something in a few weeks," Paige said. "We'd better get back to work. Once you get everything loaded on your desktop, we'll go over the website."

"Would you mind telling me who does what, so I'll know who to go to if I have questions?"

"Sure. My husband heads up design and does the photos and graphics for ads. Noah is in charge of the production and finishing crews, and I do the marketing and retail stuff. I used to maintain the website as well." She grinned. "I can't tell you how glad I am to let that go. We're looking for retail space in Evansville, and eventually we'll expand from there. We're also developing a catalog. My hands are already more than full."

"What does Ted do?" Warmth flooded her cheeks. It was a reasonable question under the circumstances, right? They were talking about what everybody did, and it wasn't like she was more interested in him than in anyone else. Because she wasn't.

"Honestly, Ted is the backbone of L&L. He's been taking care of the order processing, shipping, payroll and all of the business administration stuff." Paige's expression grew solemn. "Frankly, we've all been a little worried about him lately."

"Oh?" Cory's curiosity piqued, she straightened. "Why is that?"

"He's been unhappy. He snaps and snarls at everyone. Noah believes it's because he has too much on his plate. He's hoping having you take over a few of his responsibilities will help." She shrugged. "I think it's more than that."

"Like?"

"He's worked around the clock for the past five years and needs a break." She leaned back in her chair and stretched. "My brother had the woodworking skills, but Langford & Lovejoy Heritage Furniture was all Ted's idea. Noah agreed to form a partnership with him on the condition that Ted get his business degree. He did, plus a master's, all the while putting in a ton of hours here. If you ask me, he's suffering from burnout."

Cory pondered what Paige had shared, along with what she'd heard in the hallway on her way to the conference room this morning. Ted's issues went deeper than burnout. She was sure of it. What ate at him? "Why doesn't he take a vacation?"

"Good question."

Maybe she'd ask him once she had the chance. Then again, his problems were none of her business. As if he'd heard them talking about him, Ted appeared in the doorway with several papers in his hand. "You can fill these out this afternoon." He laid them on her desk. "Are you two ready for lunch? The crew's already headed over. Noah and Ryan are waiting downstairs."

Ready for lunch in an unfamiliar setting with a group of men she didn't know? Hell, no, but she wasn't ready for this job either. She wouldn't have taken it if Brenda's words hadn't scared her shitless. They'd ignited a tiny flame of self-preservation and whatever fight she had left in her. Brenda had been right. If she didn't take a step in the right direction now, she'd end up an agoraphobic with no life and serious hygiene issues. "Sure." She rose from her place and waited for Paige to precede her.

"Have you met the day crew?" Ted held the elevator door open for them.

The interior of the freight elevator loomed dark and sinister before her, and once again her heart raced, sending a chill down her spine. She swiped a palm over her damp forehead. "Um...I think I'll take the stairs."

Ted's face fell. "Oh, right. Sure."

She moved a little closer to Paige, relieved when they moved toward the stairway. "Bunny introduced me to the crew when I got here."

Paige snorted. "How does a guy like Wesley Holt get a nickname like Bunny?"

"It's from when we were kids. He's the oldest of five, and he had to keep an eye on all of his younger siblings. His sister and I are best friends, so I was usually included in any games they played. Wes is fast. Nobody could catch him in a game of tag or capture the flag. Somebody said he was quick like a bunny, so we all started calling him Bunny."

Ted smiled, his expression warm. "And Squirrel?"

"I was the resident tree-climbing expert. I started out as Monkey, but Wes said there weren't any monkeys native to Indiana. So the Holt clan changed my nickname to Squirrel." They left the stairs and walked into the production area. "Kid stuff."

Stuff that had given her a sense of home after the rug had been ripped out from under her when her dad died. The Holts gave her a place to belong, and even if they were a ragtag bunch, they'd stuck together and protected one another.

They joined Ryan and Noah, leaving by the front door to walk to the diner with Noah leading the way. Ryan and Paige held hands in front of her, while she and Ted took up the rear.

She checked out the town of Perfect as they walked. Nice. Well maintained and litter free, the small town had an old-timey feel to it, as if the redbrick and limestone office buildings and storefronts had seen a lot of history. They all had window boxes or planters on the sidewalk filled with a variety of flourishing spring flowers in bloom. She suspected the town had an ordinance against shabbiness and peeling paint. How had she ended up here again?

"My ancestor founded this town." Ted came up beside her, and she edged away a little. "My great-great-great-grandfather Tobias Lovejoy ended up here after the Civil War and decided to put down roots. There are a ton of Lovejoys living in or near Perfect. In fact, Noah's wife and I are first cousins."

"It's nice. Quiet." What would it be like to have a large extended family? Her mom had been an only child, and so had she. All her grandparents had passed, and it had been just the two of them for as long as she could remember.

Ted continued to walk next to her. "My aunt believes Perfect holds magical healing powers for veterans."

She flashed him a skeptical look.

"It does. I'm here to testify to that fact," Noah said over his shoulder. "Something about the peacefulness just seeps into your soul. Wait until you're living in the carriage house for a while. You'll see."

"Ceejay and Noah's house is right on the banks of the Ohio River." Ted glanced sideways at her. "By the way, Noah has an appointment this afternoon, and he asked me to give you a ride home. Are you going to be all right with that?"

Alarm raced along her nerves, and she bit her lower lip to squelch the panic. *Relax.* Paige had assured her Ted was harmless, and he'd been nothing but nice to her so far. "Sure. Thanks," she murmured.

"I know you heard me ranting about—"

"Yeah. You didn't want to hire me." She lifted an eyebrow and glanced at him. "I got that loud and clear."

"No. It's not that I didn't want to hire you. It's..." He shook his head. "It seems silly now. I'm glad you joined L&L." One side of his mouth quirked up. "This is it. Aunt Jenny's diner is a landmark in Perfect. Most days we have our lunch here. I hope you'll join us."

"We all hope you'll join us," Paige added.

She pasted a smile on her face, and remained silent. Whatever savings she'd managed to amass while in the military had been spent supporting herself and her court case for the past year.

Lunches out were not an option. In fact, she wondered how she'd make it to her first paycheck. Cory followed everyone into the retro diner. The black-and-white tile floor and red Formica tabletops looked like they were straight out of the fifties. And the smells. Lord, she'd fallen into comfort food heaven. Her mouth watered and her stomach made embarrassing rumbling sounds.

Two tables had been pushed together in the back corner. Kyle, John and Xavier—the production crew—had taken the seats against the wall, leaving the end chair in the corner free. Noah headed for the corner seat as if he owned that particular space. Ryan and Paige took the places to Noah's right. Ted offered her the chair next to Paige, which would've hemmed her in between them. "Do you mind if I sit on the end?"

"Not at all." He switched places with her and sat down.

"Hey, kid. Where's your aunt today?" Kyle asked, leaning forward to look down the table. "Is she OK?"

Ted tensed beside her, and she remembered how he'd shouted at Ryan for calling him kid earlier that morning. Was it being called kid that got to him, or was there something wrong with his aunt?

"She's spending the day with Ceejay and the kids," Noah answered. "We have our ultrasound this afternoon, and Jenny is babysitting."

"Are you going to ask about the gender or keep it a surprise?" Paige asked.

"If they can tell, we want to know." Noah grinned. "Ceejay has her heart set on a girl. So does Lucinda. I think Toby and Micah are starting to make our little girl feel outnumbered."

"Where are you two from?" Cory turned to Paige. "You don't sound like southern Indiana to me."

"We were born and raised in Pennsylvania." Paige picked up

the specials sheet. "Noah moved here five years ago, and I joined him a couple years after that."

Ryan put his arm around his wife's shoulders and gave her a squeeze. "She couldn't resist me."

"True." Paige turned an indulgent, love-filled expression toward her husband.

Cory's gut twisted, and a hollow ache spread through her. She'd never have what they had. Never. Sergeant Dickhead had seen to that. She let the conversation go on without her, noticing Ted didn't contribute either.

After her conversation with Paige about Ted, and what she'd overheard this morning, the dynamics of the group fascinated her. Hyperaware of Ted beside her, she was dying to ask questions that were none of her business. Everyone ordered the special of the day, and she did the same. Her mouth watered at the thought of meat loaf and mashed potatoes. Yep. Her appetite was definitely coming back.

After lunch with the crew, they returned to work and Cory continued to set up her computer while making small talk with Paige. The rest of the afternoon flew by, and her nerves were on edge at the thought of the ride home. She'd be alone with a guy she didn't know. Logically, she knew nothing was likely to happen. One man had raped her, and it didn't equate that all men were rapists because of that experience. And yet, here she was, a shaky, quaking mess. Logic didn't factor in.

Paige shut her computer down and straightened the piles on her desk. "What did you think of your first day?"

"Perfect seems like a really nice town, and this business is unique. I was military for eight years. It's going to take some time to get used to the way things are done, but it's great." Taking her cue from Paige, she closed things down for the day.

"We all have our routines at the end of our shifts. I clean out the coffeepot and get it ready for the night crew. I'm sure we'll come up with something for you." She stood up and grabbed her purse. "Come downstairs when you're ready to leave."

Gulp. "I'll come with you now if that's all right." Ted and Ryan had headed down the back stairs ten minutes ago. She didn't want to be alone in their office, or on the second floor for that matter. Wesley and his dog emerged from the third floor just as they reached the stairs.

"How'd it go today?" He scrutinized her.

"It went fine." He'd changed since their days in the trailer park. Wesley's face had grown more angular, more intense, all traces of youthfulness gone, replaced by a hardened maturity. His hazel eyes held a haunted look, and deep lines etched the sides of his mouth. She hadn't seen him smile once since she'd returned to Indiana. She missed his smiles.

His brow lowered. "For real?"

Gratitude flooded her. "For real. I'm glad you're here. You know that, right?"

"Same back." He pulled her in for a quick hug, releasing her before she could react. "Things are going to get better. You'll see."

She nodded. Wesley was the big brother she'd never had, and she'd missed him terribly once he'd left to join the marines. Maybe he was right, and being back home in Indiana would help her. She stepped into the production area just as the night crew began to filter in. The presence of more unfamiliar men made her anxious to leave. Wesley and Paige introduced her. She nodded a greeting and left to retrieve her belongings. She'd stashed them in the closet located between the storefront and the work space.

Ted appeared with his car keys in hand. "Ready?" He took the cardboard box she carried.

"As ready as I'll ever be." She gripped the shoulder strap of her duffel bag and followed him out to the alley. He led her to a classic Mustang convertible. "This is yours?"

"Yep." He set her box inside the trunk and turned to take the duffel bag from her. "My aunt's husband was the original owner. He died in Vietnam, and it sat under a tarp in the carriage house bay for years and years." He opened the passenger door for her and walked around to the driver's side. "Aunt Jenny gave it to me when I graduated from high school."

She hesitated before getting in. The top was down, and that helped. Plus, he'd been so courteous. Finally, she climbed in and ran her hand over the cream-colored leather bucket seat. Nice.

Ted reached back to the floor behind him and drew out a Dick's Sporting Goods bag, dropping it in her lap. "I got you something."

She jerked and stared at the bag as if it might be an IED about to explode in her face. Baffled, she asked, "Why?"

"Noah told me what happened to you in Afghanistan. I want you to feel safe at L&L. That's my first priority, helping you to feel in control and comfortable at work."

Her face heated at the way he talked so frankly about her experience. What happened to her was none of his damn business. Her neck and shoulders stiff, she poured the contents of the sack onto her lap. "Pepper spray and a stun gun?" Tears pricked at her eyes, and the tension leached out of her.

His gift was so thoughtful and considerate she could hardly stand it. No man would give a woman pepper spray if he intended to cause her harm, would he? "Thank you," she whispered.

"Do you have the keys for the carriage house?"

She nodded, unable to speak for the emotions choking her.

"Let me have them for a second." He held out his hand.

Cory riffled through her purse for the key ring Noah had given her and handed it over. She watched as he attached her keys to the ring on the end of the leather case holding the pepper spray.

"Use them, Cory. If you ever feel the least bit threatened, use them first and ask questions later." He sat back and stared at her, one eyebrow raised. "Even if it's on me."

She had to swallow several times before she could speak. "That's one of the nicest things anyone has ever said or done for me." Glancing into the warmth and sincerity of his wonderful gray eyes, she experienced another flutter, and this time she didn't mind it so much.

"I'm hoping someday you'll trust me enough not to need those." He started the engine and pulled out into the alley.

"Why would you care?" She frowned. "You just met me for the first time this morning. What possible difference could it make to you whether or not I trust you?"

"It just does. We'll be working together every day. I don't want you to be uncomfortable with that." His mouth tightened into a straight line for an instant. "I'm taking you grocery shopping before we head to the carriage house. Get whatever you need. Noah said you've been out of work for a while, and—"

Her eyes widened, and mortification burned through her. Obviously Noah had told Ted the entire story of her destitution, not just about the rape. He pitied her. Pity. Something she'd fought against all the years of her youth, and something she abhorred with a vengeance. Ted had probably given her the stun gun and pepper spray out of pity as well. Poor little poverty-stricken victim. "I'm not a charity case. I have skills well worth the salary you're paying me."

Damn. A minute ago she'd been touched by what she believed

make, and Noah's advice to tread lightly came back to him. For the umpteenth time today, the urge to protect and comfort her surged to the forefront. He turned into the parking lot of an IGA grocery store. "If you'd like, we can stop at Offermeyer's butcher shop before we leave. All the meat they sell is produced by the farmers in our community. We like to support the locals."

"That sounds good to me. Noah said the carriage house is completely furnished, including pots and pans."

"It is."

"Do you know if there's a Crock-Pot?"

"I don't know, but if there isn't, between my mom and my sisters there are about a dozen of them in the Lovejoy family. I'm sure I can get a loaner until you can buy your own. I'll bring one to work tomorrow just in case."

"That would be nice. My mom is big on Crock-Pot cooking, and it's what I know."

After loading up on the basics at IGA, he drove them the short distance to Offermeyer's. Opening the door for her, he followed her inside.

"Oh, my God, it smells good in here, like ham, bacon and sausage." She inhaled loudly and closed her eyes. "It's making my mouth water." A grin broke free, lighting up her pretty face and erasing the spooked look.

The impact hit him squarely in the region of his heart, stunning him as if she'd used the device he'd given her for that purpose. "Yeah, it always does," he muttered. "My aunt gets her meat for the diner here."

Denny Offermeyer emerged from the back of the shop. "Hey, Ted. How're you?" The butcher's curious stare settled on Cory.

"Hey, Denny. This is Cory Marcel. It's her first day at L&L. She's moving into the Langfords' carriage house this afternoon."

"No." OK, he'd failed to change her train of thought. "I've never served in any branch of the military."

"Oh." Her tone held an unmistakable note of relief. "I thought maybe you knew Noah from the army, and that was the connection that brought him to Perfect. If he grew up in Pennsylvania, how'd he end up here, anyway?"

"Noah's stepbrother died around the same time he got out of the VA hospital. Noah came here to find his stepbrother's family—Ceejay and Lucinda. He rented the carriage house, fell in love with Ceejay, and the rest is history."

"How about his sister? Why'd she come to Perfect?"

"She came here shortly after she finished school. We offered her a job, and she ended up staying."

"Ryan was already working at L&L?"

"He started about a month before Paige did. Ryan was in the same Humvee as Noah when they got hit by a suicide bomber in Iraq." He watched as she took it all in and made the connections in her mind. Ted turned into the Langfords' gravel driveway lined by huge walnut trees on one side and the fully blossomed orchard on the other.

The house came into view, and Cory sucked in her breath. "It looks like something out of a magazine."

Ted tried to see the old Lovejoy home from her perspective. He and Noah had restored the square limestone house to its former glory, with its wide veranda, columns and the second-floor three-season porch. A rush of pride swelled his chest.

His aunt sat at the wrought-iron table on the porch with Micah on her lap. Lucinda and Toby were perched on the steps next to Sweet Pea. "That's my aunt Jenny." Ted parked and shut off the car. He hopped out and grabbed two of the four bags from

"Paige said the idea for starting the business was yours. Is that true?" She set her bags down on the concrete slab in front of the door, fished around in her purse and pulled out her keys.

"It is. I took one look at that cradle and knew what I wanted to do with my life." He chuckled, remembering the way he'd pestered Noah. "Noah and I were both kind of lost back then. Neither of us knew what to do with ourselves. We were working together on the big house, which was a wreck, and I hounded him to go into business with me." He trailed off, aware that he'd lost his audience.

Cory's attention and demeanor had shifted. Her posture held a defensive tension, and the shuttered expression returned to her face. He got it. She didn't want him inside. He set his two bags down on the concrete slab. "I'll go get the stuff from the trunk, and when I come back, let's go take a look at the river."

She released an audible breath, and some of her tension eased. *Damn.* She feared him, and that stung. Ted backtracked to his Mustang. Best to give her a few extra minutes to put her groceries away. "Hey, Aunt Jenny," he called as he opened his trunk. "What's new with you?"

His aunt walked toward him, slowing her pace to accommodate Micah's short legs. The little guy held tightly to two of her fingers. "Not much. What do you think of our new tenant?"

He chuffed out a breath and shook his head. "She's been hurt bad. Did Noah tell you what happened to her?"

"No. Ceejay did." Jenny patted his cheek. "You can help her, Teddy. You were always such a sweet, sensitive boy, and you've grown into a fine young man. You can help her regain her trust."

"I don't know, Jenny." Did he want to get tangled up in her emotional issues? They were beyond him. He lifted the army-issue duffel bag and the single cardboard box containing Cory's

sound of semis and cars on the freeway. And then there were the floodlights and diesel engines from the trucking company next door." She shook her head. "No peace or quiet there."

"Where did you grow up?" Ted tried to imagine living with that kind of constant disturbance. She didn't answer, and one look at her told him this was another touchy subject. "No matter where it was, it can't be as bad as where I grew up."

"Wanna bet?"

"Yeah, I do." He barked out a laugh. "Let's make a wager."

Her brow creased. "What kind of wager?"

"You take a look at where I grew up, and we go see where you grew up. We'll compare, and whoever had it worse wins."

"I don't think so." She tensed up again, and he caught the panic in her eyes as she cast him a furtive glance.

"It's not like that, Cory. We're coworkers. I'm just trying to be a friend here and help you feel welcome." It bothered him way too much that he made her nervous and afraid. "I would never do anything to harm you. You can keep your finger on the pepper spray for the entire trip. What do you say to a wager between friends?"

She relaxed a bit. "What's the ante?"

"The loser buys the winner lunch at the truck stop outside of town. They make the best burgers and shakes. Jenny's diner can't compare when it comes to the truck stop's burgers and fries." Cory bit her lower lip, and the gesture tugged at the corners of his heart.

"I'm *going* to win, but can it wait until I get my first paycheck just in case you grew up in a chicken coop or something?"

He laughed again. "It's worse than a chicken coop. I'm going to win, and sure—we can wait. Not a word about it until you're ready." He held his hand out. "Shake on it?"

She hesitated, staring at his hand. He kept it extended and

At first he thought she was teasing, but one look into her wide eyes, and he knew she was serious. *Idiot!* He should've quit while he was ahead. "Uh, I don't know. I suppose you can ask." *Don't ask.* Ted wanted her to stay right where she was. He wanted her to let the magic of this place heal her the way it had Noah and Ryan. He wanted that for her in the worst way.

"Don't mention it. If you need anything else, let me know." Ted gestured to the patio doors. "Let's go in through the back. I want to say good-bye to Jenny and the kids."

"You go on. I'm going to put my stuff in the carriage house first."

"I can wait."

"That's OK. Go on without me. I'll see you tomorrow at work." *Please take the hint. Please go away.* They stopped at the carriage house door, and she hoisted her duffel bag to her shoulder. "Thanks again for all your help." He sent her another one of his I'm-confused looks. Or was it disappointment she saw in his expression? Pity? Probably pity.

"Right." He backed away, keeping her in his sights. "See you tomorrow." Finally, he turned and headed for the house.

Heaving a sigh of relief, Cory opened the carriage house door and nudged the cardboard box through with her foot. She locked the door behind her and took her duffel back to the bedroom. The carriage house was the nicest place she'd ever lived. She could hardly believe her good luck. Hardwood floors, great leather furniture, a nice flat-screen TV mounted on the living room wall with a recliner set up in front of it—and she had the place all to herself. For the first time in her life, she had a place of her own.

Someone had cleaned recently, because the apartment sparkled and smelled fresh and lemony. She dropped her duffel on the old-fashioned chenille bedspread and pulled the blankets back. The sheets felt new to her touch, and the scent of laundry soap and dryer sheets floated up around her. Sweet.

A wave of gratitude washed through her. The Langfords didn't know her at all, and yet they'd come to her aid at one of the lowest points in her life. She had to come up with a way to

They ended the call, and after taking one more look at her new digs, Cory headed to the main house. She knocked, and Lucinda slid the patio door open for her. The garlicky scent of Italian food filled her senses. "Smells good in here. Can I do anything to help?"

"Keep an eye on Micah, so I can put everything on the table." Jenny put the toddler down. "He's at that age where he gets into everything."

"I'm setting the table," Lucinda announced. Her chestnut hair had been pulled into a wavy ponytail. "Toby's upstairs washing his hands. I already washed mine."

"Thank you so much for inviting me to eat with you." Cory followed the towheaded little boy around the kitchen, ready to intervene if he got into something he shouldn't.

"You're welcome." Jenny's warm gaze settled on her. "What do you think of the carriage house?"

The older woman bore an uncanny resemblance to Ted. They had the same kind eyes and curly hair, though Jenny's had turned mostly silver. "It's really nice." The toddler swatted her hand away as she tried to keep him out of the dog's water dish. "I love it. Somebody cleaned in there recently. Do you know who I should thank?" She glanced toward Lucinda.

"Me and Mommy." The little girl beamed, and her large brown eyes sparkled. "Mommy did most of the work, but I helped. I dusted and swept."

"I sure do appreciate all your hard work." Cory lifted a squirming Micah and brought him over to his high chair. "Does he have a bib handy?"

"I'll get one for him." Lucinda headed for the kitchen drawers next to the sink.

Jenny placed a large ceramic bowl of spaghetti and meatballs

"You're pretty," he blurted.

"And you're a charmer." She ruffled his hair and took her seat.

"You *are* pretty," Lucinda confirmed.

Her breath hitched. She didn't feel pretty, nor did she want to. She shoved the unwelcome thoughts away. "Everybody has been so kind since I arrived."

"Perfect is a special place." Jenny set a small dish of food on Micah's high chair tray. "All you have to do is be open to what comes your way, and things will change for the better."

"I don't know about the place. I only know about the people. I have a great job and an amazing apartment, not to mention wonderful neighbors." She grinned at Lucinda and Toby.

That's all there was to it. If Jenny's words were in reference to the supposed magic this place held, Cory didn't want to hear it, not the falling-in-love part anyway. Healing would be good, but she had nothing to offer to anyone in the love department. She was already a shipwreck with an empty cargo hold. She didn't need more holes in her hull.

"How was your first day at work?" Jenny asked.

"Good." She helped herself to salad. "We had lunch at your diner today. It's really cool. I love the retro look."

"Retro?" Jenny laughed. "That diner has always looked the way it does now. I've just never updated."

"Ryan said it's a tradition to take new hires there for lunch."

"That's true. The L&L crew eats lunch there on a regular basis, and Wesley comes in for breakfast most mornings. I think he has a little thing for my assistant manager." The laugh lines around her eyes creased. "At any rate, Noah and Ted's business has certainly stimulated Perfect's economy. When they have one of their sample sales, the whole town benefits."

"L&L is definitely one of a kind. I'm glad to be there." So

time with Toby, Micah and Lucinda. You have a lovely family." Ceejay shared Ted's country good looks and had similar coloring. Although her hair had way more red in it than Ted's sandy blond, they both had the Lovejoy curls.

"Are you all settled into the carriage house?" Ceejay asked.

Considering all her possessions fit into one cardboard box and one large duffel...there wasn't really anything to settle. "Pretty much. The apartment is..." Overwhelmed with gratitude, she cleared her throat, trying to dislodge the lump that had formed. "It's great, and thank you so much for having it all ready for me to move in."

"Mommy, did you find out if we're having a brother or a sister?" Lucinda interrupted, placing her hands on Ceejay's baby bump.

"It's a girl," Ceejay announced, threading her fingers through her daughter's chestnut locks.

Lucinda pumped her fist in the air. "Yes!"

"That's wonderful news," Jenny added. "Another little girl for me to spoil and dress up."

Cory backed toward the sliding doors, ready to make her exit. She had no place in their family celebration. "Thanks for supper, Jenny."

Ceejay's brow rose. "You don't have to rush off."

"I don't mean to eat and leave, but it's been a long day, and I'm tired." She slid the patio door open.

"Harlen is waiting for me." Jenny gathered her things. "I'm ready to go home too." She turned toward Cory. "I'm glad we had the chance to visit. Don't be a stranger. Come on down to the diner any time, even if it's just to say hello."

"I will." Cory started to slip out the back.

"Wait a sec." Noah walked to the counter where their phone was situated. He grabbed a pen and wrote something down on a Post-It. "We have satellite Internet. H

handed her the paper. "You also have c

your rent."

"But…" She frowned. "I'm not payir

"You will once you're back on you

mouth quirked up. "See you tomorrow."

"Thanks." She nodded and left. Noa

reason to reach out to her, yet they had

kind of generosity from total strangers

way to make it up to them. Letting her

ment, she thought of things she could d

and beyond her list of responsibilities.

her work, make that her focus, and ever

It took her all of twenty minutes to

away. How pathetic. It had taken her les

completely moved in. Her thoughts kn

head like rocks in a cement mixer. No

the quiet.

After constant background noise f

the army and in the trailer park, the tota

her. Cory made her way to the living roo

control and turned on the TV. She didn't

but the noise calmed her. She snatched

and settled herself in the recliner. After

with the password Noah had provided

searching for any news from the law cli

Unfit to serve. Her chest tightene

rebelled. The words lodged in her sou

she couldn't reach. Her inbox held not

She made short work of answering the

friends still in the army and set the la

nine o'clock yet, and she was ready to go to bed. After being so inactive for weeks, following a schedule, learning a new job and being around a group of strangers had exhausted her.

She got ready for bed, set her alarm clock and slipped between the brand-new sheets, her mind straying to thoughts of Ted—the satisfied smile lighting his face after he'd installed the deadbolt, his earnest expression as he gave her the stun gun and pepper spray. If she'd met him any time other than now, would they date?

Her insides clenched, and bitterness brought tears to her eyes. Taking a deep breath, she forced her mind to other things, like defragging all the computers at L&L and reorganizing some of their systems and processes to increase efficiency. Exhaustion tugged at her. She yawned, turned to her side and curled up, slipping into sleep.

Sergeant Barnett pinned her against the back wall, his hand pressed tightly across her mouth and nose. The pungent smell of his sweat filled her with revulsion. She couldn't get enough air into her lungs, and terror clawed its way up her throat. Don't panic. Think. You're a trained soldier! Cory fought, gouging and poking at his eyes with her thumbs, until he was forced to back off. The second he did, she kneed him in the groin.

"Stop, bitch." His fist connected with her mouth. "Don't make this harder than it has to be. You know you have this coming."

Her lip split, and stinging pain raced along her nerves. The salty, metallic taste of her blood filled her mouth, and rage turned her vision to hot red. No one had this kind of shit coming. Taking advantage of the momentary freedom, she tried to scream for help. His hand came back to cover her face. She twisted and turned, fought for all she was worth. His second blow caught her right eye, and her head snapped back against the wall hard enough to make her dizzy. Spots swam in front of her eyes, and the throbbing ache brought tears to her eyes.

The snap of his belt being pulled free from his pants sent panic streaking through her. NO! She went slack, sliding down the wall, feigning unconsciousness in an attempt to get him to follow. If he'd only follow, she could catch him with a head butt.

"I tried to go about this the right way, but no," he said through gritted teeth. "You wouldn't have anything to do with me. Bitch, you should've put out for me months ago. You don't know your place, and I'm going to teach it to you today. I own you."

He backhanded her, but he didn't follow her down. Dammit. The minute she raised her arms to protect herself, he grabbed her wrists. Still dizzy, in pain and close to passing out, she made a desperate effort to gather her resources enough to fight. Despair and helplessness swamped her.

He flipped her around and used his belt to bind her wrists. She struck out at him with a boot. He grunted, and a flare of triumph bloomed in her chest. A vicious kick to her ribs robbed her of breath, sending more spots dancing around her head. The small bit of triumph dissipated. She couldn't stop what was happening, couldn't fight him off bound as she was...

His hands were all over her, tugging at her clothing, rubbing against her bare skin. Disgust and bile rose in her throat at his brutal touch, his unwelcome probing and pinching. His hot, heavy breathing filled the silence as he unfastened his pants. Forcing her legs apart with his knees, he lowered himself...

"No!" she cried, flinging the blankets off. Disoriented, she gasped for air, struggling to remember where she was. A cold, clammy sweat covered her body, and a shudder pulsed through her. Dirty, violated, ugly—all that was good had been hollowed out of her, everything she had been, leaving nothing but rage and fear behind. Nausea roiled through her.

She sat up, swung her legs to the floor and began rocking herself back and forth with her arms wrapped around her middle. Not here. This horror had no place in her new home with its coziness, its magic and healing powers. She clenched her jaw so tight it ached.

Sergeant Dickhead could not have this place. He could not fill the carriage house with his ugliness and violence. He'd already taken so much. She couldn't let him take this as well. Angry tears coursed down her cheeks as she rocked back and forth. Finally the trembling stopped, and she got up on shaky legs and headed for the bathroom. She turned on the shower to scalding hot, stripped and stepped under the spray.

Scrubbing her skin until she couldn't take any more didn't erase the disgust. Her attacker's filth lived inside her, in a place so deep she couldn't reach it with soap and a washcloth. Still, she stood under the nozzle, praying the water would wash her clean, trying to shut out the words echoing through her head.

"You tell anybody this was anything other than consensual, and I'll make sure you never receive another promotion for the rest of your career." Sergeant Barnett put himself back together. He loomed over her where she lay broken and battered on the concrete floor. *"Next time I expect your full cooperation."* He took a step back and studied her swollen and bruised face. *"If anyone asks, you tripped and fell into the metal shelving in here. You got that, Corporal?"*

Damn him to hell.

❦　❦　❦

Ted sat next to Cory at her desk, close enough to catch a whiff of the soap she used, along with her own unique feminine scent. He drew a deep breath into his lungs and guided her through the shipping process. She smelled so damn good, like fresh air, sunshine and sweet clover.

The week had flown by, and Cory had proven herself over and over. She'd already taken over the web maintenance and ordering, handling both like she'd done the job for months. "We have several trucking companies we work with, and who we use depends upon the region for delivery and their availability." He brought up the file with the links to the companies they used on a regular basis. "Once an order is completed, you have to check with their dispatchers to see if they have a truck already going to a particular area. Once you choose a carrier, you fill out the paperwork, a packing slip, and let the guys know when the pickup is going to take place. They'll crate everything up and have it ready to go."

"That sounds easy enough."

"It is, but it's time-consuming."

She glanced at him. "Have you given any more thought to my suggestions for updating the ordering process? I still think bringing a piece of paper down to a basket on the wall is archaic. We could do it all electronically with a computer or tablets."

"Uh, no. Let's keep it as it is for now." Dollar signs flashed in front of his eyes. Tablets weren't cheap. "It's simple, and it's worked for us up till now."

"Welcome to L&L." Paige smirked from her desk. "We like to keep things low-tech."

"It's time to update." Cory's eyes held a challenge. "There should be a computer in the production area."

"There used to be," he told her. "When it was just the four

of us, Ryan liked to keep his desktop in the workspace. Now it's in his office. We needed the extra room to accommodate the increase in production."

"What if we mounted a screen on the wall? We could send the orders, and each guy in production could have a separate file. You back everything up, don't you?"

He took in another breath, savoring the Cory-scented air filling his senses. "Um…you'd have to ask Paige. Technology isn't really my thing. I know how to navigate the software, and that's about it."

"Yes. We back everything up." Paige raised her eyes from her computer.

"That's good." Cory grinned at Paige like they shared some big technological secret he didn't get.

True. He didn't get it, and he didn't care that he didn't. Ted shifted in his chair. Her nearness, the way she smelled and seeing her grin—it all worked on him until he couldn't think straight. He wanted more time with her. Alone. "Are you prepared to lose our bet?" She'd be more likely to think the whole thing was no big deal if he opened up the conversation in front of Paige, right? "We can start with my place this weekend."

Paige straightened, peering at him over the top of her computer screen. "What's this about?"

"I bet Cory where I grew up is worse than where she grew up."

"Oh." Paige laughed. "Ted's gonna win that one."

"Don't count on it." Cory raised an eyebrow, and her eyes held a competitive glint. "What did you have in mind?"

"Come to my parents' house for Sunday dinner. The whole family gathers there once or twice a month, and one more mouth to feed won't make a difference."

She tensed and averted her gaze.

"It's no big deal. Jenny and her husband will be there, and maybe Noah, Ceejay and their brood. They prefer to keep their Sundays to themselves, but they do join us every few months or so. If you aren't comfortable with me picking you up, I'm sure Jenny and Harlen would be happy to swing by for you if Noah's family isn't coming."

Cory looked to Paige, her expression unsure.

"Ted's folks are the nicest people ever," Paige told her. "Even if they do live—"

"Don't say it." Ted flashed her a warning look. "This is a wager between me and Cory, and I don't want her to…uh…*get wind* of my situation. She might pull out if she finds out what she's up against."

"I see what you mean. If you want, I can be the final judge if it comes down to a tie," Paige volunteered. "You can each give me your impressions of each other's situation, and I promise to be fair."

Cory looked between them, her brow furrowed as if she was trying to figure something out. "All right." Her chin rose a determined notch. "You can pick me up."

"Great." He tried to keep his expression neutral, even though he wanted to jump up and down and throw his fists in the air like he'd just scored the winning touchdown in the last game of the playoffs. "I'll be by around eleven thirty. We generally eat at noon or shortly after."

"Should I bring something?"

"Naw. Between my mom, my sisters and my aunts, there's always way more than enough to feed the entire town."

"All the Lovejoys are great cooks too," Paige added. She glanced at Ted. "We'll have to make sure Cory is included for the Fourth of July pig roast."

"Absolutely." Ted flashed her a grateful look.

"I don't know." Cory frowned. "I'm just an employee here. I don't want to intrude."

"It's not like that. The Fourth of July celebration is open to the entire town of Perfect," Ted said. "The Lovejoys host the event every year because our ancestor is the town's primary founder. Everybody brings a dish to share, and we all camp out on Ceejay and Noah's lawn to eat and watch fireworks across the river."

"Anyway, Noah should've made it clear before you accepted the job," Paige added. "No one here is just an employee. As soon as you signed on the dotted line, you became part of the L&L family. Just ask the guys. In fact, as soon as we're done painting our bare walls, Ryan and I are planning a company picnic at our new place." She turned to Ted. "You wouldn't mind picking her up for that, would you, Ted?"

"Not at all."

"I don't want to be a burden. Maybe Bunny can come for me."

"It's in the opposite direction for Wes, and I don't mind. You're on my way." A twinge of jealousy shot through him. He didn't like the idea of Wesley being her go-to guy. He wanted to be that man for her. "You're not a burden."

"I can always catch a ride with Noah and his family."

He caught the look of frustration Paige slid his way as she spoke. "Let's wait until we have the day planned, and we can figure it out then."

He shot Paige a wry grin. She'd tried, and he was grateful for the help. He rose from his chair and stretched. "We've done enough for today. There are a few orders ready to go. Tomorrow we'll walk through the process together. I'll let you deal with dispatch while I sit next to you in case any questions come up."

Paige put her things away and shut her computer down. Cory

followed suit. She glanced at the clock. "Wesley's sister is picking me up at five. I'd better head downstairs. I told her to come in through the alley."

"Oh?" Ted stepped back so she and Paige could walk out of the office ahead of him. "Are you two going out on the town tonight?"

"Hardly." She chuffed out a breath. "She's coming to the carriage house for dinner. Thanks again for the Crock-Pot, by the way."

"Sure." By the time they got to the stairs, the sound of voices and laughter drifted up. One of them decidedly feminine.

"Brenda's here." Cory grinned and hurried down to the first floor. "Gotta go protect the production crew."

Huh? Curious, Ted followed. He stepped into the room to find a gorgeous, curvy blonde in the midst of a circle of enraptured men. Kyle Reeves leaned against his workbench as if his legs wouldn't hold him, and he wore a stunned look while two of the finishing crew teased and flirted with the newcomer.

"Hey, Bren," Cory interrupted. "Did you meet everyone?"

Brenda's glance brushed over Kyle and swung back to the guys who were flirting with her. "TreVonne and Kenneth introduced themselves when we came in together, and I met the other two production guys as they left. This one's kind of shy, though." She shot Kyle a wry grin. "He hasn't said a word."

Kyle's Adam's apple bobbed, and he turned to rearrange the tools on his workbench that didn't need rearranging. Ted felt sorry for the guy. He knew the feeling. "That's Kyle. I'm Ted Lovejoy, and this is Paige Malloy. You're Wesley's little sister?"

"Yep." She gave Ted a dazzling smile and held out her hand. "I'm Brenda Holt. It's nice to meet all of you. I was just telling the guys here I'd be happy to give them a veteran's discount on haircuts."

Ted shook her hand. "That's nice of you."

Brenda fished around in her purse and pulled out a bunch of business cards. "I'm happy to do it." She placed the cards on the edge of the table saw next to where Kyle worked. Her eyes flitted over the flustered guy for a second and then darted away just as quickly. She turned to Ted. "Call me for an appointment anytime."

Ted stuffed his hands into his pockets, once again feeling like the odd man out. "I'm not a veteran."

"Doesn't matter." Brenda's gaze swept the room. "My offer is meant for everyone involved with Langford & Lovejoy." She turned to Paige. "I'd really love to get my hands on your hair. It's gorgeous."

"Thanks." Paige reached for one of the cards. "Did you style Cory's hair?"

"I did."

"I really like the cut. It's perfect for her."

"That's my specialty, finding the right cut to bring out my client's best assets."

"Are you ready to go?" Cory slung her purse strap over her shoulder. "I'm starving."

Brenda turned her dazzling smile on the guys one more time. "It was great meeting all of you. Tell Wes I'm sorry I missed him." She followed Cory out the back door.

Kyle snatched one of her cards from the table saw and stuffed it in his pocket. Ted grinned. "Are you going to get your haircut at"— he picked up a card—"the Hair Apparent Salon in Evansville?"

"Maybe I am, kid." Kyle shrugged without meeting his eyes. "She's Wesley's sister. We all gotta get our hair cut now and then. May as well give her the business."

"What's that about my sister?" Wesley stepped into the room with Rex at his side.

"Brenda came by for Cory. You just missed her," Ted answered. "She offered L&L employees a discount on haircuts."

"Humph," Wesley grunted. "She does mine for free."

The remaining day crew left, and Ted went out the doors with them, heading for his Mustang. He had a date on Sunday. Cory didn't think of it as a date, but he did. With someone as wary and skittish as she was, he'd have to find ways to circumvent her defenses, gain her trust and work his way into her heart before she even knew what was happening. The challenge gave him a new focus.

He wanted to replace her bad memories with good, coax more of those heart-stopping smiles out of her and erase the hurt from those pretty brown eyes once and for all. Was he crazy? Probably, but he'd been far less restless at work since she'd joined them, and being around her did something to him. Every hard-earned look of trust she aimed his way turned his insides to mush and stole his breath.

Watching her spirit ignite when she argued with him about updating their systems sent his pulse soaring, and the glint of competitiveness he'd witnessed when they talked about their bet gave him glimpses of the feisty woman she'd been before that asshole stole her fire.

L&L was the perfect place for Corinna Marcel, and he intended to be there for her each step of the way as she returned to herself, full of confidence and ready to take on the world.

❦ ❦ ❦

Like every other Friday, Ted worked on payroll, hurrying to get it done. He couldn't wait to see the pleased expression on Cory's face when he handed over her first paycheck. Hell, he couldn't wait to pick her up on Sunday to take her to his folks'. He turned up his iPod dock and moved the ruler down to the next line on the spreadsheet.

"Hey, kid." Kyle stood in his doorway with his shoulders bunched forward. "I have a favor to ask."

"You're much more likely to get that favor if you'd stop calling me kid," Ted muttered to his desktop.

"Huh?"

Ted blew out a long breath and turned the volume down on his iPod. "What's the favor, Kyle?"

"I...uh..." He cleared his throat. "I asked Brenda Holt out for a date."

"Yeah? Good for you. What's that got to do with me?"

"She said she'd only go out with me on one condition."

Puzzled, Ted abandoned his spreadsheet and frowned. "And?"

"It has to be a double date with Cory, and I thought you could be the fourth."

"Why me?" Ted leaned back in his chair, his thoughts spinning.

"I don't want any of the other guys on our crew along. You saw how they acted around Brenda." His brow furrowed. "And you—"

"I'm the safest choice?" Like he couldn't possibly compete? Ted's jaw clenched, and the familiar ache of inferiority twisted his gut.

"No. It's not like that. You didn't seem interested in her, is all. Help me out here, will you? We're talking bowling and pizza—completely casual."

"I'll talk to Cory about it this Sunday." Hell, what difference did it make? He should be grateful for any chance he caught to spend time with her. "I can't promise anything."

"Sunday?" Kyle's eyes lit up. "What's going with you two this Sunday?"

Heat crept up his neck. He shouldn't have let that slip. Speculation and gossip at work would not help his cause. "I'll do you this favor if you'll do one for me."

"Yeah?" Kyle's eyes filled with amusement. "What's that?"

"Cory is coming to dinner at my folks' house this Sunday. It's not a date, just a friendly gesture to a newcomer. I'd—"

"Just a friendly gesture, eh, kid?" Kyle smirked. "I'm a newcomer. You've never asked me to have dinner at your folks'."

Ted glared. "You want me to arrange this foursome or not?"

Kyle's smirk remained firmly in place. "Yep."

"Then keep that bit of information to yourself."

"Done." He straightened up off the door frame.

"And stop calling me kid."

"Sure, kid." Kyle sauntered away.

Ted chewed on this newest development while he finished payroll. No way could he disguise an evening out with another couple as anything other than what it was: a date. His heart skipped a beat. What if she said no? Aw, hell. What if she said yes?

He hit print and sat back in his leather chair while the printer did its job. Visions of Cory looking at him with trust and something more lighting her brown eyes played through his mind, sending heat curling through him…

"Hey." Noah came in and sat in the chair in front of Ted's desk. "You about done with the paychecks? I thought I'd give Cory a ride to the bank in town before it closes, so she can open an account."

His fantasy cut short, Ted pulled his chair up to his desk and straightened. "I'll take her."

"It makes more sense for me to do it," Noah said. "She rides home in my truck."

Heat crept up Ted's neck again. He moved to the printer and started separating the serrated edges of their paychecks. "Right."

"Unless you really want to—"

"No, that's OK." It wasn't, but he didn't want to push the issue. "I'm giving her the check, though."

"If you insist." Noah pushed himself out of the chair. "Do it soon. I want to get going a little early."

They all had their pay direct deposited, so distributing the stubs was no big deal. Cory's was the only actual check. Ted signed it and headed for her office. "I'm on my way."

"I'm right behind you," Noah said.

Great. An audience, when all he wanted was a moment alone with Cory. He wanted to savor the pleased expression on her face when he placed the check in her hands. Swallowing the disappointment, he walked into her office with Noah on his heels. Cory and Paige both looked up from their work.

"I have something for you," Ted said, handing Cory the check. "Your first L&L earnings."

"Oh," she said, taking it from him. "Thank you."

The smile she aimed his way hit the bull's-eye tattooed on his heart, and the impact sent an electric buzz humming through his veins. "You want a ride to the bank? There's enough time to open an account if we hurry."

"Uh…" Her eyes clouded, and her brow creased.

"We can stop there on our way home." Noah squeezed Ted's shoulder as he edged around him to enter the small office. "You about ready to leave?"

Cory's face cleared. "Sure." She grabbed her purse, shut her computer off, and got up to leave. She spared him a glance as she passed.

Ted watched her leave, embarrassment and disappointment chasing through him.

"Well." Paige put her stuff away. "That was painful, huh?"

"A little."

"Go slow, Ted. Baby steps. She's—"

"Yeah, I know. I just got caught up—"

"In her smile?" Paige chuckled. "I noticed, but I'm not sure Cory did. She's too wrapped up in her own protective shell to see what a great guy you are. Give it time."

"I offered her a ride to the bank—a public place with a security guard. It's not like I asked her on a date. I don't think time is going to make a difference." He plowed a hand through his hair. His attraction to her was a one-way street to heartache, but he couldn't manage to steer his bus in another direction. Her smile and the way she'd looked at him flashed through his mind, sending his heart racing. *Shit.*

Where his heart was concerned, he was a sucker for lost causes.

CHAPTER FOUR

CORY STARED AT HER REFLECTION in the tiny bathroom mirror. Steam from her shower still obscured the edges, framing her face in silvery drips. Should she wear makeup today? If she did, would Ted take it as a sign that she was interested in him? Her mind shied away from the thought. If she didn't wear makeup, would his family think she didn't care enough to look her best for them?

A compromise—foundation, a little blush and mascara—not enough to draw attention, and not so little that she'd come across as disinterested in her own appearance. She snorted. Like anybody would care either way.

Reaching for her toothbrush, she considered her clothing options: baggy old army fatigues or jeans and a blouse. Hmm. She'd like to do something about her limited wardrobe, but after paying Ted a portion of what she owed for groceries, and forcing Noah to take half a month's rent, she didn't have enough left for a shopping spree. Not if she wanted to continue eating, which she did. And not if she wanted to buy a car at some point. Which she also did.

She could've tucked a little of her paycheck away. Noah didn't expect rent for the first three months, but it just wasn't in her to take charity. As a child she'd had no choice. As an adult with an education and skills, it didn't sit well with her. She had a job; she'd pay her way.

Once she finished drying her hair and putting on a little makeup, she moved into the bedroom and dressed. As ready as she'd ever be, Cory made the rounds, locking all the windows and making sure everything had been shut off. Her stun gun rested in its place on the bedside table, and she had the pepper spray with her. Check. Slinging the strap of her purse over her shoulder, she left the carriage house to wait for Ted on the Langfords' veranda.

It was one of those rare days where the temperature and humidity were in sync, warm but not overwhelming. Lazy white clouds drifted across the clear blue sky, and a light breeze lifted the hair around her face. Rounding the corner of the big house, she found Ceejay sitting at the wrought-iron table by herself. Sweet Pea lay sprawled half under the table, half out, like he didn't realize he was too big to fit.

"Good morning." Ceejay held a mug in her hands, and her feet were propped up on another chair.

"Hi. It's awfully quiet around here. Where's the rest of your squadron?"

"Noah is taking Lucinda to our neighbor's for a play date. Then he has a few errands to run, and Toby wanted to go along for the ride. Micah is napping." She ran her hand over her belly and grinned. "Once this one is born, moments to myself are going to be difficult to find." She swung her feet down and started to rise. "Would you like a cup of coffee? It's decaf, but—"

"No, thanks." Cory gestured for her to sit back down. "Stay where you are. I don't want to disturb your peace."

"You're an adult. I always welcome adult interruptions. What brings you to the big house this morning?"

Cory lowered herself to the top step and leaned back against

the column. "I'm waiting for Ted. He's taking me to his folks'
place for Sunday dinner."

"Oh?" Ceejay's brow shot up, and her glance sharpened.

Embarrassment flooded her. "It's not what you think. We
have a bet going, and it's his turn for show and tell." Which
reminded her—she'd have to do the same soon. She cringed at
the thought of bringing him to the shabby trailer park where
she'd spent her childhood. At least she'd win their bet and get a
free lunch out of the humiliating bargain.

"My cousin is the sweetest guy you'll ever meet. He used to
pester me to death when we were kids, but if anyone tried to bully
or push me around, he was always the first to step up and protect
me. He's more a brother than cousin."

"Yeah, but he's still a guy." Cripes. She hadn't meant to blurt
that out loud. She turned away. "I mean—"

"No need to explain. I can't imagine how difficult things
must be for you right now."

Cory shrugged. She had no words to describe what it was
like. The constant anxiety, nightmares and fear, the disgust—the
weight of all that emotional drag gave her no peace. She frowned
as an unfamiliar pickup truck bounced along the gravel driveway. *Who's this?*

"Here's Ted." Ceejay sighed. "Look, I understand how you
feel about men right now."

Cory flashed her a doubtful look.

"But he's my cousin, and I love him. Don't be too hard on the
guy just because he's a man. He'd never do anything to hurt you
or anybody else."

"I know that." Ceejay's words stung. "You see me as someone
who—"

"No. I don't believe you'd intentionally hurt him. I just

know Ted." Ceejay stared into her coffee cup. "Gah! Don't listen to me. I'm pregnant, overemotional, and driven by my out-of-control hormones."

Ted parked the truck and got out. His smile blazed a trail straight for her. Caught in all that warmth, all Cory could do was stare back. Ceejay had warned her not to hurt him. She saw her as a threat. *Am I a threat?* Her throat tightened, and her eyes stung. Sergeant Dickhead had turned her into someone to be avoided, or suffer the collateral damage only the truly screwed up could inflict.

Ted stopped in front of the steps. He wore tight jeans and a button-down light-blue shirt that made his eyes look more blue than gray. He looked relaxed, fit and at home in his own skin. Cory's heart turned over and she forgot how to exhale. Ceejay had it all wrong. Ted wasn't in any danger. She was. How could she deal with the pull he exerted on her heart, when terror and revulsion pushed right back?

"Hey, cuz." He turned to Ceejay. "How're you feeling?"

"Good. Really good. I'm past the morning sickness phase and now we're on to the growing-larger-than-a-barn part." Ceejay patted her tummy. "How are you?"

"I'm good." He turned his high-wattage smile on Cory. "You ready to get tromped in our bet?"

"I keep telling you not to get your hopes up." She stood and smoothed her jeans down, trying to cover up the way he made her breathless. "When are you going to take me seriously?"

"Not today."

This was a bad idea. *Don't be too hard on him just because he's a man.* What did that even mean? He had all the power. Her eyes darted to the cab of his truck. Such a small space...too small. Trapped between Ceejay's warning, Ted's warm gaze and her own irrational, unreasonable fear, her heart pounded out a hazard warning, and her palms started to sweat. "I…uh…Maybe I should take a rain check on today."

Concern clouded Ted's expression. "What just happened?"

"Crap. This is my fault." Ceejay rose. "Forget I said anything, Cory. Please don't let my pregnancy-induced stupidity ruin your day."

Cory sucked in a breath and fought the unwanted sting of tears. *Do not cry in front of Ted. Do not.* She didn't need to appear any more messed up than she already did.

"What did you say to her?" Ted's voice was tinged with anger.

Great. Now she had guilt to add to her bag of crazy. No way did she want to come between Ted and his cousin. "She didn't say anything. It's just…" She glanced at the truck again and sucked in a breath. "The cab of your truck. It's…"

"It's just me, Cory." Ted came around to peer into her eyes. "Do you have your pepper spray?"

She nodded.

"Let me see it." He held out his hand.

She fished around in her purse, pulled out the leather-bound canister of safety and handed it over. He uncovered the nozzle, took her hand, and wrapped her fingers around the cylinder, placing her thumb over the top. She didn't recoil. Where was the instant revulsion, the disgust? Instead, his protective touch sent a rush of warmth through her—disorienting confusion hot on its trail.

"God, I'm sorry. I triggered this, and I know better." Ceejay placed her hand on Cory's shoulder. "What can I do?"

"You didn't *trigger* this." Cory shook her head and moved out of reach. "I…I don't want to keep going on about this. Please…"

"Right. Got it. Say hi to everyone for me, Ted." Ceejay headed up the stairs. "Tell your mom we'll make it to Sunday dinner next month for sure." She disappeared through the front door.

"Sit," Ted ordered. "And it might help if you breathed a little."

It might. Then again, it might not. She sat back down and concentrated on drawing breath.

Ted moved a safe distance away and placed his hands on his hips. "No rain checks. Today is the day. I'll wait right here until you're ready. Keep the pepper spray in your hand for the entire trip, and we'll open the windows in my truck so you don't feel closed in."

Oh, how she wished he didn't see her for the basket case she truly was. Wouldn't it be nice to be a normal woman basking in his attention? She might even flirt back if that were the case—but it wasn't. Sergeant Dickhead had broken her into a thousand dysfunctional pieces, and she had no idea how to put herself back together again. There was no glue for her kind of broken, and Ted deserved so much more, so much better. Any attraction she might feel toward him needed to be squelched right now. "You must think I'm crazy."

"Nope. I see you as traumatized. There's a big difference." He studied the gravel under his feet. "Noah and Ryan both went through therapy at the VA center. Do you think maybe seeing a therapist might help you?"

"I'm sure it would." Shame twisted her into a knot, and heat rose to her face. *Unfit to serve.* She swallowed hard.

"Noah and I are all about flexible hours to accommodate therapy, Cory. If you want—"

"I don't qualify for veteran's benefits. Thanks just the same." Her jaw clenched, and she couldn't meet his eyes.

"How do you not qualify?" He moved closer. "This is service related. Didn't you spend like, what, eight years in the service? I think that's what Noah said."

"Yes. Eight years." She shot up off the stairs. "Let's go. I don't want to make you late for your family's get-together." She hurried toward his truck, way too aware he followed close behind. She opened the passenger door and climbed in before he could help her, tracking his every move as he came around to the driver's side.

He started the truck down the gravel driveway and turned onto the two-lane highway. "You OK? Because a minute ago you were—"

"Sure," she lied and held up the hand with the pepper spray. "I'm all better now."

"So..."

"Let it go."

"Nothing that happened is a reflection on you, Cory. Putting your assailant behind bars proved that. Why don't you qualify for veteran's benefits?"

Her chest ached, and the familiar surge of outrage and hurt exploded in her gut. "Because according to the US Army, I have a *personality disorder*. I must have a personality disorder. Why else would I fight like hell to put my CO behind bars?" A choked, twisted laugh escaped. "After eight years of exemplary service, my country found me *unfit to serve* because I pushed to prosecute the man who raped me. I was less than honorably discharged. With a less-than-honorable discharge on my record, I don't qualify for benefits." She glared at him. "Satisfied?"

"Man, you were—"

"Yep. Screwed—in more ways than one." A few rebel tears escaped, and she turned her face toward the passing rural landscape. "I gave up my military career to put that rat bastard behind bars, and you know what?"

"What?"

"It was worth it. I wasn't about to let him hurt another woman the way he hurt me."

"You did the right thing. You have a lot of courage, and I

admire that. I'm glad he's in prison for what he did, but what are we going to do about getting you some help?"

"What are *we* going to do?" She sneaked a swipe at the escaped tears, hoping that her mascara hadn't smeared too badly. "Who is this *we*? I'm not your responsibility."

He glanced at her, his expression inscrutable. "*We* as in L&L."

"Oh. Right. Like the groceries." Her heart didn't just drop. Oh, no. It fell—hard enough to bounce off the carpeted floor of his truck. Not personal. This was another employee issue, a problem to be solved. She should feel relief. She didn't. "I have a team of law students working to get my army records straightened out. Once that's taken care of, I'll get my benefits back. I'm not L&L's responsibility either."

"How long will that take?"

"I don't know. A year. Twenty." She chuffed out an exasperated breath. "This is the US Army we're talking about. My case will get passed from desk to desk for as long as it takes for the problem to go away on its own." She sounded bitter, even to her own ears. They'd turned onto a dirt road, and she caught a glimpse of a farmhouse, a red barn and a number of outbuildings ahead. "Is that your parents' farm?"

"We could—"

"Stop, Ted. I don't want to talk about this anymore. I want to concentrate on winning the bet and sharing a meal with your very large extended family without freaking out."

"Hey, my family freaks me out all the time, so don't worry about that." One side of his mouth quirked up. "And you're going to lose this bet. Just wait."

She studied the surrounding fields of corn, soybeans and alfalfa. Pastoral and serene, she saw no evidence to support his claim. "Huh. I'm thinking I already won."

"We're upwind."

"Upwind?"

"Exactly." The white two-story farmhouse had a circular driveway in front, and several trucks and SUVs were already parked in a haphazard way. Ted pulled his truck behind an SUV and shut off the engine. "Ready?"

She nodded and started to get out of the truck. That's when it hit her—a stench so strong and pungent, her eyes watered. Covering her nose with her hand, she turned to him. "What is that awful smell?"

"Hogs." He flashed her a triumphant grin.

"I had no idea they smelled this bad."

He snorted. "What did you think pigs smelled like?"

"I don't know." She laughed. "Like smoked ham or maple-cured bacon?"

"Not hardly." He shook his head. "Speaking of ham, we'd better go inside. They're probably waiting on us to start eating." He walked toward the house. "I win, right? Imagine my adolescence. There weren't any girls in my high school interested in going out with a pig farmer's son. I suffered more than my share of taunts and rejection. Believe me."

"I'm not conceding anything." Cory stopped to survey their surroundings. A tributary to the Ohio River ran along a split-rail fence behind the house, where a profusion of trees, berry bushes and brush added to the lush green backdrop. "This isn't so bad. It's pretty here, and peaceful. Looks like a great place to grow up if you ask me."

"Yeah? I'm glad you think so." He opened the front door for her. "Prepare yourself for mayhem."

The house smelled wonderful, like Thanksgiving and Christmas all rolled into one. The savory smell of a roasting turkey, some kind of fruit pie and other mouthwatering scents erased the awful stench of the hogs. Off to the side of the entry-way, a parlor held a large TV with video game equipment. Kids of varying ages lay sprawled on the floor or slouched on the sectional couch. Some of them played cards or board games while others concentrated on the video game. She counted eight.

"Some of my nieces and nephews," Ted whispered in her ear, just as a chorus of greetings arose.

He guided her through the house, introducing her to his sisters, brothers, uncles, aunts and a few of his cousins. She greeted them all, but none of the names stuck. They finally ended up in the kitchen, where Jenny, her husband and two other women were setting platters and dishes of food on a long counter.

"There you are," a woman with salt-and-pepper hair cut in a stylish bob greeted them. She held a platter piled high with sliced turkey and set it on the counter beside a ceramic bowl of mashed potatoes and a matching pitcher filled with gravy.

"Cory, this is my mom. Mom, this is Cory Marcel."

Ted placed his hand at the small of her back, sending a shiver through her—a pleasant sensation, not one of disgust. Disconcerted, she moved forward a step. "It's nice to meet you, Mrs. Lovejoy. Thank you for including me today. Is there something I can do to help?"

"We're happy to have you. For starters you can call me Mary." The corners of her soft brown eyes creased. "Then you can help gather the throng. We're ready to eat."

As if on cue, Ted's family drifted into the kitchen, jostled into some semblance of a line and loaded their plates. Gradually, they all found spots at the long dining room table. A couple of card tables had been set at either end for the overflow, and Cory found a spot at one of them. Surrounded by Ted's family, by the good smells, constant banter and laughter, she couldn't prevent the surge of envy that overtook her.

What would it be like to be surrounded by a large loving family like his, with uncles and aunts, cousins, nieces and nephews? For as long as she could remember, it had always been just her, her mom, and their one constant companion: hard times. She'd never been to a family dinner like this. Ever. She faced Ted, who sat beside her, and whispered, "You lose."

🐏　🐏　🐏

Ted looked deep into Cory's doe eyes. His insides melted—right there in the folding chair in his parents' dining room for everyone to see. Longing slammed into him like a sucker punch to the gut, and all he could manage was to stare stupidly back. Man, he wanted to kiss her—wanted to put his arms around her and hold her close until everything was right in her world. "Why is that?"

"Look around you, Ted. You grew up with all of *this*." She tilted her head toward the crowded table. "I don't care how the place smells, you have no idea how good you have it."

He followed the path of her gaze as she looked around the table. Yeah, he had a large, noisy, nosy family, but it did little to assuage the gaping hole in his center. He yearned for something more, something intimate shared with one woman. His woman.

Being around Cory sharpened that yearning to an unbearable point. Was it simply having someone beside him that set it off, or was it *Cory specific*? He hardly knew her. More than likely loneliness triggered his reaction, and he'd feel this way no matter who sat beside him. He'd been alone for too long. That's all.

She leaned closer to grab a saltshaker, and he felt her warmth and caught a whiff of her clean, sweet scent. His eyes trailed along the graceful line of her neck to the delicate curve where it met her shoulder. Had he thought her merely pretty? Because right now, with her hair framing her face in feathery wisps, and her expression open and friendly, he realized his mistake. Corinna Marcel was beautiful. His groin tightened and his pulse raced.

Nope. She wasn't an *idea*. Something about her called to him, and he couldn't tear his eyes away. She glanced at him sideways, frowning when she caught him staring.

"Are you my uncle's girlfriend?" his ten-year-old nephew, Ben, asked from across the table. The room grew quiet as all ears strained to hear Cory's response.

"Um…" Her face turned a lovely shade of pink.

Ben stared at her. "He's never brought a girl home for Sunday dinner before."

Every eye in the room fixed on them. Ted leaned close and whispered, "You lose."

She shot him a disgruntled look and turned to Ben. "I just moved to Perfect. I work for your uncle at Langford & Lovejoy, and he's been kind enough to help me get to know the area." She met the curious looks around the table. "We just met."

Ben's eyes narrowed with that dog-with-a-bone look Ted had seen a few too many times. His nephew wasn't going to let it go.

"Yeah, but he's never brought a—"

"Benjy," Jenny called down the table. "Pass the peas, and put your mouth to better use. Let our guest eat in peace."

The tension in the room dissolved, and Ted shot his aunt a grateful look. He settled back, played with his food and watched Cory devour hers. Good. She needed the calories. The rest of the meal and the ensuing cleanup would take way too long as far as he was concerned. He wanted alone time with Cory, and it couldn't come fast enough.

After dinner, she pitched in with the rest of his family to help with the cleanup. His eyes kept straying back to her as he folded up the card tables and lowered the extensions on the dining room table. She, Jenny, his mom and his sisters were chatting up a storm as they put leftovers away and loaded the dishwasher. He'd never seen her so relaxed, and relaxed looked good on her. Hearing her laughter and seeing the happy expression lighting her eyes—it did his heart good to see her enjoying herself.

"She seems like a nice girl." His dad came up beside him. "Are you two dating?"

"Not really." Ted grabbed the two card tables to take them to the storage space under the front stairs.

His dad followed. "But you'd like to. Am I right?"

"Yeah, but I don't think she's interested in dating." He placed the card tables in their customary place and shut the door. "It's complicated."

"So I heard. Jenny shared a little of Cory's story with your mom and me. It's plain to anyone bothering to notice that she likes you, son."

"Dad." Ted straightened. "I'm pretty damned tired of being *liked*." Whoa. Where had that come from? He and his father were close, but Ted never shared how lonely and unhappy he sometimes felt.

"I know." His father's mouth turned up. "Still, for a woman who's gone through what she's been through, like is a good place to start, right?"

"Sure." He sighed. "I'd better get her home. I'll be back to help with chores later this afternoon."

"Take your time."

Extricating Cory from the covey of Lovejoy women took some doing. His mother made it clear she expected Cory to come again, and Jenny reminded her to visit the diner anytime. They packed leftovers for her, insisting she accept them. His sisters, mom and aunts said their good-byes and he finally managed to get her out the front door.

"You have a wonderful family, Ted. They're all so down-to-earth and friendly."

"They are. Sometimes too friendly. This was only part of the Lovejoy clan. Noah and his bunch join us every couple months, and I have relatives who live a distance away. They make it home every six months or so. We're a tight-knit group." He turned to survey their surroundings. It had been awhile since he'd given it much thought. This was home, that's all. He couldn't imagine living anywhere else. "Are you interested in seeing the piglets while we're here?"

Her face lit up. "Sure. Let me leave my stuff in your truck first."

He opened the door and took her things, placing them in the backseat. "The building off to the left is where the sows with new litters stay, and the next one over is for the weanlings." Fighting the overwhelming need to take her hand, he continued to tell her about the farm. "We grow corn, soybeans and a mix of alfalfa and clover. The corn and soybeans provide a lot of the feed for the hogs, and we sell the hay."

"When you say *we*, do you mean you help with the farming?"

"I do. My folks are getting older, and they need the help. All my siblings have families and jobs, and they don't live close enough to help on a regular basis. They help out when they can, but it's mostly just me and my dad, and occasionally a hired hand or two."

"Let me get this straight." Her brow creased. "You work more than full-time at L&L, you just finished your master's degree, *and* you help your dad keep this farm going?"

"That's right."

Her eyes widened. "How do you do it all?"

"I don't know. I just do." This was his life, and he'd never known anything different. It just was. He opened the sliding door. "This is called the farrowing barn. It's not so bad in here smellwise." They walked through the rows of aisles where piglets had free access to the sows lounging around in their stalls.

Cory approached one of the pens, knelt down and reached out a hand with a look of wonder on her face. The piglets hurried over, nosing her outstretched hand, looking for some tidbit she might offer. "Oh, my God, they are so cute." She turned her face up to beam up at him. "It's hard to believe something this tiny and adorable grows into something so big and stinky." She scratched a particularly bold piglet behind the ear. "Can I pick one up?"

"Go ahead and give that a try." He chuckled. "Good luck."

She reached for a piglet, only to have it squeal and run back to the protection of its sow. Trying to catch a different one and then another yielded much the same result, until the sow stood up to put an end to the disturbance. Cory laughed, rose from the floor and dusted off her jeans. "I guess not. *Charlotte's Web* made it look so easy."

"That's why they call it fiction. Are you ready to go?"

"Yeah, I guess." She sighed. "I had a great time this afternoon, and I'm more sure than ever I'm going to enjoy lunch at the truck stop on your dime."

"We'll see."

"That's right, we will, and it's a done deal in my favor." She slid the door open and stepped out into the yard. "Do you commute to the farm from town?"

"Nope." He pointed to another small building. "Noah and I built an apartment over the machine garage over there. Do you want to see my place? It's pretty nice, considering it started out as a storage space." As soon as the words were out of his mouth, Ted realized he'd blown it.

Cory's face went into wary mode, and her mouth tightened into a straight line. "Uh…"

Damn. He'd forgotten. She'd been so happy, so relaxed, and he'd ruined it for her. Angry at himself, and even angrier at the man who'd hurt her, he swore under his breath. "It's just *me*, Cory."

"What do you mean when you say that?" she snapped. "You say it like you think you don't count or something."

"I don't. You heard Paige. I'm harmless." He raked his fingers through his hair and turned away. "I'm no threat to you or to anybody else. You see how it is at work. I'm the *kid*, the one person nobody has to take seriously—or respect." *Damn, get a grip.* First his outburst with his dad, and now this. He'd just blurted his worst insecurities to the one woman he wanted more than anything to impress. *Great job, kid.*

"Oh." Her eyebrows rose.

"Oh?" That couldn't be good. Her tone said she'd just figured something out. What? What did she know that he didn't, and why did he get the feeling he'd blown any chance he'd ever had at being *the man* in her eyes? "What does that mean?" She stared out over the field of soybeans, and he could almost see her mind putting puzzle pieces together. What puzzle? There was nothing puzzling about him. Nothing. His mouth went dry, and his armpits had the opposite reaction.

She glanced up at him. "If it makes you feel any better, I see you as a threat."

"Hell, no, that doesn't make me feel better." He jammed his hands deep into his back pockets and headed for his truck. "You're the one person I don't want to see me that way," he muttered.

"What?" She picked up her pace until she strode along beside him. "Why?"

Shit. Good question. "Because…because, um—"

Cory stopped in her tracks. "Because I'm the troubled employee—your work problem to solve? You don't want my fear to affect my *productivity*. Is that it?"

"What the hell are you talking about?"

She shrugged and averted her eyes. "Like the groceries, the stun gun and pepper spray. Hungry, frightened employees are less productive."

Her eyes rose to meet his for a heartbeat, and the hurt he glimpsed there went right through him. "I—"

"It's all right. I get it." Starting off toward his truck, she squared her shoulders. "I'm not as flighty or as fragile as you might think. Or I didn't used to be, anyway. I'm suffering a delayed reaction to everything that happened because I haven't had time to process it is all. That's fairly common with PTSD." She swung his truck door open and climbed in. "I'm not going to freak out or run away, and you don't have to walk around on eggshells when you're with me. Don't forget. I was a soldier for eight years."

"Ah, yes. The exclusive I'm-a-veteran-and-you're-not *club*." Sunday dinner felt like a brick in his stomach. "I'm familiar."

Once he settled into the driver's seat, she flashed him a disgruntled look. "That's not what I meant, Ted."

"Whatever." The knot tightening his chest made breathing difficult. The day had started out so well. How had it gone to hell so quickly? Why were things spewing out of his mouth like he had a busted filter?

"I just meant I'm tougher than you think."

"I'm sure you are." He gripped the steering wheel. "The groceries and stuff? I wanted to do those things for you. Just for the record, Noah said you wouldn't accept them if I made it seem personal. If it were up to me, you wouldn't be paying me back for any of it." He glanced at her. Color rose to her cheeks, and her mouth formed a surprised O. Was she pleased or dismayed? He couldn't tell. "How tough are you?"

Her brow furrowed. "Why do you ask?"

Might as well go for broke, since he'd already ruined the day. "Kyle asked Brenda out for a date."

Confusion clouded her face. "Yeah, so?"

"Brenda said she'd only go out with him if it was a double date with you. Kyle asked me to be your date." He turned to catch the play of emotions dancing across her face. None of them resembled *tough*. "Any idea why she'd do that?"

Cory looked everywhere but at him. "Because she's a bossy, meddling, pushy friend who *thinks* she's helping me." Her lips compressed into a straight line. "It's something we used to do when we were in high school. I'll explain, but only after you've seen where I grew up. Don't want to tip my hand in the big wager and all. You don't have to do this, Ted. I'm sure Kyle and Brenda will do fine without us." She propped an elbow on the window frame and rested her chin on her fist, turning to face the countryside.

"But I want to. We're going bowling. I enjoy bowling immensely. So, again—how tough are you?"

"I don't want to date you...or anybody." She tensed. "It's not you, it's just—"

"Fair enough. I get it." Even if it did suck the *hopeful* right out of his Sunday. "We can go as friends. I never said anything about wanting to date you either. Kyle asked me to do this favor, and I said I'd talk to you about it."

"As friends, then. Nothing more."

Damn. He'd just set himself up for an evening of torture. "Right. Nothing more."

CHAPTER FIVE

HER AFTERNOON WITH TED STILL fresh in her mind, Cory sat on the couch in her apartment and held her cell phone to her ear. Might as well get the bet thing settled once and for all. After she made arrangements with her mom, she'd have the rest of her Sunday for laundry and getting ready for the coming week. "Hey, Mom, how are you?"

"I'm good, baby. You still enjoyin' that new job?"

"I am." She realized with a start that she meant it. She really liked her job and the freedom L&L gave her to do it her way. "It's challenging, and the people I work with are great. In fact that's one of the reasons I'm calling. I have a favor to ask."

"Oh?"

"Would you be interested in having some company for dinner one evening this week? It would be me and a friend." Her mother's resources were limited, and asking for anything sent guilt pinging through her. "I'll pay you back for whatever you spend, and once I get my next paycheck, I want to take you out to dinner somewhere nice."

"You don't need to pay me back, honey. I gotta eat anyway, which also means I gotta cook. Besides, I'd love to have you home for supper, and I'm always happy to meet your friends. Is she someone from work?"

"He. It's a *he*, Mom." She braced herself, knowing her mom would jump to the wrong conclusion.

"Well, that's even better." Claire's tone rose to an enthusiastic pitch. "I'm off this comin' Wednesday."

"Ted is my boss. We're just friends." Even if she longed for more, it wasn't meant to be. "I owe him. He gave me an advance on my salary so I could stock up on groceries, and…um." Did she really want to tell her about the pepper spray, the stun gun, or the bet? No. Especially not the bet part. Her mom had done the best she could, and Cory didn't want to hurt her feelings. "He's been really welcoming and helpful. I want you to meet the man who started Langford & Lovejoy Heritage Furniture, and I want him to meet you." With another start, she realized this was the truth. "I'll bring dessert."

Her mother was the sweetest, most generous and hardworking soul in the world, and she'd raised her only daughter right. Claire Marcel hadn't had access to higher education, and it wasn't her fault she'd lost her husband in a war overseas. She'd been left a single parent struggling to make ends meet, moving to Indiana to be close to Cory's paternal grandparents. Her mom had hoped her in-laws could help her out, but they hadn't been much better off. Babysitting had been the only support they could offer, and they did so willingly, glad to spend time with their only grandchild, especially since they'd lost their only son.

"All right. I know just what I'm gonna make. I'm lookin' forward to seeing you and this new friend of yours." Her voice wavered. "It does my heart good to know you're nearby and doin' so good."

"Don't worry about me, Mom." The backs of her eyes stung.

"Things are going great, and I'm feeling better every day. If Ted is free that evening, we'll be by around six. I'll call tomorrow and let you know." They said their good-byes and hung up, and Cory busied herself with cleaning and preparing for the week ahead, keeping occupied until bedtime.

She settled on the recliner and opened her laptop to check her e-mail, looking for any word from the Yale law clinic. Her nightly ritual—she ended each day hoping for news that would... what? Free her? Not likely, but checking every day had become her obsession, and every day she hoped for good news, news with the power of vindication.

She shut her laptop and leaned back, closing her eyes. Nothing today. *Unfit to serve.* The bitter disappointment darkened her otherwise bright, shiny day, one of the best she'd had for a long, long time. Steering her mind in another direction, she pictured the piglets she'd tried to hold. Their wiggly bodies darting zigzags through the barn brought a smile to her face. Ted's smug expression, his gray eyes alight with amusement flashed through her mind. Her breath caught. Such a great guy, if only she weren't damaged goods.

Her thoughts started to drift, and she rubbed her tired eyes. She should get up, get ready for bed. Instead, she remained where she was, her mind taking her back, going over everything for the thousandth time. Lord, she wished she could've changed the outcome...done something differently...The memory took hold, and she was back in Afghanistan, back in base camp with its neverending grit blowing into everything...

"Go out with me, Marcel. I'll treat you right." Staff Sergeant *Barnett crowded her space, backing her into a corner of his cramped office, running his hands up and down her arms while his eyes raked over her with lascivious intensity.*

Shivers of revulsion followed the path of his gaze, and goose bumps covered her forearms. "We've had this discussion before, and I haven't changed my mind. Thanks, but no." She tried to slip by, tried to put some space between them. "You're my commanding officer. It wouldn't be appropriate."

He grabbed her wrist before she could get away. "That's right. I'm your goddamned CO, so you gotta do what I tell you to, soldier. I'm telling you I want you. One way or another, I'm going to have you. Now, you can make this easy, and we can have some fun, or you can make things difficult for yourself. What's it gonna be?"

"No, thank you, SIR!" She jerked her wrist out of his grasp. "Leave me alone." Not waiting for his reply, she hurried toward the commissary, a more populated area on base. Note to self: carry your handgun with you at all times, and always move around camp with someone you trust. Barnett had a reputation—all bad. She'd seen what happened to women who reported abuse—passed up for promotions, demoted, given the lousiest possible assignments or worse. The best she could do was to be prepared, and stay far, far away...

Cory jerked back to the present, guilt and shame pulsing through her. She hadn't followed her own advice. Sergeant Dickhead had left her alone, and she'd believed he'd moved on, targeting easier prey, or at least focusing on someone more willing.

Wrong.

Her skin crawled, and her stomach lurched. She shot up and beat a hasty path for the bathroom, barely making it before the dry heaves hit. Leaning over the toilet, she tried once again to purge herself of the violation. No good. Heaving didn't help. His vile pollution remained intact and dead center—the fulcrum of her life.

She straightened, turned on the shower full blast, stripped

and stepped under the scalding spray. What would Ted think of her now? How would he react if he saw her bent over the toilet, retching her guts out? She had no business spending time with him. The army had it wrong. She wasn't unfit to serve. She was unfit to relate. Unfit to carry on in any kind of **normal** way with the rest of the population.

Once the bet and the bowling night were done, she'd explain to Ted what a mistake it would be to continue putting himself anywhere in her proximity. Yep. That's what she'd do. The sudden, burning constriction in her chest brought tears to her eyes. No matter. They merged with the rest of the water pouring down the drain—one more failed attempt to rid herself of the fetid reminder of the violence infecting her soul.

"How was yesterday's dinner with the Lovejoys?" Paige swept into their office. Dropping her purse into a drawer, she took her seat. "Overwhelming and smelly? Did Ted win the bet?"

"Not by a long shot." Cory snorted. "Ted has an amazing family, and their farm is really pretty. I loved it despite the stench, and after awhile, you don't even notice the hog smell. There are so many good things about his home and family, the hogs don't carry much weight. He's lucky to have grown up where he did."

"Huh." Paige pursed her lips. "If you say so. Were Noah and Ceejay there?"

"No." Ceejay's warning came back to her in a rush of hurt pride.

"Hey," Paige murmured. "What's wrong?"

She hesitated, wondering how much she wanted to share. At the same time, it would be good to get another perspective, and Paige knew everybody so much better than she did. "Ceejay warned me not to hurt Ted. It kind of came out of nowhere, and…" It still stung.

"Oh." Paige flashed her a sympathetic look. "There's history there, and it involves L&L. Ted was only twenty-one when I moved to Perfect. He had a crush on me back then. He kept asking me out and trying to convince me we'd be great together. And—"

"You fell for Ryan."

"Yeah, I sure did. I couldn't help myself. It's that whole cowboy thing he's got going on and those tortured blue eyes of his." Her hand splayed over her baby bump, and she sighed.

"Tortured?" Cory frowned. "I've never seen him looking anything but cocky and content."

"He's fine now, but he was in pretty bad shape when he got here. He'd lost someone very important to him before he enlisted, and then his best friend died before his eyes in the same bombing that took Noah's leg. One morning I found Ryan passed out with a gun and a suicide letter on the coffee table beside him."

Shocked, Cory sucked in a breath. "Wow, you'd never know it to see him today. How…" She had to take another calming breath before she could continue. Knowing Ryan had been to the point of suicide, and seeing him today, sent a flare of hope burning through her. "How'd he get better?"

"He started therapy and fell in love." Paige's eyes filled with a dreamy look. "If you ask me, mostly it was the falling-in-love part."

"Humph." The flare of hope sputtered out. She couldn't afford therapy, and love wasn't going to happen for her. How could it? Even the thought of physical intimacy made her nauseous and anxious. A shudder racked through her.

Paige raised a single perfectly shaped eyebrow. "Don't under-estimate the healing power of love, Cory."

"My situation is different." Her jaw tightened, and she had to bite back against the familiar rage that always sprang up with claws extended whenever the subject of her rape came up. Her hand balled into fists where they rested on the desk.

"No doubt, but don't close yourself off to..." Paige glanced at her for a second before continuing. "Anyway, Ted took it pretty hard. I feel bad about the whole thing, but I never encouraged him in any way. In fact I made it very clear I had no interest in him that way." She shrugged. "Ted is the kind of man who falls hard and fast. You're new to L&L, and other than me you're the only female here. Plus, you're a knockout. I'm sure Ceejay is just being overly sensitive on his behalf, but he's a grown man. He doesn't need his cousin looking out for him."

"You're probably right." Concentrating on her breathing, she forced herself back into calmer territory. "Ceejay said her hormones are wacky and not to listen to her." Still, she couldn't shake the hurt. She'd never been the kind of person to toy with anyone's emotions.

"It's true. Pregnancy hormones can be a bitch. I'd love to see Ted happily involved with someone. We all would. Anyway, he and Ryan didn't get along back then." Paige brightened, her face relaxing into an easy smile. "The situation caused a lot of tension between them, but that's all in the past."

Is it? More of the puzzle clicked into place, and a surge of protectiveness for Ted welled up out of nowhere. "Do you and Ryan spend a lot of time with him socially?"

"Sure. We all spend time together." Her expression turned pensive. "For work events, anyway. Come to think of it, outside of employee get-togethers, not so much. A bunch of the younger couples in Perfect play poker once a month. Ryan and I go, and so do Ceejay and Noah. Ted never comes, even though we invite him all the time."

"Probably because it's a couples' thing."

"Yeah, probably." Paige set the catalog proofs in front of her to begin copyediting.

Cory settled back into uploading the new furniture photos to update their website. Footsteps in the hall drew her attention, and she glanced up just as Ted stopped at their door.

He leaned against the door frame, and the warmth in his eyes aimed straight for her heart. "Good morning, ladies." He nodded to Paige, and brought his gaze back to her. "Have you recovered from yesterday's Lovejoy overload?"

"I had a great time." Heat crept up to her face, and her pulse raced. "And if you're free Wednesday evening, I think we can declare a winner to our wager this week."

His eyes widened for a second, and one side of his mouth twitched up. "It just so happens, I'm free this Wednesday."

"Good. In that case, we're having dinner with my mother. I told her we'd be there around six."

"I'm looking forward to meeting her."

"Just so you know, my mother is amazing. She's not the issue. It's where I grew up that is going to win the bet for me." Oh, Lord, could she sound more defensive?

"Just so *you* know." He straightened off the door frame. "It never entered my mind that your mom is anything but great."

His tone had taken on the calm, even cadence he always used when she had one of her minimeltdowns. She didn't know whether to feel grateful or mortified. Her cheeks flamed even hotter, and all she could do was nod.

"Staff meeting in ten?" He turned back to Paige.

"Yep. I just have to print out the agenda."

"See you in a few." He continued on down the hall to his office.

Cory blew out the breath she hadn't realized she'd been holding.

Paige frowned at her. "What was that all about?"

"Defensiveness."

"What on earth do you have to feel defensive about?" Paige's eyes lit up and she let out a laugh. "Ted grew up knee-deep in hog poop."

"He lives on a little slice of heaven surrounded by a large, loving family. Have you ever seen a piglet? They're so cute, you just want to pick them up and hug them." Cory studied her computer screen. "I grew up in a shabby trailer park on the seedy side of town, the product of multigenerational poverty in a single-head-of-household family."

"And yet you turned out great. It's going to be a tie, and you're in luck." Paige grinned. "I get the tiebreaker vote, which is totally swinging your way. You and I have got to stick together in this testosterone-laden environment."

"Or we could just leave it a tie and forget the whole thing."

"Not going to happen, kiddo."

"Probably not," Cory conceded. Paige's good humor and warmth radiated toward her, and the bunched muscles between Cory's shoulder blades relaxed. "Do I have to go to the staff meeting, or is it mostly for employees with fancy titles?" She'd attended for the first two weeks, only because she still needed to learn the extent of her responsibilities. Most of what they discussed now had nothing to do with her, and she had better things to do with her time. More productive things, like call Brenda and set her straight on her tendency to meddle.

"It's optional. Mostly it's to keep the lines of communication open between departments. Someone has to keep things coordinated and moving in the same direction, and as it turns out, I'm that someone. Project manager is another one of my many titles here. I make sure everyone gives an update and that everything continues to move in the right direction. The guys wouldn't know who was doing what otherwise."

She rose from her chair and gathered the papers spitting out of the small printer they kept in their office. "It's something we started when I came on board, and I suspect it'll lapse while I'm on maternity leave." She frowned. "Maybe I'll bring that up this morning. Would you be willing to see to it that the meetings continue while I'm gone? By the time I go on leave, you'll be comfortable with everything, and you can be the project manager for a while."

"Sure." This would give her another way to contribute, and maybe by the time Paige went on her leave, Cory could push a little more for her own agenda. She wanted to be the one in charge of updating their systems and procedures.

"Great. I'll let the guys know." Paige stopped at the door. "I'm glad you took this job, Cory. Having you here has made a huge difference for me, and it's really nice having another woman to talk to during the day."

Warmth filled her, and she smiled back at Paige. "I'm glad too. Thanks." Once Paige left, she pulled her cell phone out and hit speed dial. Brenda didn't start her workday until eleven in the morning, and Cory wanted to settle a few things before they went on their double date. They weren't teenagers battling the trailer trash stigma anymore.

"Hey, Cory." Brenda picked up on the third ring, her voice raspy with sleep. "This better be important, because I haven't had any coffee yet."

"It is. What are you up to?" The other side of the line went quiet for a few seconds. "Well?"

Brenda yawned loudly. "It's too early in the morning for this, and my crystal ball is cracked. What is it we're talking about again?"

"I'm referring to this double date business with Kyle."

"Oh…he actually came through on that?" She sounded way too pleased with herself. "I didn't think he would."

"Again. What are you up to?"

"It's time you got back on that proverbial horse, Cory. Plus, Kyle is so shy with me, I'm hoping having another couple along will help him relax. I'm *up to* killing two birds with one stone." Another pause stretched between them. "I'm trying to help."

"I don't need that kind of help." A lie, straight out, but dammit, she needed time to get her head straight. Once she had her benefits back, she'd sign up for therapy at the VA center. Maybe in a year or two she'd be in a place where her center of gravity had returned, and she could think about dating then. Not now. "Don't do this again, Brenda. You've put me in an awkward position."

"Who did Kyle ask to be your date?"

"Ted Lovejoy, and it's not a date for us. We're doing it as a favor for Kyle, and because Ted enjoys bowling."

"Yeah? Is he the hottie with all that curly blond hair?" Brenda sounded plenty awake now. "The nonveteran I met the afternoon I picked you up, right?"

Cory frowned. She didn't like all that enthusiasm for Ted coming from her best friend. "Yes, and he's my *boss*. I don't want to mess anything up with my job, so this is a one-time deal. Got it?"

"This is perfect. If things don't work out between me and shy guy, I'm going for Ted." She chuckled. "Good job, Kyle."

"Absolutely not!" Cory's heart leapfrogged to her throat, and her palms itched. "Ted Lovejoy is off-limits."

"Why? I'm single. He's single." Brenda huffed. "I'm twenty-seven years old and ready to settle down and start a family. I'm tired of the singles scene. Ted is a business owner, and he seems like a really nice guy. Nice guys are hard to come by." Another pause. "You just said you don't want to date him, so...what's the problem?"

Jealousy and panic chased around inside her like a dog after its own tail. Hadn't she sworn to tell Ted she didn't want to spend so much time with him? What plausible reason could she give Brenda that wouldn't reveal her own jumbled feelings? Thinking about Ted dating anyone else sent her into another kind of melt-down altogether, and she wasn't prepared to deal with it. Damn, she was in all kinds of trouble—too scared to connect, and too desperate to let go.

"There's no problem, other than this job means a lot to me. I don't want any awkwardness or hard feelings. If you date him, and it doesn't work out, it'll make things difficult for me and Wesley. He needs this place as much as I do." Oh, that was lame, bringing Brenda's brother into this. She took another long breath to steady the nerves playing bumper car in her middle. "Do me this favor, Brenda."

"I don't know, Cory. You're asking a lot. What if he's the one? What if I date Ted and things go really well? It could happen. Don't assume the worst."

No! "Maybe Kyle's the one. Have you already written the poor guy off just because Ted is *my* date for bowling night?"

"Huh. A minute ago you said it wasn't a date. Now it is?"

"I've got to get back to work. I'll talk to you later." Her heart racing, and her mouth as dry as a saltine cracker, Cory hit End Call on her very best friend in the world. *Wonderful.*

❦   ❦   ❦

Now that Cory had taken over shipping, Ted had more time on his hands. He'd missed the production end of things, the deep satisfaction that came from creating something of value with his own two hands. The artistry and craftsmanship part of this business was what kept him going. He wrapped up what he'd been working on and headed down the front stairs, eager to take on a new project.

"Hey, kid," Kyle greeted him. The rest of the production crew nodded and smiled before going back to what they were doing.

"Hey." Ted took the most recent order out of the wall-mounted tray. A cradle. Good, and this one was in the sleek, new contemporary style—deceptively plain, but a challenge skillwise. Just what he wanted, a project he could get lost in. He eyeballed the bins holding their lumber supply. They had just enough bird's-eye maple to fill the order. "I thought you weren't going to call me kid anymore."

"I forgot. It's habit." Kyle leaned closer, lowering his voice. "So…how'd it go yesterday?"

"It went great." Payback was a rare commodity for him, and he planned to stretch it out. He moved away, heading for the sliding trays where their patterns were stored. After placing the cradle pattern on the drawing table, he gathered the lumber, choosing his pieces carefully and oh so slowly.

Kyle followed, fidgeting with the mallet he held in his hands. "And?"

"And what? We ate, I took her to the barn to see the piglets, and then I drove her home. No big deal." Ted glanced at Kyle over his shoulder. "Are you interested in what we had for supper? My mom roasted a turkey, and we had mashed potatoes, gravy, peas with pearl onions—"

"I don't care about what you ate." Kyle frowned. "Did you ask her?"

"My mom?" He raised his brow. "Ask her what?"

"Damn, kid." Kyle looked like his world was about to end. "Don't tell me you forgot."

Ted bristled. Hadn't he just mentioned the kid thing? "I didn't *forget* anything."

"What'd she say?"

Oh, it was tempting to keep him guessing, but Kyle really was an OK guy, and he had enough on his plate without Ted adding to his misery. "Cory agreed to go out for bowling and pizza."

Kyle's shoulders sagged with relief. "Great. I'll set it up."

"Not for this weekend. I'm tied up." A lie, but he didn't want Cory to feel pursued. Wednesday with her mom right after Sunday with his family was already pushing it. Come to think of it, they were doing things all backward. Usually a couple dated for a while before introducing their families. But…she didn't know they were dating, so it was all good.

"How about the following weekend, like Saturday night?"

"Sure. That'll work." He laid the lumber out on the drawing table and began tracing the pattern. Kyle continued to hover in his space. Ted straightened, frowning at him. "Don't you have work to do?"

"Yeah." Kyle shifted his weight but stayed put. "I was just wondering…" Another shift. "Did Cory say anything about Brenda? You know, like…anything that might be good for me to know?"

"Nope. Believe it or not, you two were *not* our primary topic of conversation. Cory was more interested in the pigs than she was in your budding romance with her friend." Ted chuffed out a laugh and shook his head. "Go back to work."

"Right."

Kyle stomped off, leaving Ted free to think about his own budding romance. Lord help him if Cory realized that's how he saw what was going on between them. Stealth. He needed stealth and a light tread. So light she wouldn't even notice the direction his steps were taking. Somehow, he'd work his way around her defenses and gain her trust before she even realized what was happening. A stupid smile broke free. Wednesday couldn't come fast enough.

"Uh-oh." Ryan stepped into the room with a new pattern in his hands. "I've worn that look a time or two, kid."

Damn. Ted's smile disappeared. "What the hell are you talking about now? I'm just happy to spend some time in production. Sitting at a desk all day is wearing."

"Sure." Ryan cocked an eyebrow and snorted. "I hear you brought L&L's newest out to meet your folks yesterday. Must have gone well for you to wear the I-can't-keep-the-dumb-ass-grin-off-my-face look this morning."

"As usual, you're full of shit." Every eye in the room fixed on him. So much for stealth. "Where's Noah?"

"He and Paige left for Evansville about a half hour ago." Ryan slid a shelf out and laid the new pattern down with care. He slid the slip of card stock out of the metal bracket on the front of the shelf, wrote the pattern name and number on it with the Sharpie they kept on top and slipped it back into place. "Remember? They're checking out a few retail sites today, and then he's picking up a load of oak and maple before they head back."

"Oh, right." Of course he remembered. All purchase orders went through him.

"What're you starting?" Ryan moved closer to peer at the pattern. "Nice. That design with bird's-eye maple is going to be stellar. Let's take a few pictures before we ship this one."

"Good idea. This will be the first project for me in the new contemporary line." Happy that he could redirect Ryan so easily, he threw in a bit of insurance. "Great design work, by the way."

"Thanks." Ryan's eyes lit up, and he warmed to the subject. "Have you taken a look at the new bedroom suite prototype we just finished? It's still set up on the third floor. It has the same deceptively simple lines as the contemporary children's furniture."

"I saw it in production, but not all put together. I'll be sure to take a look." Relieved, Ted turned back to his project. Ryan circulated, sharing a few words with each of the guys before heading back to his office. Once he left, Ted let the dumb-ass grin break out again, his thoughts focused on the real project on hand—Corinna Marcel.

"Don't get your hopes up about supper." Cory buckled her seat belt and leaned back into the passenger seat of Ted's pickup. She placed her hands on the plastic box on her lap, holding it down like it might make a leap for the window. "My mom is not a gourmet cook. She's mastered the art of the slow cooker, and that's about it."

Her brow was scrunched into worry creases, and Ted fought the urge to place a reassuring hand on her knee. "I'm sure whatever she's made will be fine. What's in the container?"

"I told mom I'd bring dessert." She lifted the box slightly. "I made lemon bars last night."

"I love lemon bars." He backed the truck out of his spot behind L&L and inched down the alley toward the street.

"Do you?" Her brow unscrunched. "Me too. They're my favorite. I have a whole collection of lemon bar recipes, and this is the best of the bunch."

"Great. Now I've got to worry about drooling while driving." He turned onto the main street out of town. Cory's shy grin peeked out for an instant, lighting her face and squeezing all the air from his lungs.

"I don't think we'll be pulled over for drooling over the speed limit," she teased. "Do you want one now?"

"Heck, yeah." His brow shot up. "Is that legal? Tasting dessert before we have dinner?"

"I won't tell if you don't." She tugged at the lip of the lid, and a wave of lemony scent filled the cab. "So long as we hide the evidence, I think we'll be fine."

"Got it. No crumbs on this shirt, ma'am." He accepted a rectangle of gooey goodness dusted with powdered sugar and took a bite. The tartness of fresh lemons topping the sweet cookie crust burst inside his mouth in a symphony of flavor. "Oh, yeah." He shot her an appreciative look. "You can cook."

"Lemon bars, anyway." She stuck her tongue out, sliding it along her lower lip to catch a few crumbs from her own bit of indulgence.

He followed the path her tongue took, imagining the sweet, warm moistness of the inside of her delectable mouth. Right now she'd taste lemony and tart. Ted's blood raced, setting a course straight for his groin. *Not good.* If she caught a glimpse of his reaction to her, she'd freak and that's the last thing he wanted. He popped the rest of the bar into his mouth, focused on chewing and studied the road straight ahead of him. *Asphalt. Broken white lines. Gravel...*

"You were going to tell me about the double-date thing you have going on with Brenda." *Don't look at her, don't look at her, don't...*She stuck a sticky finger into her mouth and sucked.

Drooling for an entirely different reason, he watched out of the corner of his eye, fascinated and turned on beyond belief.

If just watching her eat a lemon bar affected him this much, what would it be like to hold her in his arms, to kiss those delectable lips, feel the warm smoothness of her silken skin against his? A breathy sigh of satisfaction escaped her. He swallowed the answering groan rising in his throat, and shifted in his seat to relieve the growing pressure. *Lord, help me out here.* "I have a few fast-food wipes in the glove box."

"Thanks." She opened the compartment and fished out a couple of the foil packets. Tearing one open, she handed it to him. "You don't want a sticky steering wheel."

He nodded. If she kept on being so sweet, relaxed and so damn pretty, it was going to be a long frustrating night. "So, you were going to tell me about your deal with Brenda."

"You're kind of relentless."

No. More like *kind of desperate.* "I'm curious is all, and we're heading to your mom's anyway."

"True." Another sigh escaped, this one not so satisfied. "I guess you're going to see soon enough. I grew up in a seedy trailer park on the south side of Evansville. It backs up against Interstate 164, situated next door to a huge, ramshackle trucking company that's about a zillion years old."

She glanced at him, and then turned away. "Growing up poor and living in a trailer park carries a stigma. You've got to be loose. Your mama had to be loose. Trailer trash is synonymous with sluttiness in the minds of most of the adolescent boys I came into contact with in school."

"Oh." He searched his memory for any impression he might've had from back then. Nothing came to mind. "Huh. I guess I was too wrapped up in my own hogginess stigma back then to realize." She shot him an amused look, and he was inordinately pleased that he could entertain her.

"Well, it's true. Brenda and I had big plans for our futures. We were serious about school, and serious about fighting the trailer trash stigma, so we teamed up. Neither of us ever went out alone with a guy. We always doubled. That way we could watch out for each other." She shrugged. "Neither of us really did a whole lot of dating in high school other than group things, often including one or two of her big brothers. I had one semiserious boyfriend my senior year, and that was it. I enlisted in the army the day I turned eighteen."

Something niggled at him—something he needed to pay attention to. Later. He'd think about it later. Right now he wanted her to keep talking. "What happened to Mr. Semiserious?"

"We corresponded for a while, but then it kind of fizzled out. He's married and has a couple kids now."

"All right. I get the teaming up as teenagers part." He glanced at her before taking the ramp onto the highway. "So why now?"

Her lips compressed into a straight line, and the worry creases reappeared. "She thinks she's helping me out, like it's important for me to get back into dating. Brenda believes if she goes into the teaming-up mode, I'll ease into it."

"Isn't it important to you?"

"No."

"Cory, you're young, intelligent, and attractive." He kept his eyes on the road. She tensed up beside him, gripping the plastic container in her lap so tight, he worried for the lemon bars inside. "You're not going to let what happened one day in the entire span of your life ruin your chances at happiness, are you?

Maybe Brenda is right. Maybe if you start out with people you know and trust—"

"You don't have any idea what you're talking about," she snapped, and her lungs worked away like a bellows.

"Explain it to me."

"Don't you think I'd love to date, fall in love, and all that?" she huffed.

"How should I know? Do you?" His heart stopped midbeat, awaiting her reply.

"Of course I do, but I can't. Even the thought of…of…"

"You don't have to say the words. I know what you mean."

"It makes me nauseous. I get the dry heaves, and my skin crawls, and…and I have nightmares. Not exactly what a guy wants in a girlfriend, is it?" She glared at him. "I can't stand the thought of physical intimacy. There. I said it."

"You didn't always feel that way though, did you?"

"No." She made a strangled, choking sound, but the grip she had on the box eased a smidge. "I used to be fairly normal."

"What if you replaced the bad memories with good ones, like one at a time? Start out small."

Her brow furrowed. "I don't know if that's possible. Rape is such a violent intrusion. Any illusions I ever had of…of being secure, or…safe…" Her lips compressed again, turning down at the corners. "It's all gone, shattered into a million splintery shards. Everything in my world changed that day, and I don't even feel like the ground I walk on is solid anymore. That center of gravity that keeps us all grounded? I've lost it." Her voice hitched. "And I have no idea how to get that back."

"I'd like to help if you'd let me." *I'd like to be the one to replace the bad memories with good ones.* He wanted to give her a brand-new center of gravity. He wanted to be the one she could rely on when the nightmares came to haunt her.

Her breath caught, and her eyes widened a fraction.

"What?" His own grip tightened on the steering wheel.

"You're the first person I've ever said all that to."

"Thank you for trusting me. I'm always willing to listen, and I promise to keep everything to myself."

"Why?"

Because I think you could be the one to fill this gaping empty place in my heart? Yeah, not going to say that. "Why what?"

"Why are you always so nice to me? Why are you willing to listen to me go on about my personal demons?"

"I like you. Is that so difficult to accept? Now and then I get glimpses of the firecracker you were before that asshole broke your world." He shrugged. "I'd love to see you regain your center of gravity and your sense of security."

"Hmm." She studied him, her eyes roaming over his face, frowning when they tarried a fraction of a second on his mouth. "Thank you. I appreciate it."

Her pupils dilated when she lifted her eyes to his. Hadn't he read in one of his sister's magazines that our pupils do that when we're attracted to someone? Yeah, this was a good sign. He grinned. "You're entirely welcome."

"Oh, crap."

Damn. What'd I do now? He raised his brow in question.

"We just passed the turnoff to my mom's."

"No big deal. I'll just get off at the next exit and turn around." He wouldn't mind if they kept on driving all night if it meant she'd continue to open up to him.

"Yeah, see, that's the problem. Because of summer road construction, the next exit with a turnaround is about ten miles west of here." She fished her cell phone out of her purse. "Take exit 170 and hang a left. That'll take you to an eastbound ramp. I'll call my mom to let her know we might be a few minutes late."

"I think we'll be fine." He nodded toward the clock on his dashboard. "We were a little early anyway."

She set her phone on top of the box of dessert bars and relaxed into the leather seat. Also a good sign.

"Do you want to hear something really sick?" she asked, biting her lip. "I get it."

He blinked, confused. "Get what?"

"I get why rape happens in the military."

"It shouldn't happen."

"I know, but when you consider the type of person attracted to the armed forces, and the type of soldiers the armed forces actively seek—aggressive with an overload of testosterone—"

His eyes widened. "Are you all of those things?"

"No. People enlist for all kinds of reasons. Some just want the benefits and access to training and education they couldn't otherwise afford. Some have a highly developed sense of honor and patriotism, a certain percentage are unemployed and have nothing else to do, but..." She propped her elbow on the window frame and rested her chin on her fist. "Ultimately, the army wants men who are driven to fight...men who want to shoot at an enemy."

She turned to face him. "Like any other slice of society, the good, the bad and everything in between are represented. There are some enlisted personnel who are pretty close to criminal to begin with, especially the bullies. Put those men who already teeter on the edge of criminality into a dangerous situation where they're under fire, stressed out and on an adrenaline rush twenty-four-seven, and something's going to snap."

"That doesn't excuse what happened to you." His jaw clenched. Right now, he was the one who wanted to strike out at an enemy, and the man who had hurt her topped his most wanted list.

"I know that," She blew out a shaky breath. "It hasn't been that long that women have been a part of active combat duty alongside the guys. The army is a behemoth, slow to turn when it comes to updating their collective consciousness, or...or accommodating change, no matter how necessary that change might be. Rape should *not* happen—ever. No matter what side you're on. But historically, it's always been a part of war, just not...it should never be..."

It didn't help. This *understanding* she described didn't help the anger roiling in his gut on her behalf. "No one should be assaulted by someone who is supposed to be on the same side."

"No one should ever be sexually assaulted, no matter what, but yeah. Exactly. It really does a number on your head." She pointed ahead. "There's our exit."

CHAPTER SIX

THIS BARING OF THE SOUL left Cory with a giddy sense of relief, and she didn't want it to end. What was it about Ted Lovejoy that made it so easy for her to open up? He made her want to put her unsorted feelings into some semblance of order, and then put them to words. She glanced at him as he focused on getting them back on track toward her mom's. Her eyes fixed on his hands where they rested on the steering wheel. He had nice hands, masculine and strong, confident—if hands could be described as confident. Maybe not. Masterful. Yeah, that was better.

Ted had the hands of a workingman, yet he was so much more. Not only did he help his family out on the farm, he also created high quality, handcrafted furniture and ran a successful business. The man was too capable and too good for words, and that was sexy.

He cleared his throat, and she lifted her eyes to find he'd caught her staring. All the heat pooling in her middle shot up to her face. She turned away.

"Do you mind if I ask a question, Cory?"

"No, I don't mind. Go ahead."

"I've been doing some reading about rape in the military,

and from what I've gathered, a majority go unreported, or if they are reported, nothing comes of it. What was it about your case that drew so much attention?"

"After I reported the assault, my superiors brushed me off no matter how high up the hierarchy I went. I pushed the issue and threatened to take my case to the media if they didn't do something. So they did...something. They decided I have a personality disorder." She studied the dashboard of his truck, avoiding the pity she feared finding in his expression. "Reporting my CO's sexual assault against *me* resulted in my less-than-honorable discharge." The familiar band of tension tightened around her chest. "That really ticked me off." She risked a glance and noticed his jaw twitching before she turned away again.

"It makes me angry just hearing you talk about it."

"Thank you." No pity. Just anger on her behalf, and that warmed her heart. "There's a lot of shame and blame involved with rape, and it's a threatening situation all the way around. I'm sure that's why most victims just disappear into the woodwork. I couldn't let that happen. It's not right." All the anger and helpless rage she kept mostly under control surged, and her grip on the lemon bars went postal again.

Memories of the past year flooded her, the frustration and isolation, the overwhelming sense of betrayal she'd suffered. She pushed them all back into the far recesses of her mind. She didn't want to turn into a quaking mess in front of Ted. "There are a number of organizations trying to address the problem in various ways. I have a friend who is very involved with the Service Women's Action Network, and I contacted her."

She forced herself to ease her grip on the box in her lap. "SWAN is working to draft legislation and get laws passed that will make things safer for women in the armed forces." She looked at him, and this time her gaze was steady. "They put me in touch with the Yale Law School Veterans Legal Services Clinic. They're working with SWAN to draft the new laws, and they took my case pro bono. In exchange, I agreed to testify in front of congressmen and senators about what happened to me in order to help the cause. SWAN did several press releases, and the next thing I knew, I was in the middle of a media feeding frenzy."

He turned to face her, a look of comprehension covering his features. "I can't even imagine how difficult that must've been for you. Especially after everything else you'd already gone through." He shifted, turning back to the road. "You're a brave woman, Cory. I hope you know that."

"I don't know about bravery. Mostly I was motivated by rage, and I had no idea what I was getting into." More memories rushed back—the lack of privacy, cameras flashing in her face during the trial, seeing her personal horror headlined on a daily basis. She'd hated having her life laid bare to the world. As far as she was concerned, the media circus was another kind of rape, another violent intrusion into her personal life. "Brenda says I'm the poster child for rape in the military. I only did what I did because I hoped it might prevent someone else's life from being destroyed."

"No doubt you are the poster child, and I'm certain you've helped a lot of women come forward with their own stories."

"Maybe." A shudder racked her. "I don't *ever* want my name to appear in a newspaper, magazine or on the Internet again. The whole experience…" The sudden sting of tears took her by surprise. "It was horrible," she whispered, wishing she could bear having Ted's arms around her.

She pointed ahead, struggling to get a grip on her emotions. "There's our exit. We'd better not miss it a second time. Turn right at the stop sign, and the road will take you straight to the trailer park. Just look for the Pine Glen Mobile Homes sign on the left."

He made it onto the off ramp and pulled to a halt at the stop sign. "I'm sorry you went through all of that. You're getting regular paychecks now, and plenty of therapists work on a sliding scale. Have you given any more thought to—"

"There's a principle involved here." *Dammit.* Didn't he get it? "I served my country for eight years." She glared at him. "Eight years with a perfect record. I intended to make the military my career for the next twenty. I shouldn't have to *pay on a sliding scale.* I want back what was stolen from me."

Her heart pounded so hard her ears rang. *Unfit to serve.* That was the thorn that festered in her like a boil, and only one thing could make it go away. "When my record is straightened out, the first thing I plan to do is sign up for therapy. I didn't ask to be raped, and I sure didn't deserve to be treated the way I was by the institution I pledged my loyalty and service to for all those years."

A barrage of hot, angry tears flooded her eyes, and she swallowed hard as embarrassment filled the vacuum left by the receding flash of anger. "I...I'm sorry. You're not to blame for any of this, and—"

"Don't apologize. It doesn't bother me when you let all that anger out. Use me as a sounding board whenever you feel the need." He pulled onto the frontage road. "So, it's just you and your mom, huh?"

He didn't leap out of the car and run from her tirade, and once again his even-tempered, calm demeanor soothed her. What did he really think? Did he see her for the box of nuts she truly was? She hoped not. Forcing her tone out of the shrill and crazy range and back into normal, or as normal as she could pretend to be, she answered, "Yeah. Pretty much."

She rooted around in her purse for the small package of tissues to wipe the smeared mascara from under her eyes. Her mother already worried enough. Cory didn't want to show up for dinner looking like she'd been crying. Even if she had. She drew in a deep breath, let it out slowly and brought her nerves back under control. "There it is. Home."

The dilapidated sign with the half-dead pine trees planted on either side came into view. Truly cringeworthy. "Head left. We're the fourth one down, the double-wide with the small wooden deck built onto the front." They passed the rusty playground and the graffiti-covered wooden fence separating the park from the trucking company next door. "I win."

Ted shook his head. "It's old and a little run-down, yeah, but other than the graffiti on the fence, which is obviously nothing more than adolescent self-expression, I'm not seeing a ton of booze bottles littering the ground, or rusted-out cars and junk lying around in anyone's yard. The park is neat, just worn." He pulled into the gravel parking spot next to her mother's car. "It looks to me like it's a pretty decent community."

Cory thought about her mom and the neighbors she'd grown up with, especially the Holts. True enough. They were a community of hardworking folks who didn't quite make middle class. Sure, there were a few oddballs who were social dropouts and rebels in their own minds, but they all looked out for one another and had been there for one another during tough times. "It's true. I remember trick-or-treating here on Halloween. Our neighbors went out of their way to make it special for the kids who lived here. Lots of the moms made homemade treats for us, popcorn balls, caramel apples, and fudge. It is a tight community. I think that's why my mom stays. Her friends and support system are here."

"Exactly. Worn but not beaten." Ted grinned before climbing

out of the truck. He came around to her side, opening the door for her. "I think we have a tie on our hands."

"Maybe," she conceded, just as the loud rumble of a semi down-shifting on the interstate filled the air. "Don't forget the noise."

"Don't forget the smell."

"Don't forget the trailer trash stigma." Her chin came up.

He shot her another grin. "Hog farmer here."

The front door of the trailer opened, and her mother's warm smile beamed their way. "You two come on in now. Supper's ready."

Cory hurried up the steps of the deck and gave her mom a quick hug before turning to introduce Ted. "This is Ted Lovejoy. Ted, this is my mom, Claire Marcel."

"Call me Claire," her mom said as she stepped back so they could enter. "Welcome."

"It's nice to meet you, Claire." Ted inhaled audibly. "Mmm, it smells delicious in here."

It did smell good, and the mouthwatering scents weren't coming from the huge slow cooker permanently positioned on the kitchen counter. Cory looked at the stove, where a few pots and pans with lids simmered on low. A covered basket sat in the middle of their dinette table, which had been set with place mats and wineglasses. Wow. Her mother had gone all out. "What did you make?"

"Chicken Marsala, fresh green beans and garlic mashed pota-toes," she trilled. "Cory, honey, there's a bottle of Chardonnay in the door of the fridge. Will you get that for me while I transfer all of this to the table?"

"Sure." She set her lemon bars on the counter, opened the refrigerator door, and took the bottle from the bottom com-partment of the door. "When did you go all gourmet on me?"

Snatching the corkscrew from the counter on her way, she brought them both to the table and opened the wine, then filled the glasses around the table.

Her mom grinned at her from where she stood by the stove. "We have a new cook where I work. He used to be a chef at a fancy restaurant in town, but when the recession hit, the place went under. He's lookin' for a new job, but in the meantime, he's workin' at the truck stop and teachin' me how to cook."

"You're dating?" Cory noticed Ted studying the shadow box mounted on the living room wall. Her father's military portrait, the flag that had been draped over his casket and the medals he'd earned had been mounted on a backing of navy-blue velvet. "That's my dad."

He turned to look at her for a second before going back to the portrait. "I can see the resemblance. You have his dark eyes and hair."

"That's my Joe. His grandmama was Cherokee, like that Johnny Depp fella," her mom said as she placed a steaming platter on the dinette. "My husband made the ultimate sacrifice for our country durin' the Gulf War, and not a day goes by that I don't still miss that man." She glanced at Cory. "And yes. I'm dating the chef, but it's not serious."

"It wouldn't bother me if it were serious, Mom. There's no reason you shouldn't remarry." This was a well-trod discussion, one they'd had many times during her childhood. Her mother was a very attractive woman with a lot to offer. She should've remarried years ago, and though she dated plenty, she'd never settled down.

"If I ever find a man who makes me feel the way your daddy did, I will." Her mom went back to the stove and filled a serving bowl with string beans. "But that's not likely to happen. A love like the one I had with Joe is a rare thing, and only comes along once in a lifetime. Come on now, and sit down."

"How old were you when you lost your dad, Cory?" Ted walked to the dinette and settled into a chair.

"I was three." She took the place across from him. "I barely remember him. All I have left are vague impressions of being held in his arms, or being tossed in the air and caught again on the way down. Occasionally I'll hear a man's voice similar to his, and it triggers a few shadowy memories, but that's about it. We do have lots of pictures, though."

Her mom passed the platter of chicken, and Cory helped herself. "We moved here from Virginia shortly after his death. He's the reason I decided to go into the army. My dad was a decorated war hero."

"I saw the medals."

The warmth in his eyes when they met hers sent butterflies fluttering around inside her stomach. Did he understand? Wanting to be closer to the father she'd lost had been the impetus behind many of the decisions she'd made over the years. Doing well in school, keeping out of trouble, joining the army and getting her college degree—she'd done all of it to follow in his footsteps. She wanted to make him proud, wanted to believe he was somewhere watching over her.

Without a doubt, her father had loved her. They had tons of pictures of him with his arms around his family, the look of affectionate pride on his face undeniable, but it didn't make up for the years without him. Nothing could make up for that kind of emptiness.

He turned to her mother. "How did you and Joe meet?"

That question was one of her mom's favorite topics, and the two of them chatted away like old friends as they ate their dinner.

Ted showed genuine interest in the one person who mattered the most in her world, and that opened up a tight place in her heart.

"Is that a cribbage board over there?" Ted gestured toward the bookshelves holding all her mom's romance novels. Their old wooden cribbage board sat next to a deck of cards.

"It surely is." Her mom lit up like a birthday cake candle. "Do you play?"

"I do. Around my house, they call me twenty-hand," he boasted with a competitive glint. "Are the two of you interested in playing a game after we're done with dinner?"

"That sounds like a great idea." Her mom practically bounced in her chair. "We can have our coffee and dessert while I kick your butts."

"Oh, brother." Cory smirked. "You have no idea what you've just unleashed. My mom is wicked sharp when it comes to cribbage, and she's no slouch in the competitiveness department either."

"Oh?" His enthusiasm rose a visible notch. "Care to make a wager?"

She laughed. "What is it with you and wagers, anyway?" The heat in his answering gaze siphoned all the air from her lungs and sent her heart racing.

"Wagers are how I get my way." His eyes, with all their heated intensity, never left hers. "I always win."

She blinked. "Well…"

"Well what?" He blinked back at her with a heart-stopping smile.

She opened her mouth to reply, realized she didn't have anything to say, and shut it again. Wasn't this a new and unexpected glimpse into his character. Who knew? For the most part, Ted came off as affable and laid-back. But right now? He practically pulsed with determination and self-assurance. The scary part was—this side of Ted turned her on. She didn't want to be turned on, didn't want to set foot on that path, because it could only lead to monumental disaster. What was he up to, anyway?

"What kind of wager are we talkin' here?" her mom interjected, dispelling the tension.

"If I lose, I get to take you two lovely ladies out to a fancy restaurant for dinner, because I can't cook a lick."

His sheepish look stirred her insides into a gooey mess, and he searched her face as if he could read what was going on inside her head. He set his fork down and rubbed his stomach. "If I win, you two have to cook me another fantastic dinner like the one we're enjoying this evening—complete with lemon bars."

"Are my mom and I a team? If we are, that puts you at an unfair disadvantage."

"Not really." He leveled another hot look at her and lifted an eyebrow. "Either way I win."

Oh, man. I'm in trouble. She opened her mouth to decline just as her mom jumped in.

"You're on." She started clearing the dishes from the table. "Cory, make the coffee while I put those lemon bars on a plate."

This mutual attraction thing was spinning out of her control, and she had to find a way to put on the brakes. *OK. Rein it in.* It was just dinner, and her mother would be there, for crying out loud. She spooned coffee grounds into the filter and started the coffee machine.

Ted was one of those people who possessed an overabundance of compassion. Plus he was a really nice guy who tended toward random acts of kindness. He obviously enjoyed her mother's company, and he was just being friendly. That's all. The heat she glimpsed in his eyes? Probably all in her overactive imagination. Right? *Gulp.*

His friendship was important to her, and growing more so every day. She didn't want to wreck what they had by crossing a line. She couldn't cope with anything more intimate than what they now shared. Right after their bowling night, she'd lay it all out for him. Surely he'd understand.

❦ ❦ ❦

He'd blown it, come on too strong, and now Cory wouldn't look at him. She fussed around the kitchen as if she didn't know what to do with herself. Time to dial it back. He needed to fly under her radar or she'd freak, but dammit, he couldn't help himself. He was still on a high from the way she'd opened up to him earlier, and he loved seeing her here with her mom. Tonight he'd gotten to know a relaxed, affectionate side of Cory as she sat across from him to share a meal. He wanted more, and he wanted to be on the receiving end.

He was bound to slip up and let his feelings for her show. Especially after a few glasses of Chardonnay. Better quit with the wine. Ted stood up, gathered the remaining dirty dishes, including his wineglass, and brought them to the sink. "That was an excellent dinner, Claire. Thank you."

"My pleasure." Claire patted his shoulder. "You're welcome to come for supper anytime. Thank you for putting a smile on my girl's face."

"Mom…" Cory's cheeks turned an attractive shade of dusky rose.

"Can I help with the dishes?" he asked.

"No. They'll keep. Once I put these leftovers away, we'll play cribbage." Claire nodded toward the bookshelf. "You can get the board."

"Yes, ma'am." He fetched the cards and board and set them on the table.

"Do you want coffee?" Cory approached, holding three steaming mugs by the handles.

"Sure." He accepted the cup she handed him. "And I'd love one or two of those lemon bars."

"Help yourself." Claire set the plate of bars and a stack of napkins down before taking a seat. "Let's play. Cut for crib."

The next hour flew by, and Ted enjoyed the banter while he let the two Marcel women believe they could best him. He hadn't decided yet which would be better: another home-cooked meal in an environment where Cory could relax, or impressing them both by taking the two out for an expensive meal at a classy restaurant. When it got right down to it, their financial circumstances helped him decide, plus, he couldn't wait to spend more time alone with Cory as he drove her home. He threw potential points to the crib hands and let Cory and her mother win. "That's it. You won."

"Did we?" Cory shot him a skeptical look. "For all that bragging you did earlier, I'd expect you to know better than to feed us points in the crib the way you did those last few hands."

He shrugged, stood up and stretched. "You want a rematch?"

"Not tonight. It's getting late, and in case you aren't aware, I have to work tomorrow." She grinned. "Don't wanna upset my boss by oversleeping and showing up late."

"Good point." He turned to Cory's mother. "Mrs. Marcel, thank you again for a wonderful evening. I'm looking forward to taking the two of you to dinner. Talk to Cory and figure out a date that works for the two of you, and I'll make the reservation."

"I surely am looking forward to that myself, and I enjoyed the evening too." Claire rose from her place and brought the plate of lemon bars to the counter. "Cory, I'm keeping two of these bars and sending the rest home with you. Otherwise I'll eat them all."

Cory grabbed her purse from the edge of the couch and accepted the plastic container from her mom. "That's fine. I'll bring the rest into work tomorrow for the production crew." She gave her mom another hug. "Dinner was amazing. Thanks."

"You're welcome, baby." Claire hugged her back. "I'm glad we did this tonight. Let's do it again real soon."

"We will. Good night, Mom."

Ted followed Cory to the front door. Once they were on their way, he turned to smile at her. "I had a wonderful time, and your mom is great. I like her a lot."

"We're even." She grinned back. "I like your family too."

"So I guess we'll split the check at the truck stop. Maybe Paige and the rest of the crew would be interested in joining us. Does Friday sound good?"

"I'd like that. Friday works fine." A happy sigh escaped her, or at least it sounded happy to him, and she settled into her seat for the ride home.

Satisfaction and triumph thrummed through him. The evening had gone far better than he'd hoped. Cory had opened up to him, and right now she sat beside him without needing the windows of his truck open or the pepper spray in her hand. All good. If this were a normal date, he'd kiss her good night. The thought sent his blood rushing, heating his insides to a feverish pitch.

"What are you thinking about, Ted?" she asked. "You look as if you're concentrating pretty hard over there."

Hard? Oh, yeah. He was hard all right, and desperately trying to change the direction his thoughts were taking. "I was just thinking about how much I enjoyed seeing you so relaxed this evening." He slid her a sideways glance. "Happy looks good on you."

"It was fun." A half smile lit her face. "Thanks for being so nice to my mom."

"You don't have to thank me. I really did enjoy her company. Her accent is different. Where's she from?"

"She grew up on a farm in the Appalachians near Wheeling, West Virginia."

"Ah, that explains it. I'm looking forward to taking the two of you to dinner. It's not every day a guy like me gets to show off two pretty women on the same date."

"It's not a date." She tensed. "It's a wager, like the truck stop."

Damn, she turned prickly at the speed of light. "I was trying to pay you and your mother a compliment." Ted gripped the steering wheel and cast a frown her way. "Would dating me be so horrible?" Her chin lowered, and she worked her lower lip between her teeth. His heart rolled over and played possum. Dumb question. He didn't really want to hear the answer. "Forget I said that."

"No, Ted. I want to answer." She swallowed a few times and lifted her anguished eyes to his. "Under normal circumstances, dating you would be a dream come true."

His heart turned over again, soaring this time.

"But these aren't normal circumstances, and you deserve better." Her voice hitched. "I...I don't have anything to offer. I'm messed up. I can't even consider dating anyone right now."

"Don't I get a say?"

She shook her head and turned to face the window. "Don't waste your time waiting for me to make it to normal."

Damn. His heart couldn't take much more of this flip-flopping around. He felt like a fish on the bottom of a rowboat, bruised and gasping. "You aren't a waste of time, Cory. You've only been with L&L a little over a month, and already you're much less skittish and more relaxed. Time." He nodded to him- self. "You just need more time."

The Langfords' driveway came into view, and he turned onto the gravel, pulling up alongside their minivan. He hurried out so he could open the door for her. "I have an idea."

She climbed out without his help. "Oh, yeah? What is it?"

"You said you can't stand the thought of physical intimacy, and I know you can't tolerate being hemmed in."

"Right."

"Kiss me."

"What?" Her eyebrows shot up. "After everything we've dis- cussed, you want to—"

"No, Cory. I'm not going to kiss you. You're going to kiss me. My hands will be in my back pockets, and they won't move. You'll be in complete control with nothing binding you. Set the lemon bars on the hood of my truck and get that pepper spray out of your purse. Put your finger on the nozzle and pucker up."

"I don't think so." Now her brow lowered, bringing back the worry grooves she wore far too often.

"Remember I talked about replacing the bad memories with good? This is a step. I'm trying to help." He wanted to convince her to take the chance like his life depended on it. "I'm safe. You can trust me." He raked a hand through his hair. "You do trust me, don't you, Cory?"

"I...I do, Ted, but I don't want to risk ruining our friendship."

"You won't. I swear. No matter what, I'll always be there for you. If friendship is all you can manage, fine." He'd never be sat- isfied with anything platonic where she was concerned, and now he'd turned into a liar for the sake of getting her past their first kiss. Yep. *A fool in the making, that's me.* She scrutinized him, her gaze roaming over his face, finally focusing on his mouth—which suddenly went sawdust dry. "Let's pretend."

"What are we pretending?" Her frown deepened.

"From this point on, you're a born-again virgin. This is your first kiss, and you have no bad memories."

She sucked in an audible gasp and stared at him as if he'd lost his mind. He held his breath, certain she'd refuse. Several tense seconds stretched between them. He filled the gap by kicking his own ass. He'd pushed too hard and too soon. *Dumb! Baby steps.* He could hardly believe it when she set her purse and the plastic container on his truck.

"You swear you'll keep your hands to yourself?" she whispered.

"I swear." He jammed them into his back pockets and backed up against the door of his pickup. "Have at me. I'm all yours."

She stepped closer, leaned in, and tentatively brushed her lips against his, immediately backing away. The brief contact set off grand-finale fireworks inside him, all of his nerves firing up at once. "That's it? That's all you got?"

She shot him a disgruntled look, but took the bait. She stepped closer, her lips connecting with his more firmly. He melted, kissing her back, letting her take the lead. It worked. Her tongue slid into his mouth for a brief exploration, then withdrew. He couldn't resist chasing the lure and tried to follow. She let him. Good Lord. She let him in, and he fell under her spell completely.

His entire world narrowed to the single point of contact, her mouth on his, the most erotic experience he'd ever had. The kiss consumed him. His knees went wobbly, his heart thundered, and he couldn't catch his breath. Keeping his hands to himself was the hardest thing he'd ever done.

Her palms came up to rest against his chest, and then it was over. She pushed away from him, her chest rising and falling as rapidly as his. Only with her he had no clue whether it was from panic or arousal. No matter how much he wanted to reassure her, the link between his brain and his mouth refused to connect. He was on overload, hard as rock, achy and wanting. All he could do was stare into her lovely brown eyes with all the longing he couldn't hide. Bad move.

"Good night, Ted." She turned on her heels and hurried off to the carriage house.

He watched as she disappeared around the corner of the big house in the dimming light, wondering if he'd just made a huge mistake, or…Scrubbing his hands over his face, he tried to draw enough air into his lungs to calm his raging lust. One kiss. The only things touching were their mouths. What would it be like to hold her in his arms?

Once he regained control over his rubber-band legs, he climbed into his truck and headed home, his mind still lust buzzed and fogged. Twenty minutes later he pulled into his parking spot, climbed the stairs to his lonely apartment over the machine barn and flopped down on his couch. There he stayed, staring at the ceiling, and then around the home that wasn't really a home at all. It was far too empty for that.

He and Noah had custom built his two-bedroom apartment. The kitchen with its center island spanned the entire width of the great room, which included the living room with the exposed timber framing and a small fireplace. A short hall led to two large bedrooms, with one nicely sized bathroom at the end of the corridor and a laundry room next door. He'd furnished the place mostly with L&L scratch-and-dent returns and samples, with the exception of his bedroom furniture. That he'd custom designed and built with his own two hands.

He wanted someone living here with him, someone to wake up beside every morning, making this a home instead of just the space where he lived. The stainless steel appliances, granite counters and custom cabinets in the kitchen had been designed with that faceless feminine someone **in mind**. He had a face to put with the longing now, and he hoped like hell that for once things would work out in his favor.

Their kiss had shaken him like a pair of dice in a cup, and there was no turning back for him. He wanted Cory, and it was the deep kind of want that wasn't going to go away, only grow stronger.

What was she doing right now? What was she thinking and feeling? He didn't know how he'd face it if she'd been more disgusted than turned on. That would be a setback of monumental proportions. He leaned his head back and groaned. *Born-again virgin?* Who said stuff like that? What the hell had he been thinking? Well, the deed had been done, and she'd kissed him back. Whatever shook free from tonight would shake free, and there wasn't a thing he could do about it now.

He rubbed his eyes, sat up, and searched around the couch cushions for the remote control. Might as well attempt to get his mind off Cory's delectable lips, the sweet taste of her mouth and the breathy little sounds she'd made that had gone straight through him. Otherwise it was going to be a long, frustrating night. He flipped through the channels until he found an action movie in full swing, hit Enter, and stared without really seeing while counting the hours until work tomorrow.

CHAPTER SEVEN

CORY LEANED CLOSER TO TED, *tentatively placing her mouth against his. He tasted sweet, and the softness of his lips against hers sent a delicious tingling current cascading through her. She stepped closer. Intoxicated by his unique scent and the warmth radiating from him, she placed her palms against his chest and deepened the kiss. His heart raced under her palm, and the sudden intake of his breath thrilled her. She ran the tip of her tongue over the seam of his mouth. He opened for her, and she slid her tongue over and around his, reveling in the groan her actions elicited from him. Ted kissed her back with heart-stopping tenderness, demanding nothing, offering everything. She moved closer, craving more…*

His arms came around her. Roughly pulling her against him, he turned her around and pressed her against…the wall? The sour smell of Staff Sergeant Barnett's sweat assaulted her. His rough, callused hand came up to cover her mouth and he leaned close enough for her to smell what he'd had for lunch on his breath.

"You have this coming, bitch."

No, no, no! She twisted and turned, fought him with everything she had. Desperation and panic clawed at her gut, and bile burned the back of her throat. She couldn't breathe. Rage exploded into a red haze in her brain. This wasn't right. Not fair. Not fair at all…

Cory cried out and sat up in bed. Sweating and shaky, she sucked in bucketfuls of air and wiped her face. "Oh, God." Wrapping her arms around herself, she began the all too familiar ritual rocking. Once she'd worked herself into some semblance of calm, she swung her legs over the edge of the bed and made the trip to her small bathroom. One more hot shower that would do little to assuage the horror.

Tears pricked at the back of her eyes. The nightmare echoed exactly what had happened a few hours earlier. At first, kissing Ted had been wonderful, tender and sweet beyond belief, filling her with tantalizing sensations. But then his earnest image morphed into her attacker's, and everything went to hell. Panic banished all the good stuff, replacing it with revulsion and white-hot rage. She'd fled, leaving him with that familiar hurt and confused look on his face.

Cory stepped under the scalding-hot water and scrubbed away at the panic and fear. She toweled herself dry and put on a clean T-shirt and boxers. Not ready to return to bed, she headed for her laptop. She sat on the recliner and searched through her e-mail for any word from the Yale law clinic. Spam, a few messages from military friends, something from Brenda, and that was it. Nothing from Yale. She slammed the computer shut, got up, and kicked the chair. Twice. *Not fair at all.* Her chest banded so tightly she could hardly breathe.

Frustrated, she took a swing at the chair's overstuffed headrest. The smacking sound reverberated through the living room. How could she face Ted tomorrow? How could she tell the greatest guy she'd ever met that kissing him made her want to vomit and beat up furniture?

Unfit to serve. Hell, yes. Unfit pretty much covered it, and she was so damned tired of feeling this way. Damned tired of the rage, the nightmares, the fear and the twitchy, skin-crawly desire to jump out of her own body when touched. The black, miasmic pit that had taken up permanent residence in the center of her soul exhausted her. *Smack.* Her fist connected with the leather again.

Maybe Ted was right, and she should find a therapist in Perfect who worked on a sliding scale. She hadn't done anything up till now, and look where that had gotten her. Nowhere. On the other hand, the army owed her. All she had left of her military career were her principles. Sergeant Butthead had been found guilty. Changing her record should be a slam dunk. So what was taking so long?

Aiming all of her rage at the innocent La-Z-Boy, she slammed her fists into the chair again and again, imagining Sergeant Barnett's face in place of the smooth brown leather. *Take that, asshole.* After sucking in another huge breath, Cory let it out slowly and stopped her assault. After all, the furniture was innocent in all of this, and it wasn't hers to destroy.

She walked to the kitchen toward the roll of paper towels and tore off a few to blow her nose. It wouldn't hurt to at least look into getting help sooner rather than later. Having a backup plan didn't mean she'd given up on her principles. Right?

Returning to her computer, she sat down and Googled therapists in Perfect. There weren't any. She tried a few more keywords and found the closest clinics willing to work on a sliding scale were all in Evansville—forty-five minutes away, and she had no car. Despair ate away at her resolve, and a fresh deluge flooded her eyes. Now what?

She'd have to save every penny she earned and buy a cheap vehicle ASAP, that's what. The alternative was to beg rides, and that she couldn't do. She had her pride. Being dependent on Noah for rides to and from work was hard enough. Asking him to stop at the grocery store was no picnic either. He had a family to get home to, and taking more of his time twisted her into knots. She was twenty-seven years old and still living like a teenager with no real independence. That sucked.

I could ask Ted. No, no, no. As soon as the thought entered her head, she rejected it. No doubt he'd help, but she already owed him so much, and helpless and dependent were not the characteristics she wanted him to associate with her. Besides, did she really want to be anywhere near him after a session? She'd be chewed up, raw and extremely vulnerable. Who in their right mind would want anyone to see them like that? Not her, that's for sure.

Cory pressed her palms against her eyes. She had no choice but to work toward buying her own car, and that would take months. She'd have to wait—wait for enough money to support a car, wait to get word from the law clinic, wait to leave her personal hell behind so she could start living again. And it certainly wasn't fair to expect Ted to wait with her. More than ever she needed to put some distance between them. No more evenings out or time alone, and no more kisses.

Crap. They already had Friday's lunch at the truck stop, dinner with her mother and the bowling night planned. At least those dates involved other people. After that she'd tell him they had to stop spending so much time together, and that would be that. Putting an end to whatever this was between them was going to hurt like hell, but it had to be done.

"Hey, Squirrel. You're looking kind of haggard this morning," Wesley told her as they met on the stairs.

She nodded. Something in her expression must have tipped him off, because his forehead furrowed, and his gaze sharpened. "I was on my way to the Perfect Diner for breakfast. Come with me. I'll buy."

"I already ate. Besides, I can't take a break. I just got here."

Wesley ushered her back to the production room. "Noah, do you mind if I take Cory to the diner? We have some catching up to do, and we're on opposite schedules."

"Go ahead." Noah lifted his safety goggles to peer at them. "You can make up the time this afternoon, Cory. I have to leave late anyway. I have a meeting with the finishing crew."

"Thanks." Heat filled her cheeks as the rest of the guys raised their heads to watch her leave with Wesley. They walked down the alley toward the sidewalk, and she had to lengthen her stride to keep up. "Are we in a hurry?"

"Huh?" He glanced at her, as if just now realizing she was beside him. "Oh, sorry. Habit, I guess." He slowed his pace. "I usually eat breakfast alone at the diner before I hit the sack."

"I heard."

"This is the first time I've ever invited anyone else along."

"Really?" Her eyes widened. "You don't hang out with the rest of the crew?" Wesley had always been very social and friendly when they were kids, and thinking he might be isolating himself now disturbed her. "Aren't you happy here in Perfect?"

His expression closed up and turned inward. He'd probably seen more than his share of horror and had his own personal demons to fight. "For the most part, sure. I'm content."

"Do you…" She cleared her throat. "Are you seeing a therapist?"

"Naw. Not anymore. I did when I first got back, though, and I still meet with my group. I'm not about to give that up."

"Did the therapy help?"

"Bad night, Cory?"

"Yeah, I guess you could say that." After that first nightmare, she'd tossed and turned all night long, and every time she managed to fall asleep, more bad dreams woke her. And they'd all been triggered by the best kiss she'd ever experienced.

They reached the diner, and Wesley opened the door for her. "I always sit at the little table back in the corner. Is that OK with you?"

"Sure, so long as I can sit on the outside."

"Definitely not a problem." He shot her a wry look. "I prefer to have my back to the wall anyway."

"Good morning, you two." Holding two mugs and a coffeepot, Jenny led them back to the corner table. She set down the mugs and poured their coffee while they took their seats. "It's nice to see you again, Cory. How're things going?"

"Fine, thanks." The diner always smelled so good, and at this hour, the overriding aromas of bacon, sausage and maple syrup filled her senses. Cory took an appreciative sniff. All she'd had for breakfast was toast and coffee.

"Are you sure you don't want something?" He pulled a laminated breakfast menu from the clip at the back of the stainless steel condiment holder.

She took a menu as well. "I guess I could eat."

"Good. My treat. You're still too thin."

"Morning, Wes." Jenny's assistant manager set flatware wrapped in napkins in front of them, her gaze firmly planted on his face. "I see you brought someone with you this morning." She spared Cory a smile that held the unmistakable hint of something besides curiosity. A pinch of uncertainty? Jenny believed

Wesley had a thing for—she checked the woman's name tag—
Carlie. Maybe Carlie felt something for him in return.

"This is Cory Marcel. Cory, this is Carlie Stewart."

"Nice to meet you." Carlie's assessing stare slid over her. "I
see you here with the L&L crew all the time. Do you work there?"

"I do, thanks to Wes. He's like my big brother." She smiled.
"We grew up together."

Sure enough, there was no mistaking the flash of relief that
crossed Carlie's face. "Welcome to Perfect. Do you know what
you want, or do you two need a few minutes?" She took out a pad
and pen from her apron pocket.

"I'll have number two with the eggs scrambled, whole wheat
toast and bacon." Wesley tucked the menu back in its place
behind the ketchup. "Can you ask Bill to toss some onions in
with the hash browns?"

"Sure, Wes." She turned to Cory.

"I'll have the same, only I want my eggs over easy, and a short
stack instead of toast."

"Got it. I'll be back in a minute to refill your coffee." Carlie
walked away. Wesley watched her every step, his face filled with
unmistakable longing.

"Have you asked her out?"

"What?" His face reddened, and he studied the contents of
his coffee mug like he might find the Loch Ness monster in its
black depths. "No. What made you say that?"

"Because of the way you two look at each other. There's all
kinds of chemistry going on." She snorted. "Didn't you notice
how unhappy she was to see me here with you?"

"Was she?" His head snapped up.

She rolled her eyes. "You can't be that oblivious, Bunny."

"Sure I can." His eyes went back to his mug. "So, what has

you looking so rough around the edges this morning, and what's with all the questions about therapy?"

She studied her own coffee. "I get so tired of all this weight dragging me down all the time. I can't seem to shake or break it. Know what I mean?"

"I have a pretty fair idea."

She sighed. "It's been more than a year since…since it happened, and I still have nightmares. I can't tolerate being closed in or…*touched*. I'm angry all the time. I…I haven't dealt well with any of the fallout." She bit her lip. "Ted suggested I stop waiting for my veteran's benefits to be restored and get help now, but—"

"Ted suggested?" His focus intensified. "You're spending a lot of time with him, aren't you? What's going on between the two of you?"

She picked at a chipped spot on the red Formica tabletop and shrugged. "I wouldn't say *a lot* of time. He's been helping me get acclimated is all. We're just friends." She forced herself to meet Wesley's gaze. "He's right. I do need to get help, but even if I do decide to do something now, there are no therapists in Perfect, and I don't have a car."

"I sleep during the day. You can always take my truck if you want."

Her eyes widened and a flare of hope ignited. She still hadn't made up her mind about which direction to turn, but at least she knew she could get somewhere if the need arose. "Really?"

"Sure. No problem." He glanced toward the assistant manager making her way toward them before turning back to her. "Just let me know what you decide to do and when you need to be somewhere. Is your driver's license current?"

"Yep. It is." She grinned. "I made a point of keeping it up to date. Thanks."

"No problem."

Carlie delivered their food, sending a lingering look Wesley's way. "Do either of you need anything else right now?"

"Nope. This looks great. Thanks." Cory's stomach rumbled, and she unwrapped the flatware.

"More coffee when you get the chance." Wesley smiled at Carlie. "Don't hurry, though. I know you're busy."

"Got it." Carlie patted his shoulder and left.

"She likes you. You should ask her out." His only response was a grunt. He'd changed so much, and Cory's mind went back to their earlier years—the easy way they'd teased each other, the way he'd always looked out for his younger siblings, including her in that circle. "What do you know about Carlie?"

"Only that she took this job and moved here shortly after a divorce. She has a son."

"You know your way around kids, that's for sure." She took a bite of her pancakes, and their fluffy, buttery sweetness made her stomach rumble again. She swallowed and cut off another bite. "Did you know Kyle asked Brenda out?"

"All right." Wesley set his fork down, put his elbows on the table and fixed her with a stare. "As long as we're following this track, let's talk about Ted."

She choked on her pancakes and had to cough a few times. "What about him?"

"He's a great guy. You could do worse." A single eyebrow rose. "We've all seen the way he looks at you, and there's a lot more than *friendly* going on there."

Appetite gone. She stirred the runny yolks of her eggs around her plate while a lump clogged her throat. "I know he's a great guy. He's..." She swallowed hard. "He deserves the best, and—"

"And you're messed up?"

She nodded. Great. Now the tears. She tried to blink them away and failed.

Wesley snatched an extra napkin from the dispenser on their table and thrust it her way. "Give it some time, and give yourself a chance. Somehow I have a feeling Ted's the kind of guy who's willing to take things real slow."

"You don't understand." She jerked her hand away.

"Don't I?" His look drifted across the diner to where Carlie chatted with a couple of old codgers in bib overalls and beat-up John Deere caps.

"OK. Maybe you do, but our situations are entirely different. What if Ted and I date, and it turns into a disaster? I don't want to hurt him. It would break my heart to hurt him."

"And what if you give it a shot, and it works out? Are you willing to pass up the chance at something good without a fight?" Both his eyebrows rose this time. "I've seen the way you look back at him. I've known you for most of your life, and I can tell you feel something for him too. Go for it."

"Sure. I will if you will." She nodded toward Carlie and cocked an eyebrow at him.

He grunted and went back to eating his breakfast.

Cory's heart raced at the thought. Could she do it? Could she date Ted for real, see if he could help her break through the barrier of revulsion and disgust Sergeant Asshole had cast around her? Before all the bad stuff stirred up, Ted's kiss had curled her toes and melted her bones. Maybe the second time around...or the third...

"I don't know." Wesley interrupted her fantasy. "I'm almost forty, set in my ways, and Carlie has a kid. Kids and PTSD don't exactly mix."

"Noah has three children and one on the way. I don't think he'd agree with you."

"He wasn't a marine."

"No, but he was part of a heavy combat unit." Now that she had a way to get to therapy if she decided not to wait for the army to come through for her, her mind buzzed with possibilities—and Ted was foremost in her thoughts. "You'd be great with her son. I know from firsthand experience."

"A lot has changed since we were kids." The corners of his mouth turned down, and he pushed his half-eaten breakfast away.

"I'm sorry, Wes. I didn't mean to ruin your breakfast. Let's talk about something else. Don't let this great food go to waste." She loaded her fork and took a bite of eggs and bacon, as if doing so could bring them back to safer ground.

"I do love their hash browns." The tension lines around his mouth eased, and he picked up his fork. "How do you like working at L&L?"

Relieved, she swallowed her mouthful. "I like it a lot. Do you see yourself moving into production eventually? I kind of get the feeling that it's viewed as a big promotion around L&L."

"Nope. I'm already a shift supervisor. Plus, after the night crew leaves, I'm in charge of after-hours security. I really like the work I do. Finishing furniture is soothing. I also have my military pension. I'm content."

"Content sounds pretty darn good." She finished her breakfast, wondering how she'd handle seeing Ted for the first time since their kiss.

Wesley finished his breakfast and tossed a five-dollar bill on the table for Carlie. "Let's go."

She followed him to the front, where he paid the bill. They walked out the front door and headed back to L&L. Her heart thumped away, half trepidation and the other half anticipation at seeing Ted. Could she take a chance and see where things led with him? They entered through the alley, and there he was. Their eyes met and held, setting off a trip wire inside her. *Ping.* A rush of adrenaline sent her heart and stomach into a frenzied jig.

Ted's glance swung from her to Wesley—and back to her. He didn't look happy. "Morning, you two."

"Good morning," she stammered. "Wes and I just had breakfast at your aunt's diner." Why'd she tell him that? He hadn't asked, and she didn't really owe him any explanations. "I gotta get to work." Fleeing from him once again, she took the stairs two at a time and hightailed it to her office. Oh, yeah. She was great relationship material. Not.

❧ ❧ ❧

Watching Cory walk into L&L with Wesley Holt had Ted seeing through a green haze of jealousy and possessiveness. Had she read it in his face? Was that why she took off like Bambi caught in the crosshairs? Probably. Staring at the spot where she'd stood a second ago wasn't going to bring her back either.

Anxiety took a bite out of his hide. Their kiss last night had been a mistake, and now she was spooked. Which left him... where? In too deep, and she hadn't even begun to wade up to her ankles. *Damn.* He needed to go after her, talk it out and offer some reassurance. And he would've too, if it weren't for the fact that he knew how his current audience would react.

Wesley cleared his throat. "Cory and I had some catching up to do. I'm always gonna look out for her. Can't help it, bro."

Yeah, that didn't help with the jealousy. A couple of the guys smirked his way, and he ground his molars together. *Great. Everyone knows I have a thing for Cory.* "Sure. Of course. No big deal." *Jeez, shut up.* He glared at Kyle and John. The two still acted like giddy spectators. Xavier had his earbuds in and continued to focus on his work. Ted's respect for the guy rose a notch. "Don't you two have work to do?"

"Sure, kid." Kyle shot him one more amused look and turned back to the headboard on his workbench.

John straightened and stretched. "I need coffee. Anybody else want me to fill their cup?"

"Nah. I'm good." Ted turned to Wesley, curiosity burning a hole through him. What had he and Cory talked about? Had she told Wesley about last night? "Is everything OK with her?"

"Define OK." Wesley's steady gaze held his. "Untreated, PTSD only gets worse as time passes. She's stuck between a rock and a brick right now."

"I know."

"Take it easy, Ted." Wesley moved closer and lowered his voice. "She wants to get better, and that's the key. She's not self-medicating or acting out in ways that would cause her harm, and she's eating again. I'm hopeful."

Relief turned his knees to rubber, and his attention drifted toward the stairs. He wanted to go after her, find out what was going on in her head...and her heart. "Good. That's good."

"Humph."

"What?" He turned back to find Wesley studying him.

"Might wanna leave her be for now. Let her nerves settle."

"Did she tell you about last night?" he blurted before he could stop himself.

"No." Wes's brow lowered. "What happened last night?"

"Yeah, kid. What happened last night?" Ryan turned up out of nowhere, positioning himself at Ted's other elbow.

"Where'd you come from?" Ted plowed a hand through his

hair. Cory wasn't the only one whose nerves sizzled and popped like water on a hot skillet.

Ryan lifted his filled mug, his sardonic smile firmly in place. "Came down the front stairs for coffee."

"Nothing happened last night." Ted extricated himself from the Wesley and Ryan bookends and returned to his workstation. Wesley made another one of his grunting noises and left. Ryan followed, leaving Ted with his thoughts in turmoil. He tried to focus on his work, but it was no use. His need to talk to Cory overrode everything else. Noah had his monthly meeting with the finishing crew this afternoon. Maybe he could finagle a way to drive her home.

He glanced at the wall clock. Two more hours until lunchtime. After that he'd move upstairs to his office. That would give him a chance to talk to Noah before offering Cory a ride. Forcing his mind off of her, he focused on the maple cradle taking shape beneath his hands and tried once again to lose himself in his work.

The rest of the day dragged by, but at least he'd managed to arrange time with Cory. She'd agreed to let him drive her home, and now he sat in his office waiting while she made up for the time she'd missed earlier. His work for the day was done, so he busied himself organizing the piles on his desk, discarding anything he no longer needed.

"I'm ready." Cory leaned against his door frame, a half smile on her face.

What did that smile mean? Was it a we-need-to-talk-goodbye smile or an I'm-glad-to-see-you expression? His stomach bunched into a knot. "Great. Let's go." He shut his computer down and rose from his chair. "Do you need to stop anywhere in town before we head out?"

She straightened and moved out of the doorway to accommodate him. "Nope. I'm good for now. Thanks."

He caught a whiff of the perfume she wore as they walked side by side down the hall to the back stairway. Whatever she used, it blended with her own unique scent perfectly, the overall effect fresh and lightly floral. How could a woman smell so damn good? "How was your day?" *Lame.* Yep, lame, but he couldn't think of anything else to say. With his insides in a jumble, he couldn't muster enough wit to carry on a conversation.

She slung her purse strap over her shoulder and started down the stairs ahead of him. "Fine. How was yours?"

"It was OK." He wanted to place his hand at the small of her back, guide her through the production area and establish for any who might happen to look that she was his—but she wasn't. Not yet, anyway. He opened the passenger door of his truck for her, knowing better than to help her climb in. How should he start the conversation that had plagued his thoughts all day long? He slid into the driver's seat and started the truck. Once he pulled out of his parking spot and headed for the two-lane highway to the Langfords', he screwed up his courage and plunged right in. "Cory...about last night..."

She studied the dashboard and folded her hands in her lap. "What about it?"

"Do you regret kissing me? You took off so fast that—"

"No." She shook her head and glanced at him. "I don't regret it. In fact, our kiss motivated me to look into getting help now rather than waiting for the law clinic to settle things with the army."

His gut dropped. "It was that bad?"

She chuckled softly, her eyes meeting his. "That didn't come out right."

"Then…it wasn't bad?" He searched her face for some hint of what might be going on inside her head.

She turned away. "At first it was wonderful, and I really did feel like it was my first kiss."

"That's good, right?" He grinned, and his heart took off on a mad dash.

"Sure…but then everything changed, and you turned into the guy who…who—"

"Oh."

"Yeah, oh." She bit her lip, and her hands twisted together in her lap. "I'm sorry."

"Don't be." He turned back to the broken white line on the highway. "It's not your fault, and we should be encouraged. You were able to enjoy it for a few seconds, right?" His grip on the steering wheel tightened. She'd said kissing him had been wonderful, and he'd cling to that for now. Maybe the next time the good part would last longer.

She shot him a doubtful look. "Anyway, I'm going to make a list of therapists in Evansville. If I don't hear from Yale in another month, I'll make an appointment with a place that works on a sliding scale. Wesley said I could use his truck to get there."

She'd gone to Wesley for help instead of coming to him. Jealousy gnawed at him. Cory had a long history with Wes. She was already at ease with him, and even though they were around a decade apart in age, lots of women went for older guys. She'd lost her father at a very early age. Gravitating toward an older man made sense, especially considering all of her issues. Plus, they were both veterans—another thing they had in common. "I didn't think about that," he muttered.

"About what?"

Had he said that out loud? *Shit.* He scrambled for something to say. "About the fact that you don't have a car."

"Nope, and I'm no position to buy one either." She sighed. "I'm saving every dime I can, but it's going to take months."

"Listen, I have this old Chevy pickup truck just sitting idle in the machine shed. It has a rebuilt engine, and the body is in pretty good shape. I could let you have it for really cheap. No down payment required. You can give me a hundred bucks a month for fifteen months, and it's yours." That was stretching it. The engine lay in pieces around the shed. He had all the parts he needed and worked on it whenever he had the time, but with his dad's help, they could have it back together and running like new by the end of the weekend. "The tires are good too."

"Ted…" The worry lines between her eyebrows made an appearance. "You've already done so much for me, and—"

"What have I done for you? Given you rides now and then?" He frowned at her. "The truck isn't doing anybody any good sitting in the shed. Rebuilding engines is kind of a hobby of mine. I can always find another vehicle to work on."

"You're a mechanic too? Another skill to add to your long list." The corners of her mouth tugged up slightly. "Is there anything you can't do?"

"Is that how you see me?" His chest swelled, and warmth spread through him.

"Hmm." She nodded. "You farm, run a successful business that was your brilliant idea to begin with, create amazing furniture and rebuild engines. I've never met anybody like you. Maybe you don't know it, but you're pretty amazing, Ted."

"Thanks." If his chest expanded any more, he might pop a button or two. She'd taken notice, appreciated his abilities enough to comment, and that made him want to do a victory dance. "So, what about the truck?"

"Is it an automatic?"

"No, but I can teach you how to drive a stick shift." Another opportunity to spend time with her. Alone.

"I'd have to look at it first, and try it out to see if I can manage the clutch."

"I have no doubt you can manage." They'd reached the Langfords', and he turned into the driveway.

"It would be really nice not to have to depend on everyone else for rides." Her eyes lit up. "I'll think about it."

"Take your time, and let me know what you decide. The Chevy isn't going anywhere." Especially not in its present disassembled state. He pulled up to the side of the house. "Don't forget, tomorrow we're going to the truck stop. We'll split the bill since it was a tie. Noah, Ryan and Paige are coming, and I'll let the crew know." Or not. He saw no reason to include other single guys.

"I haven't forgotten." She opened her door. "Ted, about the dinner out with my mom, neither of us has much in the way of fancy clothing. I was thinking something kind of casual might be nice."

"I know just the place. Have you and your mom figured out a date yet?"

"I haven't even talked to her about it, but I will. Thanks for the ride."

"Anytime." He watched her walk around the corner of the big house until she disappeared. He loved the way she moved. Cory had an inner strength and grace that showed in the way she carried herself, despite the trauma she'd suffered. Everything about her turned him on, and the more he came to know her, the more convinced he was that she was the woman for him.

He started the truck down the driveway, his mind spinning and his cheeks aching from the smile he couldn't keep off his face. *She thinks I'm amazing.* Their kiss hadn't been a total failure, and he'd come up with a solution to her transportation problem that didn't involve Wesley Holt. Yep, all in all a pretty good day's work.

Fiddling with his radio, Ted found some tunes and turned up the volume. He tapped out the beat on his steering wheel and thought about a second kiss. He couldn't wait to finally hold Cory in his arms and show her all the tenderness she deserved. Once he pulled into the spot by his apartment, he hopped out of his truck and went in search of his dad. He'd be feeding the hogs about now, so he set out for the barn.

He slid the door open and stepped inside. His father's voice carried across the large enclosure. Ted laughed. The way his dad talked to the hogs always tickled him. His old man even discussed politics and current events with the swine while filling their feeders. "Hey, Dad. Need a hand?"

"Nope. I'm about done." His dad upended the bucket he carried and tapped the bottom so the last few remaining bits of silage dropped out. "You going to join me and your mom for supper tonight?"

"Yeah, I'm starving." He shoved his hands into his front pockets and followed his dad out of the building. "I have a favor to ask."

His dad glanced at him. "I'm all ears."

"You know the Chevy pickup I've been tinkering with? Do you have time this weekend to help me get it put back together and get it roadworthy?"

"What's the sudden hurry? It's been months since you took that engine apart."

"Cory doesn't have transportation." Heat rose under his collar. "I've offered to sell the truck to her for cheap."

"Oh?" His dad's eyes lit up. "How are things going with you two?"

He wanted to spill it all, lay his feelings out on the summer grass for his father to see, but he didn't. Just because he was falling didn't mean Cory felt the same, and he didn't want to deal with the mortifying aftermath if things went to hell. "They're going OK. She's settling into her job and seems to be doing better every day. We're just friends."

"She likes you." His dad studied him as they walked up the porch steps to the front door.

The words he'd blurted to his dad the Sunday Cory came for dinner returned to him. He'd told his father that he was sick of being *liked*. "For now." He rubbed the back of his neck. "I'm working on it, Dad. Slow but sure I'm working on it." Bit by bit, one defense mechanism at time, he intended to find his way into her heart for good.

"Sure." His dad slapped him on the back. "I can find a few hours to work on the truck. Saturday afternoon works for me, and if we need to, we can work on it Sunday evening too."

"Thanks." They both kicked off their boots and went inside for supper, Ted's cheek-aching smile back in place. "Cory thinks I'm amazing."

His dad laughed. "You don't say."

CHAPTER EIGHT

IT HAD BEEN ONE WEEK and three days since she and Ted shared a kiss—one week and one day since she'd called all the therapists on the list she'd assembled and found out it would take anywhere from six to eight weeks to get on the schedule. If she didn't hear from Yale within the next month, she'd call and make an appointment. She had a solid plan of action.

She blew out a frustrated breath and leaned in over the bathroom sink to get closer to the mirror while applying her mascara. Ted had promised to pick her up early for their bowling night so he could give her a lesson on driving a stick shift. Checking her reflection, she frowned. Her highlights needing touching up, and she had nothing to wear that he hadn't already seen. What must Ted think? Her heart gave a little flutter, and she glanced at her watch. He'd be here soon.

She'd better be a fast learner with that old truck if she wanted her transportation problems solved. She could easily afford the one hundred per month, and then she'd have a little extra cash for other things—like buying new clothes.

The notion of shopping alone sent an icy shiver through her. Malls had too many shadowy places and dark halls leading to utility closets. Shopping centers were filled with too many people who would crowd her space. Unfamiliars bumping into her—even thinking about it brought a sheen of perspiration to her brow.

She'd ask Brenda to come along. Maybe they could plan a trip to the outlet mall soon. All the Fourth of July sales would be going on. She did one more perusal of her reflection, brushed her hair and sighed. As always, Brenda would look gorgeous tonight, and she'd look like a little brown wren next to her. Nothing she could do about it.

She walked to the living room to grab her purse from the coffee table and headed out the door for the big house. Coming around the corner, she heard voices. Ceejay, her children and their slobbery dog were together on the veranda. "Hey, how's it going?" Cory climbed the first two steps and sat down. Lucinda and Toby were settled at a child-size plastic table next to the railing. "What are you up to there?"

"I'm teaching Toby how to play go fish." Lucinda raised her hand full of cards for her to see.

"I'm winning," Toby boasted.

"I'm letting you win because you're just learning." Lucinda shook her head.

Toby shot his big sister a rebellious look. "Nuh-uh. I'm winning."

"Play nice, you two," Ceejay cut in. "Where are you off to this evening, Cory?" Micah sat in her lap with his pacifier in his mouth and a sleepy, peaceful expression on his angelic face.

"Ted is going to teach me how to drive a stick shift, and then we're going bowling."

Noah came through the front door with his hands full of Popsicles. He handed them around to his family and smiled at her. "I would've brought one more if I'd known you were here. Would you like one?"

"That's OK." Seeing the Langfords doing nothing other than hanging out together on their front porch sent a pang of longing through her. And envy. They had it all, and their kind of domestic bliss was so far out of her reach she didn't even dare to try for it.

"Did I hear you say Ted is going to teach you how to drive a stick shift?" Noah handed Ceejay a Popsicle and lifted Micah from her lap, settling the now sleeping toddler against his shoulder.

"Yep. If I can manage the clutch, I'm going to buy his old Chevy pickup."

"Really?" Ceejay's eyes widened. "He's had that truck since he turned sixteen. It was his dad's for a long time before that. That old thing has got to be close to twenty-five years old." She chuckled. "His truck is older than he is."

"He rebuilt the engine." Cory jumped in to defend the pickup...or Ted. She wasn't sure which. "It has new brakes, good tires, and he swears it's going to last another twenty."

"Is Ted your boyfriend?" Lucinda glanced at her over her shoulder. The little girl's lips were blue from the Popsicle she stuck back into her mouth.

Heat flooded Cory's cheeks. "Um...we're friends." Ceejay's warning not to hurt Ted came back to her. She looked down the driveway and wished she was already on her way. Yes indeed. A vehicle of her own would definitely be a good thing.

Noah walked over to stand by the two children playing cards. "Lucinda, it's not polite to ask grown-ups personal questions."

"I'm sorry. I just wanted to know." Lucinda looked up at her dad. "Ted *needs* a girlfriend. That's what Mommy and Aunt Jenny said, and Cory—"

"Lucinda Mae," Ceejay cried. "You don't need to repeat every single thing you hear." She turned to Cory. "I apologize. *That* conversation happened long before you were hired."

"It's OK." It was true. Ted did need a girlfriend, and the fact that he was spending so much time with her was not helping him to find one. Her heart wrenched at the thought of him with someone else. How like life to place the perfect man in her path just when she was too screwed up to do anything about it.

Her throat constricted, and anger reared its ugly head. She struggled to gain control over her out-of-control emotions. PTSD. Sudden irrational anger and irritability were symptoms. She'd been reading about her condition over the past weeks. The sad thing was, PTSD didn't go away on its own. She rose from her place and leaned against the column.

"There's Teddy." Toby hopped up from his place and ran to the steps, dropping his Popsicle on the way. Their monster dog rose from his place and made quick work of cleaning up the red, sticky mess. "He's drivin' that old truck." Toby tugged at Cory's hand. "I'm gonna have a pickup just like my daddy and Teddy."

"I'm sure you will." She squeezed his sticky little hand. "You have to put on a few more years first."

"I know." He took his hand back and hopped down the stairs. "Hi, Teddy," Toby shouted and ran toward him.

Ted climbed out of the Chevy. He wore faded jeans and a navy-blue polo shirt. He looked good. "Hey, little man." He picked Toby up and tossed him into the air. "What kind of trouble are you getting into today?"

Toby giggled and shrieked as he came back down, to be caught safely in Ted's arms. "I'm not in any kind of trouble. I'm playing cards with my big sister."

"Kicking her butt, no doubt." Ted set him back on his feet.

"Yep." Toby nodded happily.

Lucinda came to stand by the railing. "I'm letting him win because he's little, and he's just learning."

Toby opened his mouth to retort, and Ted drew him against his knees and covered his mouth with a gentle hand. "You're one mighty fine big sister, Luce." He peered down at Toby. "Right, little man?" Toby rolled his eyes. Ted laughed and let him go. "Hey, Ceejay, Noah. What are you guys up to tonight?"

"We have an exciting evening planned." Noah bounced an awakened and fussing Micah and paced the porch. "First, these three are getting baths, then we're watching a Disney movie. I believe the master plan for the evening is to hit the sack early."

"That's my idea of a good time these days." Ceejay yawned and rubbed her baby bump. "Have a nice evening, you two."

"Thanks. We will." Ted turned his warm gray eyes Cory's way. "You ready for your first driving lesson?"

Her stomach fluttered. "I guess. So, this is it?" She walked down the stairs and circled the truck. It had just the right number of dents, a few scratches, a little rust and faded blue paint to give it character. The payload had obviously been well used, because it was pretty beat-up. She loved it. Inspecting each tire, she noticed that they were all brand-new. Had he bought them just for her? This time her heart fluttered. *Perfect guy; bad timing.*

Ted opened the passenger door for her. "There's a country road down the highway about a quarter mile. It doesn't get any traffic to speak of. I thought I'd take you there. It's a great place to learn."

"All right. Let's do this." Cory climbed in and buckled her seat belt. She waved good-bye to the Langfords as they pulled out. "They are the nicest people, and those kids are so adorable."

"They are. Do you want to have children someday?"

"I used to. Growing up as an only child, I always thought it would be great to have at least two children of my own."

"Used to?" Ted threw a questioning look her way.

"It's hard to have kids when…when—"

"It's not always going to be like this, Cory. You'll get better." He turned onto a narrow asphalt road and pulled to a stop. "I think you'd be an excellent mom."

"You do?" She frowned. "Based on what?"

"Based on how you are around my cousin's kids and my nieces and nephews. Based on the way Toby reached for your hand without hesitation. Children have a sixth sense about adults. He trusts you."

Her chest filled with warmth. "I used to have this fantasy…"

Ted's eyes darkened as they met hers. "Tell me."

The warmth in her chest turned to heat under his intense scrutiny, and she turned away. "My mom and I never had it easy, but she was always there for me. She had a knack for turning all of our hardships into adventures, and we had fun." The memories spilling through her mind brought a smile to her face. "Trips to the secondhand store became treasure hunts, and we were displaced royalty on the lam from enemies of the state, stuff like that."

She shrugged. "I used to dream of having a husband and a family of my own. My fantasy was to someday have a place with a mother-in-law apartment for my mom. All she ever wanted was to be a stay-at-home mother and wife. That didn't work out, and I was hoping to give her the chance to spend time with her grandkids without having to worry about working so hard just to keep a roof over her head. She'd be the best grandmother ever. I'd love to make her life easier if I could. She deserves it."

She glanced at him to gauge his reaction and lost the ability to speak. The tenderness and longing filling his eyes as he looked back stole her breath. Her heart tumbled over itself, and images of curly-headed, gray-eyed babies danced through her mind. *Fantasy* being the operative word in that scenario. Can't have babies if you can't let the man touch you.

Her heart breaking, she broke the eye contact before he could see the despair. "So, show me how to drive this truck."

"Cory…"

"Driving lesson, Ted. We came here so I can learn how to master this stick shift."

He blew out a loud breath and shifted in his seat. "OK, watch. This is neutral." He stepped on the clutch and brought the gearshift to the middle, moving it back and forth so she could see. "To the left and up is first, straight down is second." He demonstrated each shift. "Over to the right and up is third, and straight down from third is fourth. All the way over and down is reverse. Got it?"

"I think so."

"To start out, turn on the engine with the gearshift in neutral. Engage the clutch and shift into first. Ease up on the clutch while also easing down on the gas. Like this." He demonstrated, and they crept down the road. "I want you to practice shifting into first a few times before we try shifting while driving. Starting out is the hardest part." He stopped the truck and climbed out so they could switch places. Cory slid over, adjusted everything to accommodate her height and waited for Ted to get settled. He leaned close and put his arm around the back of the seat.

Distracted by his nearness and intoxicating scent, she repeated his instructions. "Engage the clutch and shift into first." She spared him a smile before turning all of her attention to coordinating the clutch, gas and driving. "The engine sounds great, by the way."

"Of course it does." He squeezed her shoulder. "Do you think

I'd put you in a vehicle that wasn't one hundred and ten percent safe and reliable?"

Heat flooded her cheeks. "I appreciate your willingness to part with it. Ceejay said you've had this pickup since you were sixteen."

"That's right." He ran his hand over the dashboard. "She's my first."

"She?" Cory laughed. "And here I was going to name *him* Freddy Dent." Easing up on the clutch, she gave it a little gas. The truck lurched and stalled out. "Well, that didn't go like I expected."

"You were too quick with the gas. Try to apply equal amounts of pressure and easing up."

"Easier said than done." She restarted the truck and tried again. This time the pickup hopped down the road a few feet before stalling out again. "Grr."

Ted grinned. "That was better. We moved a few feet."

"Third time's the charm." She bit her lower lip and started the truck again. It bucked a little, but then smoothed out and rolled down the country road. "What do I do to stop?"

"Step on the brake and the clutch, then put it into neutral."

Cory brought the pickup to a stop and practiced shifting into first gear three more times before turning to Ted. A sense of accomplishment thrummed through her, and she lifted her chin. "I did it, and I love this old truck. Thanks so much for your willingness to part with it." She ran her hands around the steering wheel. Strong emotions welled out of nowhere, the intensity blindsiding her. Uppermost were her growing feelings for the generous, sweet man beside her. Too much. These were feelings she couldn't face right now.

"Hey." Ted tucked a strand of hair behind her ear. "What just happened, Cory?"

She shrugged. "Just overcome with everything, I guess. I'm very grateful to you, Noah, and everyone else in Perfect. I'm a total stranger, and yet you've all taken me in and been so kind." *Good save.* So much better than admitting she'd fallen hopelessly in love with him. She couldn't act on those feelings. With all the crazy she carried, that path could only lead to disaster, and Ted was the last person in the world she wanted to hurt.

"You've been generous too. Don't think the extra things you do around L&L go unnoticed."

"It's my way of saying thank you." She forced her mind away from the ache in her heart. "I'm ready to try second and third gear."

"It's going to have to wait until your next lesson. We have to get going." He tapped his watch. "Beer, pizza and bowling await." He opened his door and climbed out, coming around the hood to the driver's side.

Cory slid back to the passenger seat. "Where is this bowling alley, anyway? Not in Perfect."

"Riverside Tavern and Lanes is halfway between Perfect and Evansville just outside of Rockport, which is why we need to get going." Ted backed the truck around and headed for the highway. "There's a mall and a movie theater too."

"You've been to this bowling alley before?"

"Sure. Lots of times. Believe it or not, when I went to middle school, we took bowling in gym. Riverside Tavern is where we went to practice. We also had the opportunity to learn how to polka and square dance." He chuckled. "Rural education is… different."

"I'm surprised they'd take a bunch of kids to a tavern."

"We went early in the morning. The bar was closed."

"It's been years since I've bowled." She shifted in her seat so she half faced him. "There's a place not too far from the trailer park where we kids used to hang out, mostly for the arcade and junk food."

"I enjoy the game, but I haven't been bowling in years either." His gray eyes sparkled as he smiled at her. "We're well matched."

Well matched. She peered out her window and tried to swallow away the sudden tightness in her throat. He had no idea how his words affected her.

"There you go again."

"Hmm?"

"It's like…one minute you're here with me and happy, and the next you just fall off into a sad place, and you're gone." He chuffed out a breath. "I want to follow, Cory. I want to go there with you, so I can pull you through whatever it is that takes away that pretty smile of yours."

"Add perceptiveness to your long list of fine qualities," she muttered and blinked away the sting in her eyes. "I have PTSD, Ted. Abrupt mood swings, anxiety, anger and depression are all part of the roller-coaster ride I'm on every single day." Turning to glance at him, she bit her lip and considered her next words. "I'm no good for you. I'm no good for anyone right now."

❦ ❦ ❦

Damn. He'd done it again—gotten too close. Time to back off. "I understand. All I'm asking for is friendship." *Bullshit.* "Friends help each other. I want to help."

"I worry…"

"What?" He studied her, hating to see her mouth turned down the way it was now. "What do you worry about?"

She shrugged. "I worry that you're spending so much time with me that it might prevent you from finding somebody who—"

"Don't give it another thought. I'm right where I want to be." Their eyes caught and held, and his heart stuttered to a stop. The world fell away, leaving nothing but the two of them suspended in time. He wanted to pull over to the side of the road, draw her into his arms, and kiss the sadness away, hold her until nothing remained of the trauma haunting her. The truck swerved toward the shoulder of the road, and he snapped back to reality. *Shit. Pay attention.*

"I wish we'd met under different circumstances, or at a different time," she whispered, turning to look out the passenger side window.

"We met exactly when we were supposed to meet." His jaw tightened and twitched. "And when you're ready to date, I'll be right here. I'm like this old truck." He patted the steering wheel. "Dependable. Steady. I'll never let you down or leave you stranded."

She opened her mouth to reply. He didn't really want to listen to her tell him to forget about her and move on. Too late, anyway. His heart rose and fell on her smiles and sighs, and she had no clue. "I have an idea," he said. "Let's relax and have a good time tonight. No pressure, just friends hanging out."

"Good idea." A half smile erased some of the sadness from her face. "This should be interesting. Kyle isn't shy at all when he's at work, but did you notice he didn't say a word when Brenda was there?"

"Yep. I noticed." He grinned. "I'm surprised he worked up enough gumption to ask her out."

"I wonder if they'll hit it off."

"I hope so. Kyle's a good guy." They settled into a companionable silence, and he let his mind wander, imagining a future with Cory—imagining a time when physical affection, holding hands, and loving came easily to her. Once she began seeing a therapist, how long did it take before she started to get better? He glanced at her. She seemed to be as lost in thought as he. "What are you thinking about?"

She startled and blinked. "Nothing in particular."

"Humph. I'd pay good money to see what goes on in that head of yours."

She rolled her eyes. "That would be a waste of perfectly good cash."

The mall came into view, and the intersection where he had to turn onto the frontage road was just ahead. He was tempted to miss it, like they'd missed the exit to her mom's place. They could keep on driving, and he'd have her all to himself. Downshifting, he switched to the left lane and put on his blinker.

"Ted…" Her voice held a strained note.

"What is it, honey?" *Oh, shit.* Another slip, but she didn't seem to notice. He turned into the Riverside Tavern's parking lot and pulled into the first spot he found. He noticed she'd gone pale, and her forehead glistened.

"Don't…uh…" she stammered.

Tension pulsed through the cab, and he caught the wild panic flashing through her eyes. She swallowed several times, and her breathing came in short gasps. Her struggle broke his heart, and more than anything he longed to comfort her. "We'll stay right here, Cory. Take your time and don't forget to breathe."

Her hands fisted in her lap. She drew a long breath, then another. "Don't leave me alone in there."

"Didn't I tell you I'm like this old truck?" He risked running his hand over her shoulder, relieved when she didn't flinch away. Did she even realize she rarely pulled away or flinched anymore when he touched her? "I won't let you down. I'll stick by your side tonight. You have my promise. Nobody is going to get between us."

"Sucks." She gave a slight nod. "PTSD sucks."

"I know it does." He made no move to climb out of the cab. Letting her take the lead was important. "Breathe now."

She shot him a disgruntled look, and he bit the inside of his cheek to keep from grinning. She wouldn't be disgruntled if she wasn't coming out of her panic.

"It's not like I can stop myself." She inhaled deeply as if to prove her point.

"Right. Sorry."

She stared out the windshield at the building before them. "This place is old. It looks like it's been around since Indiana became a state."

He glanced at the tavern. It had been built to resemble a two-storied German inn, with light-colored stucco and exposed wooden beams stained a dark brown. The bowling alley had been added years later, and the brick-fronted squat addition didn't match the tavern part at all. "Could be. The bar and grill, anyway." Just then he spotted Brenda and Kyle crossing the parking lot toward the front doors. "There they are. If you aren't ready, I'm perfectly content to sit here until you are."

"You're such a great guy."

"I know." He cocked an eyebrow. "You ought to snap me up before anyone else catches on." *Wrong thing to say.* The corners of her mouth turned down, and she fell back into that place called Sorrowful. No GPS system in the world could help him follow her there. "Come on, Cory. Let's team up and pulverize Kyle and Brenda with our combined bowling skill."

"No wagers." She shot him a pointed look and reached for her door handle.

"No promises." He climbed out, and they walked side by side toward the couple waiting for them by the large wooden double doors. "I can't help it if I have a competitive streak."

"OK, but don't bet against me, just against them."

"Deal." He wanted to take her hand in his so badly he had to force himself to keep from reaching for her. Lord, it was painful, all the loving and affection he longed to give her and couldn't. Frustration and anger tightened his jaw again, and his pulse raced. If only he could vent his anger on the asshole who'd done this to his girl. Nothing would satisfy him more.

Cory was the genuine article, sweet, compassionate and sincere—not to mention beautiful inside and out. She was smart, quick-witted and talented, everything he wanted and more, and he ached to make her his. Knocking down a bunch of wooden pins with a twelve-pound ball appealed to him about now.

"Hey, Kyle." Ted held out his hand, and the two of them shook. "Evening, Brenda. It's nice to see you again."

She flashed him a dazzling smile. "It's nice to see you too. Are you two hungry? Do we want to eat or bowl first?"

Kyle opened the door and held it. "Let's eat. I'm starving. How about you, Cory?" He smiled warmly in her direction. "Eat or bowl first?"

"Food first. I can't bowl on an empty stomach." She shot Ted a questioning look. "Do they have other stuff besides pizza?"

"Sure." Ted took the risk and placed his hand at the small of Cory's back, ushering her through the double doors. No cringe or flinch. He withdrew the touch before it registered with her. Progress? Was it possible she was growing more and more accustomed to his nearness? His pulse surged in hopeful anticipation.

Pins knocking together, the rumble of voices and blaring country music reverberated down the hall from the right. They veered toward another set of opened double doors leading to the dark interior of the bar and grill. Cory stopped in her tracks, her posture rigid with tension.

He came around to stand in front of her, leaning down to whisper in her ear, "It's OK. I'm right here, and I won't let any harm come to you."

She shot him a grateful smile, and her gaze roamed over his face. He caught a glimpse of something deep in her lovely brown eyes. Trust. Affection. Damn, it felt good to see his own emotions reflected back. Their eyes locked. His lungs seized, and for the life of him, he couldn't catch his breath or move from the spot. He didn't want it to end.

"Break it up, you two," Kyle called. "We have a table. Brenda's already ordered a pitcher of beer."

Color flooded Cory's cheeks, and she followed Kyle. The interior of the restaurant was typical for the era it had been built, with heavy dark wood, burgundy carpet, dim lighting and votive candles in glass containers on each table. The bar formed a rectangle in the center of the room, also constructed of bulky pine stained almost black. Stairs off to their left led to a second floor with more tables and a balcony overlooking the bar.

Kyle led them to a large booth in the back corner of the first floor. Menus and ice water had already been delivered. Kyle claimed the side with his back to the wall, and took his place next to Brenda. Ted slid into their side first, knowing Cory hated being hemmed in.

She sat beside him and smiled at Brenda. "It's been awhile since we've bowled together, hasn't it? What made you decide on this particular activity for tonight?"

Brenda shrugged. "It made sense. Kyle and I live in Evansville, and you two live out in Podunk. This is halfway between the two." She turned her high-octane smile his way. "What do you like to do for fun, Ted?"

Was it his imagination, or did Cory just lean a little closer to him? "I don't have a lot of free time. I put in a lot of hours at L&L, and I help my dad farm. I do have a few hobbies I enjoy, though. I manage to keep busy."

"Speaking of hobbies, I'm buying an old Chevy pickup truck he rebuilt," Cory added, her voice tinged with unmistakable pride. "We drove it here tonight. You'll have to come take a look at my new wheels. It's got a lot of character, just like Ted." She graced him with an admiring look.

OK, this is new. He forced himself to keep his expression neutral and glanced at Kyle. "How's school coming along?"

"It's coming." Kyle slid his arm over the back of the seat so that it almost draped around Brenda's shoulders. "You know how it is. School and working full-time can be a grind."

"You're in school?" Brenda turned to study her date. "What are you studying?"

Kyle nodded. "I have a few prerequisites I'm finishing up before I can apply for programs to become a physician's assistant. I was in the medical corps in the army."

New appreciation shone in Brenda's eyes. "Huh, I had no idea you were so ambitious."

"There's a lot you don't know about me." He studied her right back. "That's what dating is all about, right? We're here to get to know each other."

"Exactly."

Their server, a young man wearing black slacks, a red shirt and a white apron, delivered a pitcher of beer and four frosted mugs. "Do you need a few minutes, or are you ready to order?"

"We need a few minutes," Kyle answered. He brought his

arm back down and picked up the menus, passing one to each of them. "Haven't even looked yet."

"You're not really shy at all, are you?" Brenda asked, casting Kyle a speculative glance.

He answered with a cocky grin, "Nope, not really."

Confusion clouded Brenda's face. "But you didn't say a word that afternoon I came to L&L."

"That wasn't shyness." Kyle stared deeply into her eyes. "I was just stunned speechless by your sudden appearance in our midst. All the while you were flirting with those other guys, I was busy strategizing."

"Strategizing?" She blinked.

"Yes, ma'am." Kyle picked up his menu and started reading. "I know a good thing when I see it. I plan to make you mine."

Brenda gasped, and Cory made a choked, snorting sound.

Ted laughed. "You two want to be alone? Cory and I can move to a different table."

"Don't you dare." Brenda's cheeks grew pink, and she shot Cory a pleading look. "I had no idea…"

"So much for Shy Guy." Cory grinned back. "Read the menu, Bren. Have a beer, and let's eat. Ted and I aren't going anywhere."

Ted and I. He loved the easy way those words rolled off her tongue, the way she took it for granted that they were in agreement. It felt as if they were a couple—for the moment, anyway. "You don't want pizza, do you?" He reached for the pitcher and filled their mugs.

"Nope. I'm going to have a Reuben with fries." She told him. "What about you?"

"I'm a big fan of their sauerkraut-and-sausage pizza." He nudged her shoulder with his. "Want to share one with me? They're great."

"Hmm." Cory continued to study her menu. "Sounds like a very weird combination if you ask me."

"Chicken."

Her head snapped up, and she scowled. "Do I sense a wager coming on? Because we did talk about this on the way in."

"No." He shook his head and winked. "Not a wager. A challenge. Try something new."

Her eyes filled with amusement. "A challenge? All right. I'll share a sauerkraut-and-sausage pizza with you on one condition."

"Agreed, and I already know what the condition is."

"Do you?" She put her menu in the middle of the table with the others.

"Sure. If you don't like the pizza, I'll order a Reuben for you."

"You're a good man, Ted, and smart." She graced him with a heart-stopping smile.

"That's what I keep trying to tell you," he whispered, reveling in the way her breath hitched.

A few pitchers of beer and an equal number of bowling games later, Ted was eager to have Cory all to himself again. After her initial reaction to the new surroundings, she'd relaxed and enjoyed herself, and true to his word, he'd stuck close all night. He stood and stretched. "This was fun, but it's getting late, and I'm ready to head out. We'll have to do this again sometime."

"It was fun." Brenda gathered her things. "Next time it'll be the boys against the girls."

"Ha!" Cory straightened from unlacing her shoes, a smug expression on her face. "You just want to switch it up because Ted and I trounced you two."

"Not by much," Kyle muttered.

"We rock." Ted held his hands in the air, and Cory stood up and slapped her palms against his.

"You ready to go?" he asked her. "I've got to be up early tomorrow to help my dad."

"Good night, you two," Cory called out. "I'll phone you tomorrow, Bren. We can figure out a time to head to the outlet mall."

"Sounds good." Brenda waved them away, her eyes on Kyle. "Later."

Cory let out a happy sigh as they walked together to the counter to turn in their borrowed shoes.

"You enjoyed yourself tonight, didn't you?" he asked.

"I did. Thanks. I even liked the pizza you ordered."

"I noticed."

"I think Kyle and Brenda hit it off really well, don't you?" She placed her bowling shoes next to his on the counter.

"Sure."

"I'm glad. For a minute there, I was worried that she'd…"

"That she'd what?" He recalled the way Brenda had flirted with him earlier, and the way Cory had moved closer to his side. "Make a pass at me?" Her face scrunched up like she'd bitten into something distasteful, and he had to laugh. Her expression confirmed his wild hope.

"I've had too much beer," she grumbled. "Do not pay any attention to anything I say. I was just concerned for you, is all." She hiccupped. "Dang. I always get the hiccups when I drink carbonated beverages."

His spirits soared. "Concerned?"

"Sure." She hiccupped again.

"You don't believe Brenda is right for me?" he teased, ushering her toward the hall leading to the front door.

"I don't even want to think about that." Her expression turned pensive. The corners of her luscious mouth turned down and sadness filled her pretty brown eyes again.

He hadn't meant to steer her onto the road to Sorrowful, but it looked like she might be headed that way. He scrambled to head her off. "You sure can bowl."

Her expression brightened. "I know, huh? So can you." She slugged his shoulder. "A man of many talents."

"And you're a woman who's had a few too many beers." He chuckled as she hiccupped again. "We'd better get you home." He took her arm and led her out into the soft warmth of a southern Indiana night.

"I don't suppose we could have another driving lesson right now." She turned a wide-eyed, hopeful expression his way.

His heart melted. "Not tonight."

"Bummer. I really want that Chevy."

"I'll be done on the farm fairly early tomorrow. How about we give that stick shift another go in the afternoon, say around two?"

"Yeah. Let's do that. And afterwards, I can give you a ride home in my truck."

"Humph, an optimist." He chuckled and almost reached for her hand.

"No, just determined." She hiccupped again and sucked in a huge breath, holding it for a few seconds before letting it go.

"Does that get rid of hiccups?" He opened the passenger door for her and walked around to the driver's side, a wide smile on his face.

"I guess we'll find out."

He settled himself behind the wheel. "When we get back to your place, do you want to go down by the river to look at the stars for a few minutes? It's a clear night."

"Sure. There's too much light pollution at my mom's place. We can't really see the stars in the city."

"Buckle your seat belt, Cory," he said, putting his own on.

"Stargazing coming right up." The evening had gone far better than he expected, and his blood thrummed with the thrill of triumph. He reminded himself to continue taking it easy and going slow. "I don't know if you noticed, but I installed a new HD sound system. Go ahead and try it out."

"Cool." Cory leaned forward and turned on the radio. "There's even a jack for my iPod. You thought of everything."

"I have to be honest, I didn't put the sound system in for you. I hadn't considered selling this truck until we talked. I have a lot of sentimental feelings for this old girl, and I still enjoy driving her. I was going to do some bodywork next. If you want, I still can."

"You mean *him*, and no. I kind of like Freddy the way he is. The dents and rusty spots are part of this truck's personality."

She ran her hand over the dashboard, and he imagined her warm palm skimming over his heated flesh in much the same way. His mouth lost all moisture, and his pulse kicked up a few notches. Struggling to bring himself under control, he thought about cutting hay, mucking out the hog barn, anything that would take his mind off sex.

Cory found a radio station she liked and sang along softly with the tune. Her slightly husky, feminine voice washed over him in a sensuous caress, setting off another wave of heat. *Not helping.* He gritted his teeth and exhaled slowly through his nose. Baby steps. Patience and...more patience, followed by many cold showers. Maybe he'd take a dip in the Ohio tonight—right after he saw Cory safely behind her locked door.

"Paige told me there's a poker group in Perfect that meets once a month. How come you never go?"

The reminder did wonders to squelch his raging lust. "I used to have a thing for Paige. After she and Ryan paired up, hanging out with them just got awkward." He cast her a quick look. "I got over it long ago, but I've never gotten around to joining the group."

"Are you sure you're over her?"

"I was very young, and what I felt for Paige was infatuation. And yeah, I'm sure, but working with the two of them is a constant reminder that I don't measure up." Oh, man. He should not have said that. There was just something about Cory that drew these embarrassing confessions out of him at the oddest moments.

"What are you talking about, Ted? In what universe do you not measure up?"

Her indignation on his behalf went a long way to improving his mood. He chuckled low in his throat. "It's nice to have you as my own personal cheerleader."

"That's right, and don't you forget it." She shoved his shoulder. "I've got your six, bro, just like you have mine."

Bro? There was nothing brotherly about the way he felt about her. "My six?" One side of his mouth quirked up.

"Yeah, it's a military term meaning we've got each other's backs. If you're facing twelve o'clock, you can't see the six behind you."

"I know what it means. I've been surrounded by military-speak for the past five years." They'd come to the Langfords' drive, and he drove up to park next to the big house. "When you drive a stick shift, you have to use the parking brake, or you can leave the truck in first gear so it doesn't coast." He pulled up on the brake and shut off the engine. "Stars. Let's go see if we can pull a couple of them down tonight."

Jamming his lusting hands into his front pockets, he walked along behind her. "I love that old willow by the bank. It's got to be over a hundred years old. I imagine the generations of Lovejoys picnicking under its shade." They reached the edge of the Ohio, and he remained a few steps away from her, enjoying the view of her enticing backside.

"Wow." Cory stared up into the canopy of stars, a whisper-soft breeze playing with her silken hair.

He gazed at her, taking her in, memorizing every tiny detail. "I have an idea."

"Of course you do." She smiled at him over her shoulder.

A riot of sensations stampeded through him. "What if you were to kiss me again, only this time, we'll end it before things go bad?"

She turned to study him, her silhouette against the horizon limned with thousands of sparkling sky diamonds. The image would remain with him for the rest of his life, of that he had no doubt. "What if I put my arms around you for a few seconds? When you were upset earlier, I wanted to comfort you. What if you let me do that now?"

"I don't know if that's such a good idea." She worried her bottom lip between her teeth.

"I'm still convinced that replacing the bad memories with good ones will help." He took a step closer. "I've got your six, Cory. I won't let any harm come to you." Miracle of miracles, she stepped closer to him. They both stood perfectly still, no more than six inches separating them. His breath got stuck somewhere between his heart and his throat.

Tilting her head, she scrutinized him. "Only for a few seconds, right?" She placed her hands on his shoulders. "I'll back away when I start to feel...when things..."

"Exactly." Slowly, and ever so tenderly, he drew her close, wrapping her up in his arms. She sighed, and the warm stir of air against his lips nearly undid him. He waited, holding his breath—seconds turning to centuries. At long last, she closed the gap. When he was sure he couldn't take the tension another second, she pressed her sweet lips against his, opening to him when he deepened their kiss.

Cory leaned into him, letting herself rest against his fevered body so they touched from shoulders to knees. Her arms came up to circle his neck, and a feminine groan left her mouth to settle into his. Unable to stop himself, he tightened his hold and poured all of the love and longing he felt for her into the best kiss of his life.

All too soon, she backed away, leaving him bereft. The sounds of their breathing filled the space between them. Her chest rose and fell. His arms ached to draw her back against him and never let her go. "You OK?"

She pondered his question for a few moments before nodding. "I am. Thanks for a lovely evening. I had fun."

"Me too." He walked beside her to the carriage house. "Tomorrow we'll finish your driving lesson, and if everything goes well, you can give me a ride home."

Her smile came quickly. "I'll have that first check ready. You'll have to tell me where to go to transfer the title."

"I will. I'll keep it on my insurance until you have it covered."

"I already talked to my mom's agent. I'll call him on Monday and get it started." She stood at her door and drew her keys out of her purse. "Tomorrow at two?"

"Right." He backed away, keeping her in his sights until she was inside and he heard the deadbolt turn. How undignified would it be to run around the Langfords' yard with his arms pumping the air? He managed to keep it together until he was near his truck, then he threw up his fists and jumped for the stars. Damn, he felt good.

CHAPTER NINE

CORY POURED HERSELF A CUP of coffee. Her hand shook so badly, some of it spilled onto the counter. The nightmares that had awakened her had been the worst ever, and she hurt inside and out—in every possible way, shape and form. She'd been selfish and naive, wanting desperately to believe in Ted's crazy theory that bad memories could be wiped out by good ones. Not so. Just when she thought things had improved, her PTSD took on a new twist. Her flashbacks weren't just about the rape anymore.

She closed her mind against the fresh assault on her psyche, pushing back the memories of things she'd seen while traveling with supply units. No use dwelling on them now. The clock on the small stove showed four a.m. No chance of catching any more sleep now, and she didn't want to risk it anyhow. She'd had more than her quota of hellish dreams, thank you very much.

Her eyes felt as if they had desert sand under the lids. Exhausted, she leaned against the counter and tried to rub away the grittiness. The hollow ache of hopelessness dragged her back to the dark place she'd been before Brenda and her mom had forced her into the land of the living. She wanted to crawl back into bed, pull the covers over her head and hide from the stark reality she couldn't escape. How the hell was she supposed to face Ted today? For that matter, how the hell was she supposed to face the rest of the day?

More out of habit than hope, she headed for her laptop to check for word from the law clinic. Setting her coffee **mug** on the end table, she perched on the edge of the couch and opened it up. She brought up her e-mail and scanned for the law clinic. Nothing. Of course there was nothing. A tear trickled down her cheek, then another.

Maybe she should text Ted to cancel their driving lesson. No. Cowardice had never been her MO, and besides, it wouldn't be fair. Best to have the conversation with him that was long overdue. They had to stop pretending they were a normal couple getting to know each other. Nothing about her could be referred to as "normal." She'd kept putting the talk off because she loved being with him, loved the way he made her forget. Too bad Sergeant Dickhead wouldn't allow Ted's sweet kisses to wipe out the violence of his assault. Her heart wrenched painfully in her chest.

The birds outside filled the early morning with their calls, offering a welcome distraction. She focused on the sound for a few minutes. Drawn by their song, Cory rose from the couch and walked out the door with her coffee mug in hand. The dew-covered grass tickled her bare feet, offering another welcome distraction. She made her way to the large willow growing on the river's edge. Ducking under the veil of hanging, leaf-filled branches, she made her way to the center of the clearing beneath. She sank to the ground, leaning back against the broad, gnarled old trunk.

The Langfords' property was situated on a bend in the river, and she watched the dark water wend and swirl its way around the slight protrusion of land. Dawn lightened the eastern horizon, and the water's movement mesmerized her. She settled. Her mind went blessedly blank and still. Grabbing onto the respite with both hands, she decided to spend the entire day right here in the midst of the birds and critters making so much noise. Watching the day grow brighter in increments, she remained in the stillness. Time slid by like the river currents in front of her...

"Morning, Cory."

Cory jerked, and some of her coffee sloshed out over the side of her mug. She set it down beside her and shook the drips from her hand. "You startled me, Noah. I didn't expect to run into anyone this early."

"Sorry." He moved to stand on the river's sloping shoreline. "I come here a lot. It's calming."

"It is." *Or, it was.* He'd destroyed her small slice of peace, and she couldn't prevent a tiny bit of resentment from creeping into her voice. Noah peered at her, and she studied the ground by her feet, ashamed of her pettiness.

"I don't have nightmares so much anymore," he said, moving under the willow branches. "You never forget, though." Lowering himself to the damp ground beside her, he stretched his prosthetic out before him. "I like to check in with the river now and then. There's something about watching the Ohio flow by that takes you out of yourself. It's hypnotic."

"Like watching a campfire." Her gaze drifted back to the water. Didn't he get that she wanted to be alone? "Yeah, I just now discovered that this morning."

"I imagine it's all still pretty raw for you." He tucked his chin down to meet her eyes. "Nightmares keeping you up?"

The sudden sting of tears made answering impossible. She nodded.

"I know you've heard this before, but—"

"Don't say it'll get better, because it won't," she snapped. "Not without meds and therapy, and lately, things have gotten worse. I'm afraid to sleep at night, and these days, even looking at a shadow sends me into a tailspin."

"Wesley can't sleep at night either. If you think it would help, you can switch to the night crew. Try sleeping during the day."

"I'll…I'll think about that." Guilt swamped her. He didn't deserve to be snapped at, and she owed him everything. "Why do you do it, Noah?"

"Do what?" His eyes widened in question.

"Why do you help perfect strangers like me?"

"Hmm." His expression grew pensive, and he too looked out over the river. "I lost five men the day we were hit in Iraq. One of them was Ryan's best friend. All of them were my responsibility." His mouth tightened into a straight line. "I survived." A shudder racked through him. "Physically, anyway. I was in pretty bad shape when I landed in Perfect. Flashbacks, nightmares, a parade of ghosts…the guilt I carried for surviving while so many hadn't nearly destroyed me."

"It sucks, doesn't it?"

He chuckled. "Yeah. Definitely. The Lovejoys helped me a lot. Being here helped. Once I came through the worst, my thinking changed. I figured I must've survived for a reason. There are a lot of veterans out there who aren't as lucky and don't have a safe place to land." He shrugged his broad shoulders. "New mission. I'm a mission kind of guy, I guess."

"Good thing for me. Words aren't enough to express how grateful I am."

"Not necessary. You're doing a great job at L&L, and we're glad to have you." He paused, going pensive again. "Ceejay and I…" He rubbed the back of his neck. "We had a pretty rough start, believe me. We both had issues to work through before finding our way together." He glanced sideways at her. "It was worth it, though. Every struggle we went through was worth it in the end."

Cory pulled her knees up and wrapped her arms around them. "I'm happy for you."

"Ted played a huge part in my recovery." He shook his head and grinned. "The guy would not leave me alone, always pestering me about what I was going to do with my life and asking if we could partner up in one business venture or another." He chuffed out a laugh. "At one time, we even considered the house-painting business. I owe him. Ted means a lot to me and my wife. He's more like a younger brother than a cousin."

A wave of misery washed over her, and she rested her forehead on her arms. "Is this the part where you warn me not to hurt him, 'cause I've already heard it." Tears pricked at the back of her eyes.

"No." Noah was quiet for few seconds. "This is the part where I tell you not to give up. He's a good man, and—"

"And the more I feel for him, the worse the nightmares get." Her muscles knotted, and anger exploded in her chest. "I can't keep doing this to myself or to him. I'm exhausted." Several moments of silence stretched between them, and she made a desperate effort to pull herself together.

"No word from the law clinic?"

She rolled her forehead back and forth against her forearms. "Nope. Still unfit to serve. Still...personality disordered." The ultimate burn, worse than any night terrors could ever be.

"Listen, it's good to talk about this stuff. If you want, I can ask around at the VA and see if there's a women's group that gets together outside of the center. I meet with my group at the VFW on a regular basis."

She raised her head. "The fact that I'm *on the outside* is what gets to me the most." She picked up a twig near her feet and snapped it in half. "I appreciate that you're trying to help. I'm just having a bad morning, no doubt caused by a very bad night. I'm sure things will get better." She snorted in disbelief at her own words. Grabbing her coffee mug, she rose to her feet. "Thanks, Noah. I'll see you at work tomorrow."

"If you ever need to talk, I'm here."

Nodding mutely again, she walked away. She'd force herself to be productive today, soldier on through the heartache. Once she was behind her door, she gathered her laundry, determined to throw herself into chores. By sheer force of will, Cory kept herself busy, watching the clock the entire day.

She plugged in her new Crock-Pot, starting the chili that would feed her for the next few days. By two o'clock, a horde of butterflies ran rampant through her midriff. She grabbed her purse and headed out the door into a bright sunny day. The thought of seeing Ted's face filled with hurt and confusion sent her heart plummeting. Each step she took grew more and more difficult, until it seemed she were slogging knee-deep through mud.

Rounding the corner of the veranda, she found him leaning against his old truck and chatting with Ceejay. Her pulse surged. His smile pierced her heart, and it took every ounce of strength she had not to burst into tears.

"There you are." He pushed himself off the truck and opened the passenger door. "Ready to go?"

"Sure." She slid her hands into her pockets to hide how they trembled. "Hey, Ceejay. How are you?"

"I'm great. Noah said he found you by the river early this morning. It's nice there, isn't it? Especially at the beginning or the end of the day." She smiled warmly. "Once the kids are a little older, we're going to put a patio and some benches down by that old willow tree. Then we'll have a comfortable place to sit while we watch the sun rise and set."

"Sounds nice." Being so near Ted made it hard to breathe, and her legs went from weighted to rubberized. She climbed into the truck. "See you later."

"Later." Ceejay lifted a hand to wave and turned to walk up the veranda stairs.

Cory fumbled with her seat belt. She tried to swallow, but the inside of her mouth had turned to dryer lint. "How're your folks?"

"They're fine. Have you and your mom decided when we're going out for dinner yet?"

"No," she murmured.

He started the truck and headed down the driveway. "What's wrong, Cory?"

"I…" She brushed the hair from her face and stared out the windshield. "Your friendship means the world to me, Ted. I hope you know that." A quick glance his way was all she could handle. "I don't want to lose what we have."

"But?" His face clouded. "I'm pretty sure I heard a *but* in there. Let's wait until we pull off the highway before we continue this discussion."

"All right." She kept her eyes straight ahead, trying not to notice how his masculine workingman hands gripped the steering wheel, and how his sexy mouth turned down at the corners. She wanted to reach for him, tell him to forget about it—convince him and herself that nothing was wrong. They turned onto the same country road they had for her first driving lesson.

He pulled to the side and cut the engine, shifting around to face her. "Talk to me."

"Like I said, I value our friendship." She twisted her hands together in her lap. "But we've been drifting into dating territory." Her voice broke, and she cleared her throat, blinking hard against the tears filling her eyes. "I...I wanted to believe that good memories could replace the bad. I did so want to believe..."

"But they aren't."

"Nope. They aren't." She sent him an anguished look. "Kissing you is amazing, but it triggers...I have flashbacks and nightmares...late at night. They're getting worse, and I...I face that fallout alone. It's tearing me apart and keeping me up at night." She swiped at her damp cheeks. "I'm so tired."

"Damn." He lowered his head to the top of the steering wheel. "I'm sorry, Cory. I wanted to make things better, and instead I made them worse."

"No. Don't blame yourself." She reached for her purse to pull out a tissue. "I won't be able to bear it if you do. It's not your fault. Or mine. It just is." She wiped her nose and gazed out over the rows of corn beside the truck. "For both our sakes, I don't think we should spend so much time together. If you don't want to sell me the truck anymore, or teach me to drive the stick shift, I'll understand completely." He was quiet for so long, she finally risked glancing at him.

He stared back intently, a frown marring his features. Instead of the confusion and hurt she'd expected, his eyes were filled with compassion and concern. "Selling the truck to you has nothing to do with this, and it hurts that you think I'd rescind the offer just because you don't want to date me."

Heat crept up her neck to fill her cheeks. She did want to date him, and if she wasn't such a wreck, she would. "I'm sorry. Hurting you is the last thing I want to do."

"You're not going to lose my friendship just because you're

going through a rough patch. I'm not that shallow." He grunted. "Wouldn't be much of friend if that's how I rolled, now would I?"

She shook her head, wishing like hell she could be more to him than she was, wishing like hell she were whole and healthy. He opened his door and climbed out. Confused, she blinked a few times before taking his cue and sliding over to the driver's side.

"It's OK, Cory. Don't worry about me. Our friendship is rock solid, and I'm here for you if you ever need to talk." He settled himself into the passenger seat. "Have a little faith, would you?"

Unable to speak, she swallowed hard against the boulder in her throat. Great. Now she loved him more than ever. Grateful for the change of subject, she started the truck and put it into first gear, driving slowly down the deserted road. "Now what do I do?"

"Listen to the engine, and watch the RPMs. Give it a little gas, and as soon as the dial reaches three, engage the clutch and shift into second gear. Release the clutch right away." He kept his eyes forward. "You'll get a feel for when to change gears after awhile."

She practiced going through all the gears several times. Finally, he had her drive in reverse. "It's so much bigger than the cars I've driven in the past. I'm going to have to get used to where the four corners are before attempting parallel parking." She moved the stick to neutral and cut the engine. "I think I'm ready. Hand me my purse, and I'll give you that first check."

Ted leaned over to retrieve the small leather bag from the floor. "I'll write up some kind of agreement, and you can sign it tomorrow at work. We'll transfer the title over lunch, and then I'll give you your space." He handed her the purse.

He was right beside her, and she missed him already. The loss punched a hole through her heart, but this was necessary. She needed a break, or she wouldn't be able to function much longer.

"Thanks for understanding." She took out her checkbook and a pen and wrote him her very first car payment.

Ted took her check, folded the piece of paper in half, and stuffed it into his shirt pocket. "I saw what Noah and Ryan went through, and I do understand." He ran his hands over his denim clad knees. "Any word from the law clinic?"

"No."

"Damn. We need to do something about insurance for our employees, and we need to do it now. I know the VA only covers issues that are service related for veterans who aren't pensioned, and other than Wesley, we're a young staff. You shouldn't have to wait to get the help you need. No one should have to put off getting help because they don't have insurance." He blew out a long breath. "You want another project at work?"

"I've put off getting help because of my stupid principles concerning what is owed to me by the army, but yeah—insurance would be nice." Her brow creased. "What's this new project you have in mind?"

"We've talked many times about forming a consortium with other small businesses in town. Increasing our numbers would make health insurance more affordable for all of us. If you want, you can take on that project, get the other businesses on board, and start taking bids for coverage."

Excitement thrummed through her, and she could hardly wait to get started. Finally. She'd have a project that would benefit everyone at L&L, including herself. If she could get it up and running, it would be another way to express her gratitude for the help she'd been given in her hour of need. "I'd love to take that on."

"Great. None of us have had the time to see the insurance project through. It's one of those things that keeps falling through the cracks. I'll give you a list of places to contact. You can start tomorrow." He frowned for a second.

"The Fourth of July is this Thursday, making it a short week. Once the holiday is over, I'll help however I can, and I'm sure Paige would be thrilled to pitch in as well. Most of the staff are taking a vacation day on Friday, including me. I'll be pretty tied up with helping the Lovejoy clan get ready for the pig roast at Noah and Ceejay's. Then there's the cleanup the day after. You going to be OK on your own?"

"Yep. I'm on it." She started the truck and headed for the main road. "I need directions to your place. I didn't pay that much attention, and it's been awhile."

"Sure. Take a right at the stop sign."

Maybe she'd been all wrong about his attraction to her. He didn't seem nearly as affected by the whole not-spending-time-together thing as she was, and that stung. *Wait.* She had no right to be hurt, since she'd been the one to put on the brakes. "Are you all right with...with..." What was she supposed to say? *Why aren't you as torn up as I am about this?*

🐏 🐏 🐏

"This isn't about me," Ted rasped out, his jaw tightening. "Take care of yourself. Stop worrying about anything other than what you need to do to take care of yourself." For a split second, he considered arguing or cajoling her out of her I-don't-think-we-should-spend-so-much-time-together position, but one look at the dark circles under her haunted brown eyes and the defeated set of her shoulders, and he knew better.

He plowed a hand through his hair and turned away. What could he say?" *Hell, no, I'm not OK with this? Spending less time with you is going to be hell for me.* What kind of a schmuck would that make him? The kind of schmuck who'd already put himself first, causing her more grief than good. He'd been trying to seduce her out of her PTSD, sneaking around her defenses, pretending to be altruistic, while all along his motives had been completely selfish. He wanted her. Pure and simple. His Sunday dinner turned to a lump of clay in his gut.

"Ted." She glanced at him, her expression crestfallen.

"Hmm?"

"Stop beating yourself up. None of this is your fault. We can both blame Sergeant Dickhead for the hell I live with."

"Agreed, but I exacerbated the problem." He snorted. "I'm not going to lie, Cory. I'm attracted to you, and I was rationalizing the whole situation for my benefit. I'm sorry." He glanced at her. "It won't happen again."

She kept her eyes on the road. "I don't want there to be any awkwardness between us."

"There won't be. You have my word." He gestured to the dirt road ahead. "There's the turnoff to our farm." He couldn't decide which was worse, the disappointment or the self-recrimination. Both hammered painfully at the inside of his skull. He needed to be alone to process the emotions churning through him.

She pulled the truck up to his parents' house. "You're not alone in the rationalization department." Her sad eyes met his. "Don't you think I'd love to wipe out everything that happened to me that awful day? You are such a great guy, and you've been nothing but kind. I'm not happy with the way things are, but it's life as I know it right now."

He had no argument to offer, and his heart couldn't take anymore bruising. "Call me if you need anything." He opened the door and climbed out. "I'll see you tomorrow." The sadness he'd caused her cut him deep. He walked into the house with-out looking back. Why he went into his parents' house instead of heading for his place, he had no idea. Maybe he didn't really want to be alone after all. Following the smell of fresh coffee, he headed for the kitchen. His dad sat at the table with the Sunday paper spread out before him and a steaming mug in his hand.

Ted poured coffee for himself and took a seat. "Where's Mom?"

"She and Jenny went shopping." His dad peered at him over the rims of his reading glasses. "How'd the driving lesson go?"

"Fine. Cory took the truck." He couldn't stop the heavy sigh from escaping. "Being with me triggers her flashbacks and night-mares. She cut me loose this afternoon. Says she doesn't want to spend so much time with me anymore." Propping his elbows on the table, he scrubbed both hands over his face. "I don't know what to do, Dad."

"How do you feel about her, son? That's the important question."

"What difference does that make?" He raised his head and frowned. "She doesn't want to be around me."

"It makes all the difference in the world. You said you don't know what to do. Seems to me your choices are pretty straight-forward. You can cut your losses and move on, or you can be patient, give her space and support, and hope that she'll come around." His dad shrugged. "How do you feel about her?"

"I'm crazy about her. I pushed a little too hard too soon. We shared a few kisses." Turning his coffee mug around between his hands, he studied the pattern his movements caused. "I guess it made things worse for her."

"What did she say, exactly?"

"She said kissing me is amazing," he began. Then he relayed the entire conversation he'd had with Cory earlier.

"Humph." His dad raised a single eyebrow. "Is she worth waiting for? Because what I heard just now is that she has feelings for you, but her PTSD is getting in the way."

"Yeah, I thought of that, but what if she can't free herself from the association between me and the nightmares? Kissing me triggers them." And that would be his fault, because he hadn't waited for her to go through treatment before making moves on her. "What if she goes through therapy and decides she wants to leave behind anything or anyone who reminds her of the horror she went through?"

"I guess you have to decide whether or not you want to take that chance."

He slumped down into the chair. "I screwed up."

"How long has she been in Perfect?"

"Since the end of April." Ted ran his thumb over the smooth ceramic handle on his mug. Really, he and Cory had only known each other for about ten weeks. Maybe if he gave her some space and waited a few months, they could start over.

"Not long at all. It's too soon to tell if things are *screwed up*, as you put it. Give it rest, and give her some space. You don't need to make a decision right this minute, do you?"

"Good advice. In the meantime, I think I'll do some research on PTSD, learn what I can about what she's facing." Ted reached for the sports section of the paper. "Besides, it's easier to wait it out than to admit defeat."

"That's my boy." His dad reached out and patted Ted's shoulder. "For all you know, things could still work out between the two of you."

"Yeah?" Hope flared in his chest. "Do you think so?"

A grin spread across his dad's face. "Anything is possible. What woman in her right mind would pass on the chance to partner up with the son of a hog farmer?"

"Right," he replied dryly.

Ted surveyed the preparations for their Fourth of July gathering. The pavilions were lined up against the copse of black walnuts at the edge of Noah and Ceejay's property. Rented folding tables for the food had been draped in red-white-and-blue plastic table coverings. Large ladles, spoons and serving forks were ready to go, and the napkin holders and condiments were conveniently placed at the end of the line, along with the eating utensils and Solo cups stacked up in high towers.

The mouthwatering scent of the roasting pig and his aunt Jenny's special recipe baked beans filled the air. Somehow they'd managed to draw a perfect day out of the weather lottery—clear, hot, with a slight breeze and not too much humidity. Everything was set, and their neighbors and friends would start arriving any minute, along with Cory and her mom. His stomach did a flip at the thought.

All week he'd managed to keep things light and friendly between them. He'd brought the promised agreement and payment schedule for the truck, handed her the list of Perfect's privately owned businesses and sat through the Monday morning staff meeting with a smile pasted on his face. The rest of the week he'd done his best to stay out of her way.

It was killing him.

"Can you help me move the beverage coolers?" Ceejay asked, bringing him back to the present.

"Sure. Where do you want them?"

"On the last table next to the Solo cups."

Ted followed his cousin to the front of the house where the bright-orange coolers sat in a row on the veranda. Two of them had *sweet tea* written in permanent marker across the front. The other two were similarly marked for fruit punch. He lifted one. "These are heavier than I expected. Let's load them onto the back of my pickup. I can drive them down."

Ceejay pointed to her van. The back was already open. "I'm one step ahead of you." She went to lift one of the large jugs.

"Oh, no, you don't." Ted scowled at her. "We don't need you going into early labor for the sake of fruit punch."

"Who do you think got them to the porch?" She fisted her hands on her hips. "I'm fine. It's no different than lifting Toby or Micah."

Noah appeared from around the corner of the house with Lucinda in tow. "I've got it, Ceejay. Harlen has the boys. You and Lucinda are needed at the food tables. Jenny's orders."

"All right." She shot him a you-win look. "The keys are in the ignition. Thanks."

He and Noah made fast work of loading the van. Noah shut the back and faced Ted. "How are things with you and Cory?"

"With *me* and Cory?" *There is no me and Cory.* He stared at the neighboring field where cars were beginning to trickle in, flattening the tall grass and weeds. His dad and uncles were directing traffic, waving them along with their small American flags. "Why do you ask?"

"I couldn't help noticing she's been more on edge than normal this past week. The same goes for you." Noah rubbed the back of his neck. "I'm concerned, is all."

"She's having a rough time, and I've been pushed away. There's nothing I can do about it."

"Sure there is." Noah's intense gaze pinned him. "She told me the more she feels for you, the worse her flashbacks get. It's not you. It's the struggle. Don't give up. Remember how it was with me and Ceejay? She pushed me away on a daily basis, when what she really needed was to know that I wouldn't give up on her. Give Cory the room she needs, but stick close. She needs your help to get through this. She needs all of our help."

"Cory said she has feelings for me?" He'd suspected, hoped even, but to hear that she'd admitted it out loud...

"She did. I ran into her down by the river early Sunday morning, and we talked for a while."

"Her situation is a lot different than Ceejay's. My cousin had abandonment issues. Cory's trauma isn't about that."

"I agree, but she still needs to know you're there for her no matter what. Cory wants to get better; she just doesn't know how to make it happen." Noah rounded the hood of the van and took the driver's seat. "Once she can start therapy, that'll help. The VA has treating PTSD down to an art."

Ted climbed into the passenger seat. "Treatment is not an option for her right now." His gut twisted with anger on her behalf. "Thanks for the heads-up. Let's get these down to the table. The party is about to begin."

A half hour later, Ted took his place at the head of the food line. It was his job to slice up and serve the pork that had been roasting all day. He'd already loaded a few plates for the first families to arrive, greeting and exchanging small talk while loading succulent pieces of ham on their plastic plates. He'd volunteered for the job, knowing it would keep him occupied for most of the evening. Besides, he really did enjoy the banter with his neighbors. The queue began to grow in earnest, and everyone was in high spirits. The children were full of energy. Their faces were rosy with excitement for the coming fireworks and the chance to run around with the friends they hadn't seen since school let out in June.

"Hey, kid," Kyle greeted him.

Ted's head snapped up. Kyle and Brenda were a couple of people back in line, followed by Cory and her mom. His eyes connected with Cory's, and the jolt set off a riot in his midsection. "Hey." He couldn't quite muster a smile. "Glad to see you guys made it."

"Looks like you could use a little refreshment." The group he'd been serving moved along, and Kyle handed him a cold can of beer.

"Thanks. Just what I needed." He took a couple of swallows and held the cold metal against his overheated brow for a moment.

"You going to join us later for the fireworks?" Brenda held out her plate for him to fill.

Kyle jerked his thumb over his shoulder toward the sloping lawn. "We have a couple blankets laid out next to each other."

He set the beer aside. "Uh…" Good thing he was already overheated from serving up the hot food, or the color rising to his face would be obvious. He glanced at Cory. This time she turned away.

"We'd love to have you, wouldn't we, Cory?" Claire chimed. "I brought the cribbage board."

"Sure." Cory tucked her bottom lip between her teeth.

"OK." His heart knocked painfully around his rib cage. "I'll be here quite awhile yet. Save me a spot." *Give her space, but be there for her.* How the hell was *that* supposed to work again?

CHAPTER TEN

THE FOURTH OF JULY FIREWORKS were about to begin, and Cory was grateful for the darkness. It hid so much. Her eyes drifted over to Ted again. He lay sprawled on his back with his arms tucked under his head and his ankles crossed, claiming the space forming a seam between her blanket and the one Brenda shared with Kyle. Neutral territory—a statement.

True to his word, he'd kept his distance all week, and missing him had become the new backdrop to her life. Sharing her darkest secrets with him had been so easy. Did he feel the same? He'd told her things as well, allowed his vulnerabilities to show. All that was gone now, and as much as she wished it hadn't, awkwardness had sprung up between them like a prickly thistle plant.

And the real kicker? Spending less time with him hadn't really made any difference. Her nights were growing worse, and she slept less and less. A band of anxiety tightened her airway. Had she made a rash decision when she'd pushed Ted away? *Face it.* Rational was beyond her. How could any decision she made in her present state be anything but messed up?

Right now her struggle involved self-restraint. She longed to stretch out beside him, snuggle against his side, and wrap her arms around his waist, taking in his unique male scent. Maybe then she could sleep.

"You smell like roasted pork," Kyle teased.

"One of the perks of the job." Ted tilted his head to grin at Kyle. "Did everybody get enough to eat?"

"My, yes." Her mom sighed. "Everything was so yummy. We've never been to a Fourth of July celebration quite like this, have we, Cory?"

"No." She'd made lemon bars for the dessert table, and had been pleased to see how quickly they'd disappeared. Everyone brought a side dish or a dessert to share, and each family put something into the donation box to offset the costs of next year's festivities. When she was a kid, she and her mom always followed the crowd in Evansville to the levee by the Ohio River to watch the fireworks. It was fun, but lacked the sense of community and sharing the Langfords and Lovejoys' celebration provided.

The first pop and flare against the inky sky heralded the start of the fireworks display, and the crowd oohed and ahhed. The sound made her jumpy for a minute, until she checked her mom and Ted, grounding herself in their calm. A little one started wailing. A few more toddlers took up the cry as if they'd caught the condition from the first.

Ted chuckled. "Happens every year. I think I recognize Micah's screech in the choir. They'll settle down once they're distracted by the color and light."

Cory braced herself with her arms outstretched behind her and lifted her eyes, trying to distract herself with the color and light as well. Memories filled her head of the night she and Ted had stared at the stars together, and their last kiss. She preferred the natural beauty of the night sky to the fireworks, or maybe it was just her own sentimental thinking running interference.

What was going through Ted's mind right now? Her attention slid back to him. Did he miss her like she missed him? Had she made the biggest mistake of her life by putting a stop to their growing closeness?

No. She forced her gaze back to the sky. Ending it had been the right thing to do. She'd been strung so tight, one more ounce of pressure and her trip line would've sprung. The problem was, the tension hadn't eased a whole lot. Overwhelming sadness stole over her, followed by a flash of anger. No use in dwelling on the unfairness. Doing so changed nothing.

The display went on for a good thirty minutes, ending in a spectacular grand finale of neon-bright bursts of light and thunderous pops and booms. Sulfur-scented smoke drifted across the river, settling over the spectators in wispy, white tendrils. People began to gather their things. Parents lifted sleepy children into their arms and headed to their cars for the trip home.

"I'll go fetch your dessert container," her mom offered as she stood up and stretched.

"Thanks." Cory got up and started to fold their blanket.

"How are you, Cory?"

"I'm fine." *Liar!* Ted's voice, his nearness sent a shiver down her spine. "How are you?"

"Tired. It's been a busy week."

"This was the best Fourth of July event I've ever attended." She clutched the folded blanket against her chest. "I had a great time, and so did my mom. I'm glad we came here instead of following our usual routine in Evansville."

"I'm glad too." He shifted his weight and bowed his head. "Listen, I want you to know I'm not going anywhere. Don't forget. I'm like that old truck. If you need me, all you have to do is call or text. I'll be there for you in a heartbeat."

"I don't think—"

"You deserve the best, and I—"

Her mom called from a short distance up the slope. "Is the carriage house locked?"

Cory peered into Ted's earnest face. "Mom is spending the night with me. I've got to go unlock the door for her. Thank you, Ted. I won't forget." Choking on regret, she left him standing there with a million things left unsaid. Her mother waited by the carriage house door. Cory pulled her keys from her back pocket and reached around Claire to unlock it.

"That Teddy Lovejoy surely is a fine young man," her mother said as she preceded Cory into her apartment.

"Yes...he is." She flipped the light switch.

"Why do you sound so sad?"

"Because I am sad, Mom." She swung her arm out in a gesture to encompass her apartment. "I have so much to be thankful for: you, good friends, my job, this great place. Yet I can't get past the sadness, and I can't shake this awful anxiety."

The next thing she knew, she was being rocked in her mother's warm embrace like when she was a little kid. Tears filled her eyes and slipped down her cheeks. "I'm sad, and I'm angry. I feel like I'm stuck in the spin cycle of some crazy old washing machine, and I just want it to stop."

"I know, honey. I know." Her mother continued to rock her where they stood. "Let it out. A good cry leaves you empty, and then there's room for something better to fill the space."

"I...I told Ted I didn't want to spend so much time with him anymore. Being with him stirred up...It was making things worse." She sniffed.

"You have feelings for him?"

She nodded. "He's the greatest guy I've ever met."

Her mom let go of her and walked to the kitchen for paper towels. "Sit down, Cory." She returned and handed her a few sheets. "Things always seem the worst right before they get better."

"You always say that." She sank into the recliner. "And it's just because one notch above miserable can feel like relief, even though nothing has really changed."

Her mom chuckled. "We come from a long line of survivors. You'll get through this, baby."

She wiped her eyes and blew her nose. "I told Ted not to wait for me to get better. I have no idea how long it'll take, or if I'll ever be in a place where I'm ready to get close to anyone that way again."

"You think that's gonna stop him from waiting for you anyway?" Her mom's mouth quirked up. "I've seen the way that man looks at you, Corinna Lynn. Your daddy used to look at me the same way."

"Yeah, but you weren't screwed up." Even so, the words were a balm to her splintered heart. She squelched the tiny ember of hope coming to life in her chest. "I'm a mess."

"Things have a way of working out the way they're meant to."

"Or...we just have a way of adapting to *how* they work out one way or the other." She sighed and rubbed her eyes. A large yawn escaped. "I'm exhausted." She pushed herself up from the cushy chair. "I'll go get the extra pillow and blankets for the couch. You can have the bed."

"You take it. This is your place."

"I have to get up for work tomorrow, and you don't. It makes more sense for me to sleep out here. That way I won't disturb you." Not that she slept much these days anyway.

"All right." Her mom canted her head and studied her. "Focus on how much better you already are. You weren't eating, bathing, or gettin' out of bed much when you first got home. Now you go to work every day and you're taking care of yourself again. Maybe you can't see how much better you're doin', but I can."

"I guess." In some respects, sure. Having a routine and structure in her life helped. Guilt pinched at her. "I'm sorry I caused you so much worry,"

"Don't you think anything of it. I'm just overjoyed you're home now and doin' so much better." Her mother gave her another quick hug. "Go on now. Get ready for bed."

Her mother's tone brought the flicker of a smile to her face. Claire Marcel had used the same commanding mom voice Cory's entire life. "Yes, ma'am."

Knowing her mother was nearby reassured her. Still, it was midnight before she finally settled herself on the couch. Tomorrow there would only be a skeleton crew at work. Most of the guys had taken Friday off, including Paige and Ryan, who were in Oklahoma celebrating the holiday with his folks. Good thing she'd already made arrangements with Wesley to keep his dog with her.

The thought of being alone in that small room sent a shudder through her, but then she thought about how Ted had put the deadbolt on the door. She glanced at the stun gun she'd set within easy reach on the coffee table, and love for him flooded her senses. He'd done so much for her, and what had she done for him?

Snuggling into the soft leather cushions of the couch, she made a point of counting her blessings instead of sheep. Hopefully doing so would keep the nightmares at bay.

Cory took another swallow of coffee. She needed the caffeine to help her keep her thoughts together for this meeting. She'd make a point of stopping at the drugstore today on her way home. Perhaps the pharmacist could recommend an over-the-counter sleep aid. She stood up and passed out her progress report. "Here's where we are so far on the insurance project."

Attending the Monday morning meetings had become a regular thing for her ever since she and Paige had discussed it. "The Perfect Diner is on board, along with Offermeyer's Meats, the local hardware store, the real estate office, and just about every independently owned business in town." She sat back down, relieved and pleased with the progress she'd made. Despite her lack of sleep, she'd managed to pull things together in time for this meeting.

"We've formed a committee with representatives from each business to study the bids once we start taking them. The committee will narrow it down to three possible providers with a variety of tiers to choose from, and then we'll present it to the stakeholders for a vote." She looked around the room. "As you can see, we have substantially increased our numbers, which will help keep the costs down. We've also talked about starting a hardship fund that each business and member can contribute to voluntarily. It'll help defray costs in case some kind of disaster hits a particular family. Have you given any thought to how much L&L is willing to contribute to employee premiums?"

"I guess we have to take a look at what the costs are going to be first. Once the committee has actual figures, we'll discuss it." Noah leaned forward. "I can tell you this, though. We're all grateful for the way you've taken on the insurance project. Thank you, Cory."

Pride straightened her spine and infused her with energy. "I'm glad to do it. Everyone I talked to was eager to get going on this. I think we need something legal drafted to form an actual group for this. Don't we?" She glanced at Ted. "I don't really know how these things work. Mostly what I've done is contact employers and gathered numbers, and that was easy."

"My brother Roger is a lawyer," Ted said. "I'll talk to him today and find out what we need to do, especially if we intend to move forward with the hardship fund. I'm sure he'd be willing to take care of the legal stuff for us."

A surge of gratitude and warmth for him filled her. Their gazes locked, and she smiled. "Thank you. That would be great."

Ted stood up abruptly. "We done here?"

Noah blinked at his sudden movement. "I believe so. Why?"

"Got stuff to do." Ted left just as abruptly as he'd stood.

The echo of his footsteps in the hall worked on her nerves. "Me too. We have a shipment almost ready to go, and I have to get transport set up." Why had Ted left so suddenly? He'd seemed fine, courteous and politely distant as usual one minute, and desperate to get away the next. Cory gathered her things and headed for her office. She'd just settled into her chair when Paige entered.

"I feel *soooo* guilty." Paige plopped down at her desk.

"Why?" Cory frowned in confusion. "About what?"

"Two reasons." She grimaced. "One, I let the ball drop on the insurance stuff. It was originally my project, and it should've been done a few years ago. Two, because my dad pays for our insurance coverage through his company. Noah's family is on the Langford Plumbing Supplies insurance rolls as well."

"Don't feel guilty about your good fortune. With a baby coming, I'm just glad to hear you're all covered. You've had more than your share of work to do here. You didn't have the time to follow up on this project. Everybody knows that. Besides, I'm glad it fell into my lap. It's given me a chance to get to know more people in Perfect, and that's a good thing."

"Does that mean you're ready to join the monthly poker games?" Paige waggled her eyebrows.

The poker night consisted of couples, most of them married. "Hmm, I'll think about it. What about starting a bowling league?"

"Bowling? That sounds like fun. I've never bowled. Maybe Ryan and I will join."

"I'll look into it." It would be fun. They could compete against other local leagues. "I'm surprised you guys don't have a—" A voice raised in anger reverberated down the hall. Ted's voice. A minute later a door slammed.

"Oh, boy." Paige looked from the door to her. "What do you suppose that's about?"

"I don't know." Or maybe she did. She hadn't meant to hurt Ted, but her rejection had to sting. It had certainly affected her.

Ryan strode into their office, a perplexed expression on his face. "Man, I thought things were settling down on the Teddy score." He ran his palm over the back of his neck. "Seems like he's more agitated than ever." His eyes connected with hers. "You spend a lot of time with him, Cory. What's eating him now? He seemed so much better for a while there."

Her face filled with heat, and anxiety gnawed away at her ragged edges. She didn't want to admit she might be partly to blame. Regardless, he'd shared enough with her that she had a pretty good handle on what bothered him, and this was her chance to speak up. "Did you call him kid, by any chance?"

"Well, sure. We all do. He's the youngest guy here."

"No. Noah, Wesley, and I don't. Neither does Paige."

He scowled. "What are you getting at?"

She shot a quick glance at Paige, who gave her a slight nod. Sucking in a breath for courage, she met Ryan's gaze. "If it weren't for Ted, you and I wouldn't have this job. L&L was his idea, and he's worked around the clock to make it a success, getting his undergrad and master's all the while. He signs our paychecks."

"Your point being?" Ryan picked up a rubber band from the corner of Paige's desk, leaned against the wall and turned his attention to stretching and twisting the strip of rubber.

"Don't you think he deserves our respect?"

"I do respect him. He knows that." He pushed off from the wall, his posture stiff. "It's an affectionate nickname."

Her eyes widened. "I've heard him ask you repeatedly not to call him kid. We've *all* heard him ask. Knowing it bothers him, hurts him, even, but you continue to do so. And because you call him that, the production and finishing crews do too. That's your idea of affection? That's how you show him respect?"

Cory studied the desk in front of her. "It doesn't take spending a lot of time with him to see what's going on. All it takes is being an outsider looking in. From where I sit, what you're doing has nothing to do with affection or respect and everything to do with one-upmanship. You've done a great job of undermining his position and his authority with the guys, and you've managed to keep him feeling like an outsider. Year after year, that kind of put-down would be difficult for anyone to bear."

"She's right, Ryan," Paige murmured, glancing at her husband.

"Shit." He strode out of the room as quickly as he'd appeared.

Cory kept her attention focused on her computer screen, afraid to see the expression on Paige's face. "I'm sorry."

"Don't be. He needed to hear that from someone other than me. And believe me, I've tried to get through to him. It's residual baggage. Ted made it pretty clear he resented Ryan's presence here from the start. Their issues run deep, and when I arrived, it threw a whole new monkey wrench into the mix."

"I overstepped." Cory rubbed her tired eyes with both hands. "How long will Ryan be angry with me, do you think?"

Paige chuckled. "He's not mad at you. If I know my husband at all, I'd say he's angry with himself right about now. You said what needed to be said, and I for one am grateful."

Paige's desk phone rang, and she answered, leaving Cory to her own thoughts—which centered around Ted. He deserved so much better at L&L. If nothing else, she hoped her conversation with Ryan would have an impact, changing things for the better for the man who meant so much to her—the man she'd pushed away. Her heart protested the decision, while her head tried to convince her she'd done the right thing. The battle left her unsettled and edgy.

Ted worked on entering used vacation days into their system, moving the ruler down the list of employees as he went. Embarrassment about the way he'd left this morning's meeting still soured his gut. Cory's smile had been a dead-center hit to his soul. Frustration, anger and overwhelming helplessness at his current situation had swamped him in the wake of that smile. Was he doomed to always fall for women who were unavailable to him?

This misery was too close to what he'd gone through when he'd lost Paige to Ryan. Dammit, he didn't want to come out on the short end of the stick again. Not with everyone he saw every day witnessing his defeat yet again. He'd had no choice but to leave.

Should he have argued with Cory, fought a little harder to keep her by his side? He needed to come up with a way to help her separate the mental association between him and her attacker. If he held her in his arms long enough, maybe she'd have a break-through. Maybe not.

Selfish much?

Clenching his molars together, he forced himself to concentrate on his work. Once he completed the tedious task, he could head downstairs and work in production. Thank God for that. Working with his hands helped him clear his mind and settle his nerves. It had always been that way for him, which was why he'd been convinced early on that college wasn't for him.

He glanced at the two diplomas hanging on his wall, glad once again for Noah's insistence that he get a degree. With his credentials and experience, he could go anywhere, move on and start something new if need be. Was that what he wanted to do? He propped his elbows on his desk and raked his fingers through his hair.

"Hey."

Stifling a groan, he raised his head and met Ryan's eyes. "What now?"

Ryan took the chair in front of his desk. "I don't drink."

"No kidding." Ted went back to entering data into the program. "You came in here just to give me this news flash?"

"If I did drink, I'd ask you to go have a few beers with me sometime. But since I don't, maybe we could go grab a coffee?"

"Um, how about we head down to my aunt's diner for lunch today? Like we do almost every day of the week." What the hell was Malloy up to now?

"Yeah, I get it. You're pissed, and I don't blame you." Ryan's palms were on his knees, which were bouncing up and down at a frantic pace. "I owe you an apology, man."

"Huh?" *Man, not kid?* The guy had Ted's complete attention now.

"I won't call you kid anymore. You have my word."

"What brought this on?"

"Cory just read me the riot act, and it—"

"Say what?" His heart took a leap for his throat. "Cory did what?"

"She said some things that got me thinking." Ryan's knees kept up their frantic bouncing. "I guess I've always kind of worried that one of these days Paige would come to her senses and dump me for you, and so I—"

Ted chuffed out a laugh. "First of all, I got over my infatuation with your wife years ago, and she never had any interest in me in the first place. Second, you two have been married for more than three years now. You're about to become parents. Really, Ryan?"

"I know. Lame, huh?" Ryan's crooked grin was back, and his knees stilled. "We should hang out more."

"Sure." *Or not.* He gestured to the spreadsheet on his desk. "I've got to get this done."

"Say, you ever been to the rodeo?"

"Once or twice when I was a kid. Why?" Resigned, he leaned back in his chair.

"There's a big one coming to the Ford Center in Evansville next weekend. It's PRCA sanctioned with sizable payouts, so it'll be a good one to see. My uncle raises rodeo bulls, and he and a few of my cousins will be there with their livestock. Why don't we go as a foursome? Uncle Shawn already sent us four prime tickets in the VIP section. You and Cory can be our guests."

If he could finagle time with Cory, maybe he could convince her to see things his way—without the seduction piece, of course. That could wait. He'd even be willing to participate in the therapy with her if it would help. "You or Paige would have to ask her. If I do, Cory will think it's too much like a date. She'll say no for sure."

"You two aren't dating?" Ryan's brow creased. "I thought—"

"We were heading that way, but I guess being near me stirs up her PTSD symptoms." He shrugged. "She cut me loose."

"Sorry to hear that. It's not really you; that's just how PTSD works. You might think you're getting better for brief periods, but if you don't get help, the problems escalate. She hasn't caught on yet, is all. You're good for her, Ted. She's just not in a place to see it right now." Ryan stood up. "I think we should give it a shot anyway. She and my wife get along really well, and I know Paige would like to get to know her better. You in if we can convince her?"

"Sure, why not? Sounds like fun." *Absolutely.* He did his best to appear only marginally interested, while his pulse shot off the charts.

"Good. I'll let you know. We also have the get-together at our house coming up. You coming?"

"I've got it down." He gestured to the calendar hanging on the wall beside his desk. The last weekend in July had *Malloys' housewarming* penciled in. "Is Cory coming?"

"She said she is."

"Great. Later."

"Later, bro."

Ryan left, leaving Ted to think about what had just happened. A pleasurable thrill spread through him. Cory had come to his defense. A good sign. "Wish I could've been there to see it." He swiveled his chair around to look out the window overlooking Main Street, smiling for the first time all morning. Her image limned in starlight sprang to mind. Memories of the kiss they'd shared brought a tender ache to his heart. They were meant for each other. He was sure of it. Convincing her presented a challenge. Was he up to it?

He swung his desk chair back around, finished his bookwork, and straightened his desk before rising to leave. He took the front stairs, coming out into the storefront. Prototypes and pieces that had slight flaws were piling up. Once the *Architectural Digest* ad came out, they'd have to have another sample sale. He wove his way through the odd mix of furniture, stopping to get a cup of coffee before entering the production area.

"Hey, Ted." Noah spared him a glance before turning back to his work. "I see you're almost done with the cradle. Are you putting it together today?"

"Yep." Inhaling deeply, he took in the scents of freshly cut wood, stain and turpentine permeating the place. The back doors were wide open, and the ceiling fan whirred away above him, sending sawdust eddies scurrying to the far corners of the room. Country music poured out of the speakers mounted on two of the walls. Man, he loved this place.

Smiling again, he reached for his tool belt where it hung from the row of pegs. Surveying the various projects under construction, he made his way to his own workspace. The guys nodded their greetings or gave a slight wave and went back to work.

"How was the rest of your weekend?" Kyle came over to stand beside him, pushing his safety goggles up to his forehead.

"Pretty good. I bought an old 1970 pickup truck I've had my eye on for a while. It belonged to the farmer whose land abuts ours. I want to rebuild the engine and do some body work, restore it to its former glory."

"Another Chevy?"

"Nope. This one's a blue-and-white Ford Ranger, an F100."

Kyle's eyes lit up. "My dad is an airline mechanic. He and I used to work on engines together all the time when I was a kid. I miss having grease under my fingernails. Do you want some help?"

"Sure, that would be great. I'll let you know when I'm ready to start. I could use a hand to remove the engine block." He glanced at Kyle. "How're things going with you and Brenda?"

"Hard to tell. I wanted to see her again on Saturday after the shindig out at Noah's on Thursday, but she turned me down. She said she already had plans." He grinned. "I think I make her nervous. I haven't managed to get her out alone yet, but I'm working on it."

Ted grinned back. "She's not going to make things easy for you."

"I know." Kyle lowered his goggles and chuckled. "She's going to make me work for it, that's for dang sure. It's all about the chase, bro." He rubbed his hands together. "And I do love the chase."

Kyle put his goggles back on and returned to his space, and Ted studied the finished pieces of the cradle stacked in front of him. Today he'd assemble the pieces, and then the finishing crew would take over. He ran his hand over the headboard, pleased with the way the bird's-eye maple had turned out. Vise clamps, wood glue, a mallet and the square-headed nails that were L&L's hallmark were lined up against the wall.

He reached for the glue, setting it within easy reach, and then lined up the two dovetailed edges where the headboard would connect with the sideboard on one side. Concentrating on the task, he put the glue in each notch and fitted the dovetailed pieces together, using a couple of clamps to keep the pieces tight until the glue dried. Then he repeated the action for the other side. He relished the steadying influence working with his hands provided, losing himself in the craft and forgetting all about the passage of time.

Once the sides and end pieces were together, he stepped back to take a look. Pleased with the results, he moved the cradle in the middle of his space. Once the glue was dry, he'd start on the stand.

Ryan, Paige, and Cory spilled into the workroom from the stairs, and Ted looked up at the wall clock. Lunchtime. "Perfect Diner?" he asked.

Xavier shut off the sound system and started singing in Spanish, like he did every day. John and Ryan put their tools on the bench and removed their tool belts, hanging them back on their pegs.

Noah flipped the switch on the jigsaw he'd been using. "Sounds good to me."

"Me too." Ryan rubbed his stomach. "Ready?"

Ted nodded and took off his tool belt. Had Ryan already brought the rodeo up with Cory? They all left the building together, Ted stopping to shut and lock the doors. "Paige, are you planning a sample sale soon? It's difficult to walk through the storefront, and I'm sure the fire marshal would see it as a hazard."

"Some of those samples are slated for the retail store in Evansville. We should be signing the lease in the next week or so. I'm just waiting for the paperwork."

"Great." He managed to work his way to Cory's side. "Good work on the insurance project."

"Thanks. I've enjoyed putting it together. I can't wait until we're ready to start taking bids."

"I owe you a debt of gratitude." He put his hands in his pockets and walked along beside her.

"No, you don't." She shook her head. "I'm happy to have the project."

"I'm talking about Ryan. He and I had an interesting conversation earlier. He said you got him thinking, and he's not going to call me kid anymore." He shot her a grateful look.

"Oh, that." She shrugged. "He asked me what I thought, so I told him."

Now that he wasn't being dazzled by her smile, he couldn't help but notice the dark circles under her eyes. Pale and wan, she'd lost the healthy glow that had begun to bloom in her cheeks. "Cory, are you sleeping OK? Is our being apart helping? Because...I miss you," he whispered.

She looked up at him then, her eyes haunted and the corners of her mouth drawn down. "No, it's not helping. I'm having trouble sleeping, and I...I realize it has nothing to do with whether or not we spend time together." She swallowed a few times. "I miss you too."

He kept his hands in his pockets, even though more than anything he wanted to reach for her. "I have an idea."

"Why does that not surprise me?" A tiny smile flickered to life for a second, then went out. "You're the idea man."

"How about we back up, start over. No more kissing. No pressure. You and me hanging out as friends whenever we want. Do you think you can handle that?" He sensed some of the tension leaving her, and she sighed loud enough for the crew walking ahead of them to hear.

"I'd like that." She glanced at him, her eyes bright. "I'd like that a lot."

"Good. I'd like that too." *Yes!* She'd admitted she missed him. His world snapped back together like the dovetails he'd just glued together. Should he bring the rodeo up, or leave it to Paige? *Baby steps.* Ryan had said they'd take care of it, so he'd let them. For now, just knowing the ban on being together had been lifted was enough.

CHAPTER ELEVEN

CORY ROLLED DOWN THE WINDOW for her short drive into work. The cool air still held the early morning mistiness typical for July, laced with the sweet scent of the hay fields bordering the two-lane highway. She inhaled deeply. Noah was right. Something about living in rural Indiana soothed the soul. Temporarily, at least. Plus, the rushing air helped her stay awake.

She pulled her truck into the alley. L&L's doors were still closed. Only one car and Wesley's truck were parked in back. The rest of the night shift must've left already. She'd never arrived this early before, and she didn't want to walk in yet, didn't want to face Wesley. He'd home in on the dark circles under her eyes and start asking questions.

Stretching where she sat, she considered her options. She could head down the street to the diner for a cup of coffee or walk around the block until Ted or Noah arrived. Maybe she could just rest her tired eyes for a few minutes. She rubbed at them, trying to rid herself of the gritty dryness from lack of sleep. Leaning her head back, she closed her eyes, dropping her hands into her lap...

"Wake up, Cory."

Someone shook her shoulder. She woke with a start, disoriented and tensed for a fight. It took a few seconds for her to figure out where she was, quickly swiping the drool from the corners of her mouth.

"How long have you been sitting here?" Paige rested her arms on the window frame of the truck, her expression filled with concern. Ryan stood behind his wife, wearing a similar look.

Cory checked her watch. Forty-five minutes! "Not long." Embarrassment scorched through her, and she turned her face away. Grabbing her purse, she climbed out of her truck. She studied the pavement beneath her feet. "The doors weren't open when I got here. I was just going to rest my eyes for a second. I guess I fell asleep."

"I guess you did." Ryan held the door to L&L open for them. "It's a good thing this is Perfect, Indiana, and not some big city. Falling asleep in your truck with the windows down and your purse sitting next to you on the seat is probably not the best idea." He scrutinized her as she passed him through the door. "Trouble sleeping at night?"

"Sometimes." She'd even tried a sleep aid last night. What a waste of money.

"Been there." He propped the doors wide to let in the morning air.

Wesley pushed a broom around the production area, corralling piles of sawdust on the concrete floor. His dog rose from his bed in the corner. His tail wagging, he moseyed over for the ear scratches he had coming. Wesley stopped sweeping. "Morning."

"Hey, man." Kyle slapped him on the shoulder. "How'd everything go last night?"

"Quiet night. No problems." Wesley's gaze swung to her.

"Are you heading to the diner this morning?" Cory asked, hoping the Malloys wouldn't mention finding her asleep at the wheel.

"In a few minutes." Wesley studied her with inscrutable intensity. "You want to join me?"

"Not this morning. I ate a big breakfast at home." She inched her way toward the stairs and averted her gaze. Another lie. She'd eat a big lunch to make up for it. "I'll take a rain check. Say hi to Jenny and Harlen for me."

"Will do." Wesley crossed the room to pick up the dustpan.

Paige moved to the kitchen area to start the coffee, and Ryan headed upstairs. Cory followed him. Once she reached her office, she settled herself at her desk and booted up her computer to check her e-mails. She searched for word from the law clinic. Nothing. Working on getting health insurance for L&L employees, herself included, gave her a lifeline—a point in time where the possibility of getting better shimmered like a mirage on the horizon. Maybe she'd even begin a search for a therapist today. There had to be places that specialized in trauma counseling.

Ted appeared in the doorway. "Hey, I talked to my brother about the insurance group and the hardship fund. He's going to have one of their interns put together some nonprofit paperwork for us to file, and also a legal document formalizing the coalition. We should have them by the end of the week."

"Oh, good." Her pulse raced at the sight of him. "We're ready to take bids then. I'll spend some time today putting a list of providers together for the committee. Thank you, Ted."

"No problem." He leaned against the door frame. "Did Paige mention the rodeo to you?"

"Rodeo?" She shook her head. "No."

"I was going to bring it up today." Paige appeared behind Ted. "But since you already did, go ahead." She put her hands on Ted's shoulders and propelled him into the room so she could get past him. "Ask her."

Cory raised her brow in question. "Ask me what?"

"Ryan and Paige have tickets to the rodeo for next weekend. They want to know if we're interested in joining them Saturday night." He shot her a hopeful look. "No big deal, just friends hanging out."

"Oh. I've never been to a rodeo." Her insides fluttered at the thought of going anywhere with Ted. She rearranged the pens, a letter opener and a ruler in the ceramic jar on her desk. "Sure. Sounds like fun." Risking a peek at him, she caught the look of pleased relief flashing across his face.

"Great." He straightened and smiled. "See you two at lunchtime."

"Let's go somewhere different today." Paige took a seat at her desk. "I could go for Italian, and there's a brand-new place right outside of Boonville Ryan and I have wanted to try for a while. It's called Carrabba's."

"I'm in."

"Me too," Cory chimed, remembering her promise to eat a big lunch.

"Good," Paige said. "Ted, can you find out if the rest of the guys want to join us? I'll make a reservation once you give me a head count."

"We need a reservation for this place?" Ted looked down at his jeans and work boots. "It's not too fancy, is it?"

"I don't think so, but I hear it's popular, and we're a large party."

"Right. I'll go ask them now." He backed out of the door, his eyes connecting with Cory's for a brief, breathtaking second.

I'm hopeless. They'd agreed to keep their relationship strictly friendly. Right. Sighing, she started a Google search for insurance providers.

"Are you OK, Cory? When we saw you sound asleep in your truck, it kind of—"

"Sure. I'm fine." Not really. "I just haven't gotten much sleep lately."

"Ryan used to have trouble sleeping too. He said most of the trouble started for him once he fell asleep. Have you considered seeing a medical doctor? They can prescribe something."

"Do you have any idea what an office visit would cost? Or a prescription, for that matter? Believe me, I've looked into it, and therapy. One session costs around a hundred forty bucks, and I'd need to see someone once a week for starters." She snorted. "I'm still hoping the law clinic comes through for me soon. In the meantime, I'll tough it out until we have health care benefits." She shifted in her seat. "It's not like I don't get any rest. I do. Some nights are just worse than others."

"Speaking of lack of sleep, the coffee should be ready by now." Paige rose from her chair. "The baby keeps me up at night too. I'm supposed to limit my caffeine intake, but I really need it in the morning. I'm going to get a cup. Do you want some?"

"I can get it." Cory gestured for Paige to sit back down.

"Moving around is good for me." Paige rubbed her baby bump. "Otherwise, this baby boy likes to use my bladder as his own personal soccer ball. You stay. I'll be right back. Do you take anything in yours?"

"A couple spoonfuls of sugar. Thanks." Once she had the office to herself, Cory took her cell phone out of her purse and hit speed dial. It had been weeks and weeks since she'd done anything with her hair, and she wanted to look good when she went to the rodeo with Ted. Just because her head wasn't screwed on right didn't mean she should slip back into neglecting her appearance.

"This better be important," Brenda muttered as she answered on the fourth ring. "I'm not up yet."

"It is. I need a haircut and my highlights need to be touched up." Cory glanced at the door. "Before next weekend, if possible."

"What's happening next weekend?" Brenda sounded more awake.

"I'm going to a rodeo."

"With Ted?"

"With a group of people from work." Not totally a lie, but she didn't want to get into it with Brenda right now. "Next weekend doesn't really have anything to do with it." Another little white lie to add to her collection. "I haven't had a haircut since you forced me into it at my mom's, and it's time."

"True. You were due a few weeks ago. I'm free tonight, and you haven't been to my apartment yet. Come over after work. I'll do your hair, and we can order pizza."

"Perfect. Text me your address. I'll see you around six."

"Will do. See you later." Brenda ended the call.

Paige returned with their coffee and settled into the projects she had going. Cory spent the rest of the morning assembling a list of insurance providers and updating L&L's website with the newest photos. The morning went by quickly, and despite the lack of sleep, she managed to get a lot done.

At lunchtime, Ryan, Ted and Noah appeared at their door. "We're going to have to take two vehicles to Carrabba's," Ted said.

Paige rose from her desk. "You can follow us. We'll take Noah, since we have a few things to discuss regarding what we want in the way of product for our new retail space. Can you take Cory, John and Kyle?"

"Sure." Ted's mouth quirked up. "Lead the way."

Cory settled into the backseat of Ted's truck, glad that he

hadn't driven the Mustang today. The plush comfort of his extended cab, coupled with the air conditioning, held much more appeal than the convertible with the top down. The temperature had already climbed into the nineties, and the hazy air was downright damp. Kyle rode shotgun, and John sat beside her.

"I hear you're going to rebuild an old Ford Ranger, Ted." John leaned forward as they rolled down the alley. "That true?"

"Yeah. I haven't started yet. It's sitting in the machine shed right now."

"You bought another truck?" she asked.

"Sure did. I told you I'd find another old rust bucket to putz with." He grinned at her in the rearview mirror.

"When do you plan to pull the engine?" Kyle turned up the fan, sending cold air circulating through the cab.

"Not sure." Ted shrugged. "I'm still gathering parts."

"My brother-in-law owns a body shop, and I worked for him before hiring on at L&L." John's tone held a spark of interest. "I have an old Dodge Charger that needs some engine work. I'd be willing to swap bodywork for mechanical help on my street rod."

"I'd love to get my hands on a Charger." Ted glanced back at John. "Deal. How about you, Kyle?"

"I'm there, bro." Kyle nodded. "In fact, I'll start looking around for a project of my own to add. How much room do you have in that machine shed?"

"Plenty." Ted's grin lit his face.

Cory listened as the three men went on and on about engines, rust and custom paint jobs. Not once did either of the guys in the truck call Ted kid. In fact, no one had called him kid since her conversation with Ryan. As if he sensed her thoughts centering around him, Ted caught her eye in the rearview mirror. She sent him a huge smile, and his eyes widened.

"How are you doing back there, Cory?" He fumbled with the air conditioning vents, aiming them toward the backseat. "Are you comfortable?"

"I'm fine." Seeing him connect with Kyle and John sent a happy thrill through her, and a bubble of satisfaction expanded in her chest. She'd played a small part in the shift, and that lifted her spirits more than a good night's sleep ever could.

Cory scanned Brenda's street for a parking spot large enough for her to attempt parallel parking. She caught a glimpse of a man walking his yellow lab along the sidewalk. He wore cammies and a tan T-shirt, and his hair was military short. Unable to turn away, she stared, falling into a memory she hadn't even realized she'd held onto.

Clutching a large plastic bottle of water, Cory rocked along in the cargo truck traveling at a snail's pace across the desert. The road was barely discernible from the rest of the barren landscape. She rode shotgun with the supply unit heading for an FOB that had lost its satellite equipment in a raid. The scent of diesel fuel filled her nose, and sweat trickled down her temples and the front of her T-shirt. The unit followed the slow progress of a handler and his TEDD, a tactical explosive detection dog.

She watched the yellow lab's tail wag happily as he worked. His nose to the ground, the dog wove his way from one side of the road to the other. He wore a nylon harness around his rib cage with a long retractable leash attached to the back. The harness had pockets on either side. Even dogs had to haul their own gear.

The dog's motions became frantic. He'd caught a scent, and his handler let out more leash and signaled to the driver to halt. The lab's tail went ballistic now, and he came to an abrupt halt.

He turned around and sat, his tail brushing across the dirt. The ground beneath him swelled for a fraction of a second, then exploded in a fiery flash. Cory slid down as far as she could in her seat and covered her head.

"Shit, no!" the handler yelled, dropping to the ground. In an instant, the dog was gone. Shock waves from the explosion rocked the truck. Rocks and clods of dirt rained down against the hood and roof with a spattering sound like hail. The handler stood up and flung what was left of the retractable leash far out into the desert. Fisting his hands on his hips, he paced back and forth in front of the truck, so close Cory could see the tears pooling in his eyes.

Her heart slammed around inside her rib cage, and the water bottle she'd been holding collapsed in her grip. All she could do was stare at the rip in the desert where flames and black smoke still smoldered. If it hadn't been for the dog, their truck would've set off the IED, and—

"What are you doing?" Brenda climbed into the passenger seat.

A whoosh of air left her as she came back to herself. When had she put her truck into neutral? She had no recollection, but she'd stopped in the middle of the road with the engine still running. Unable to speak, she swiped at the sweat salting her eyes and tried to calm her racing heart.

"Jeez, you look like you just saw a ghost." Brenda rested a hand on Cory's shoulder. "You're trembling."

"Flashback," she croaked.

"Right here in the middle of the road?"

"It's not like I could put it off until I parked. It just happened, and there wasn't anything I could do." She leaned her head back and closed her eyes, scrubbing both hands over her face. "I…this is a first. Usually I have nightmares, but…"

Brenda ran her hand over Cory's shoulder in a soothing motion. "There's a small lot behind my building where you can park. Let's get you inside. You're going to have to go around the block. I don't do stick shifts. Can you drive?"

"Yeah, I think so." She slid the truck into gear. "The flashback wasn't about Sergeant Dickhead. This was different."

"What was it about?"

She described that day and what had happened. "The handler told us the dog sat on the trigger of the IED he'd located. I guess it happens sometimes. I haven't thought about that day for a long time."

She gripped the steering wheel to stop her hands from shaking. "We all know there's a chance we'll be wounded or worse when we enlist. But dogs don't have that awareness. They just want to please their handlers. I know military working dogs save a lot of lives, and I know how important they are. They're soldiers too, but they don't go into it knowing like we do."

Cory sent a sidelong glance Brenda's way. "That dog was so happy. His tail was going a mile a minute because he'd done what his master wanted him to do. He knew he had a treat and praise coming, and instead, he got blown to smithereens." She blinked against the sting in her eyes. "His handler was a wreck after it happened. It's got to be hard losing your partner like that."

She turned into the drive next to Brenda's building. "The bond between the handlers and their dogs is incredible, especially because the troops who work with military dogs don't move around with a squadron or a unit. They get sent out all over on their own. It's a lonely job, and it carries a huge risk."

More memories poured through her, like when the lab had laid its head on the soldier's lap when they stopped for a lunch break. The way the soldier took care of his four-legged partner, making sure he had enough water and breaks in the shade to stay healthy in the desert heat. The big yellow dog had even nosed her hand to get Cory to pet him while she chatted with his handler. "Dogs are so trusting, and they love unconditionally."

"So, you see using dogs to sniff out explosives as a kind of betrayal of all that trust and unconditional love?"

"No. What they do is crucial to any mission. They're soldiers too." Adrenaline flooded her system. "And yes…part of me does see it as a betrayal. It's like…" Her lips compressed into a tight line.

"Like how you were betrayed by your commanding officer?"

She pulled into a spot and cut the engine, yanking on the parking brake harder than necessary. "I'm not a dog, Brenda. I never trusted that asshole."

"I know, but you should've been able to. That's the point."

Was that why this particular scene had come back to her? Or had it been triggered because she'd seen a dog resembling the one that gave his life that day? Lately she'd been having dreams that had nothing to do with being assaulted, dreams where she'd been in one camp or another while they were under fire. Fear had been a constant, and she'd seen plenty of wounded troops, witnessed too many gruesome fatalities.

"OK, so you had a flashback about the dog. What do you think it means?" Brenda climbed out of the truck.

"I think it means I'm even more messed up than I thought." She followed Brenda to the back door of her old brick apartment building. "Let's talk about something else."

Brenda opened her mouth to say something and shut it again, studying her for a moment. "Sure. You wanna hear about me and Kyle?"

"I'm all ears." Her heart rate had returned to normal, and

talking about anything other than her issues would be a welcome relief. "How are things going between the two of you, anyway?"

"He's so hot I can hardly keep my hands off of him," Brenda gushed. "He's smart, ambitious and funny. I really like him. It's kind of scary."

"Scary? Weren't you the one who said you wanted to settle down and start a family?"

"Yes, but he has PTSD too. He's on anxiety meds, and he meets with Noah Langford's group. I've watched a few documentaries and read some stuff. What if he has a flashback in the middle of the night, and I wake up with his hands around my neck or something?"

"I think it depends on what a soldier did when they were deployed. Kyle was a medic. He wouldn't have engaged in heavy combat. Kyle's more likely to have flashbacks about troops he couldn't save."

"Oh. Right." Brenda opened her apartment door. "So I might wake up to find him giving me mouth-to-mouth resuscitation. I like the sound of that scenario a lot better."

"I'm sure." Cory laughed as she walked through the door and looked around. Brenda's apartment reflected her personality—splashes of color on the walls and ultramodern, equally colorful furniture filled the living room.

"You want to head to the outlet mall Sunday?" Brenda dropped her keys on the kitchen counter.

"Sure. That would be great." Gratitude filled her as Brenda's presence grounded her even more in the here and now.

Ted wiped his face with a towel and surveyed his reflection in the bathroom mirror. He couldn't keep the smile from breaking free as anticipation thrummed through him. He had the rodeo tickets Ryan had given him tucked into his wallet, and he'd be picking Cory up soon. They planned to meet Ryan and Paige there, since the Malloys were arriving early to spend time with Ryan's uncle and cousins. That meant he'd have Cory all to himself for the ride into Evansville.

He eyed the expensive aftershave sitting next to his bathroom sink. Would it be too obvious that he saw tonight as more than a couple of friends hanging out if he smelled like something out of a bottle? Probably. Eschewing the expensive smell-good stuff, he reached for the Western-style shirt hanging on the hook behind the door. He tucked the tails into his jeans as he went, heading to his bedroom closet for his one pair of cowboy boots and tugging them on.

He ran his fingers through his unruly curls and checked the clock sitting on his dresser. Time to go. He raced down his stairs and outside to his truck, his heart pounding almost as fast as his feet were hitting the ground.

"Where are you off to in such a hurry?" his dad called from the front porch. He and his mom sat in the love seat that had been there for most of Ted's life.

He walked closer to the house before answering. "I'm heading into town for the rodeo with Ryan, Paige and Cory."

"That sounds like fun." His mom lowered the magazine she held to her lap.

His dad's brow rose slightly. "I thought Cory cut you loose."

"Yeah. We talked about it." The grin slipped out before he could check it. "She missed me."

His mom put her reading glasses on and went back to her magazine. "Have a nice time, Teddy."

"Take it easy," his dad added, cracking a smile.

"I will. Gotta go." He hurried back and climbed into his truck, shooting down the driveway to the highway.

A few short minutes later, he pulled into the Langfords' drive. Cory was sitting by herself at the table on the veranda, standing up as he parked. He swung out of his truck and walked around the hood. She wore a slim denim skirt that fell just above her knees, and a navy-blue blouse with puffy short sleeves and a ruffle down the sides of the buttons in front. Her hair had been styled, and she even wore makeup. *For me?* His pulse raced, heating his blood.

The blouse she wore showed just a hint of cleavage. Dang. Maybe he should've used some of his aftershave after all. "You look amazing, Cory." *Sexy as hell and good enough to eat.* He wanted to pull her into his arms, muss that soft brown hair and kiss her until their knees gave out. His dad said to take it easy, and he'd make that his mantra for the night. No pressure, just a couple of friends hanging out. Parts of his anatomy vigorously disagreed with that approach.

"Thanks. So do you."

The half smile lighting her face scrambled his brain and sent heat spiraling through him. He opened the truck door for her. Hiding his body's reaction to her behind it, he waited for her to climb in. Once he'd settled himself behind the wheel, he forced himself to get his thoughts out of the front of her blouse. Then he caught a glimpse of her smooth, bare legs and had to stifle the groan threatening to give him away. Struggling to grasp onto a distraction, any distraction, he forced his mind and eyes away from the tantalizing vision beside him. "Where are the Langfords?"

"They went out for supper, and then they're going to a drive-in movie. Some new animated kids' show just opened there this weekend."

"Sounds like fun." He meant it. Someday he hoped he'd have a family to take to the drive-in. He wasn't like a lot of guys he knew. Most of the guys he'd grown up with couldn't wait to escape Perfect and kick up their heels. None of them wanted anything to do with settling down. For as long as he could remember, all he'd ever wanted was a house with a nice view and a family of his own.

The distraction didn't last long, and his eyes slid back to Cory. She looked downright delectable. Longing slammed into him like a wrecking ball. "Is that a new outfit?" Color crept into her cheeks, multiplying her sexiness exponentially. He had to turn away again. Tonight was going to be a struggle of epic proportions.

"It is. Brenda and I went shopping last weekend." She ran her hands over the denim. "I hope it's appropriate for the event. Have you ever been to a rodeo before?"

"I have, but it's been years. My mom and dad took me a few times when I was a kid. What about you?" He started down the driveway and turned onto the highway toward town.

"I've never been. I have no idea what to expect."

"There are a variety of events, like roping calves, riding bucking horses and bulls, barrel racing."

"Cowboys racing in barrels?" Confusion clouded her eyes. "How does that work?"

"Uh, no. Girls ride their horses around a course made up of three barrels. They try to beat each other's times without knocking the barrels down as they go around them."

"Oh."

"Are you interested in the rodeo?"

"Ask me after I've seen one." A corner of her mouth quirked up. "I don't know yet."

"Why'd you say yes to going tonight?" He held his breath, waiting to hear what she'd say.

"I like going out and trying new things, and this is the first time we've done anything together since I figured out being apart wasn't helping." Her eyes met his, and another shy smile made an appearance. "You never know. Maybe after tonight I'll become a big fan. Paige said she got hooked the first time Ryan took her to one. She also said rodeos are going on all over, and we should try one outdoors if we like this one."

She'd said *we*, and that set his heart into a hopeful flutter. He cast around for something else to talk about. "Are you hungry?"

"Not right now, but I'm sure I will be later."

"We can get something to eat there, or if you want, we can go out for pizza afterwards."

"Sure."

"Are you going to be bothered by the crowds?"

"Probably, but once we're in our seats I'll be fine."

"I'll stick close."

"I know you will." She twirled a strand of hair around her finger and kept her eyes on the road ahead. "That's another reason I said yes. I appreciate that about you, Ted. I hope you know that."

"I do now, and I hope you know I'm happy to help." He aimed his eyes toward the road as well. "How's the truck running?"

"Freddy runs like he's brand-new. I love that old pickup." Her grin lit up the inside of his cab. "Did you know it's the first vehicle I've ever owned?"

"I figured it might be, since you enlisted right out of high school. How's the search for insurance providers coming along?"

"It's done. We put the requests for bids in the mail Friday afternoon."

"That's good. The sooner everyone has insurance the better."

"Thank you for that, Ted. I've also been looking for a therapist who specializes in PTSD. I couldn't do that if it hadn't been for you."

"You're the one who pulled the whole thing together. We're all going to benefit from your efforts." He winked at her. "We might have to come up with an employee-of-the-month plaque or something."

She laughed, and the sweet sound settled into his soul and filled him with contentment. The rest of their ride into Evansville they made small talk and settled back into being comfortable with each other once again. Soon he followed the line of cars inching their way toward the parking ramps near the Ford Center. The sidewalks were teeming with people wearing cowboy hats and boots. Young men moved in rowdy groups, and couples holding hands walked along at a slower pace behind them. He turned in to a ramp where a man with a bright-orange flag waved him in. "You're in charge of remembering where we're parked."

She made a snorting sound and pulled out a pen and a scrap of paper from her purse. "Got it." More inching along ensued as they followed the line of traffic to the booth where an attendant collected the event-parking fee. Ted reached for his wallet and laid it on Cory's lap. "Can you get a ten-dollar bill out for me?"

"You want me to kick in for parking?" She opened his wallet, sparing a second to study his awful driver's license photo.

"Nope." He held out his hand for the ten, paid the attendant and put the receipt on the dashboard. Once they were on the sidewalk, Cory moved nearer to him as the crowd jostled her in passing. "Can I hold your hand, Cory? It'll be easier to stay close." Without a word, she slipped her small hand into his. Swallowing hard, he twined their fingers and brought her closer to his side. It felt good. No, better than good. Eventually she'd realize they were a perfect fit. He just hoped he could survive the wait.

Wending their way through the concrete halls filled with food booths and vendors, they found the VIP section. Ted placed his hands on her shoulders and guided her down the narrow steps to their box. Ryan and Paige were already there, two chairs in from the aisle. He leaned down and whispered into Cory's ear. "You want the outside seat or the one next to Ryan?"

"The seat on the aisle would be good, thanks."

"All right." He edged around her and slid into their row of seats. "Hey, Ryan, Paige, how was the visit with your family?"

"It was good. We caught up over hot dogs and pop. Glad you two made it," Ryan said, nodding at Cory.

"You look great, Cory." Paige waved.

"Thanks, so do you." Cory leaned forward to talk to Paige. "I love your cowboy hat."

He waited for Cory to sit before taking his own seat. She scanned the crowd around them, then the arena, where a shiny new pickup truck had been parked. The rodeo's biggest sponsor, no doubt. Every protective urge he owned surged for her. "How are you doing? Do you need anything?"

"I'm good," she answered just as the lights dimmed and a voice boomed over the loud speaker. A group of riders on horseback carrying American flags entered the arena at a canter. The MC introduced the group, which was local, and they began a series of intricate maneuvers around the arena. The cowboys and cowgirls who would compete were called out by name. A set of sparklers lit a path as each one took their place in line as their stats were broadcast over the sound system.

All the while introductions were made, the horseback riders

continued to perform synchronized riding formations around the competitors. Impressive. Next, the men who kept the riders safe during the competitions were introduced. Once everyone was in place, a color guard of marines marched in formation to the center of the arena. Each one held a flag representing a different branch of the military, with the middle soldier holding a US flag high. The "Star-Spangled Banner" echoed throughout the stadium.

The announcer's voice rose above it all, saying, "If it weren't for the brave men and women who put their lives on the line every day to protect our freedom, we wouldn't be here tonight to enjoy this rodeo. Let's take a minute to honor our veterans, and to thank those who serve this great nation of ours. Will all the veterans in the audience please stand?"

He'd been so caught up in what was going on in front of him, Ted hadn't paid any attention to Cory. Ryan stood straight, tall and proud, with Paige's hand firmly held in his. Cory remained seated. Ted shifted around in his seat to look at her, and his gut twisted. Her eyes were wild. She gripped the armrests with both hands, and a fine sheen of perspiration covered her brow and upper lip. Her entire body trembled. *Oh, shit.*

CHAPTER TWELVE

"WILL ALL THE VETERANS IN the audience please stand?"

The MC's words slammed into Cory, and tension grabbed her by the throat. By rights she should stand. She'd sacrificed. Maybe not like the soldiers who'd lost limbs or worse, but she'd served to the best of her ability. Yet try as she might, she couldn't move. The world spun around her in a dizzying blur, and her ears rang with the pounding of her heart. Humiliation tied her into a tight knot. *Unfit to serve.*

Eight years of her life wasted! All she'd ever wanted was to make something of herself, follow in her father's footsteps. Her hands ached from the stranglehold she had on her chair. Rage and grief choked her. She had to get out—get some air.

Cory shot out of her place, dashed blindly up the stairs and bolted through the velvet curtains. She rushed into the concrete hallway and stopped. Unfamiliars milled about or stood in lines, waiting for greasy food-booth fare and cold beer. People talked and laughed together like they believed the world was a good place. Not so. Bad things and bad people lurked in the shadows and in small spaces, like closets and…storerooms.

Staff Sergeant Barnett put his hands on her shoulders and pressed her up against the wall. "You have this coming, bitch. You should've put out for me months ago."

His fetid breath sent waves of revulsion and nausea roiling through her. Bile rose to burn the back of her throat. Panic exploded, and instinct took over. She sprang into action, going for his eyes with her thumbs. If she could gouge him, force him to back up, she could fight. The bastard grabbed her wrists, and she twisted and turned, trying to get free. "No!"

"Cory, stop."

She managed to get free, putting some distance between them. He reached for her again, and she thrust her knee up with all the force she could muster.

"Oof. Damn." He groaned. "Cory, it's only me."

Confused and disoriented, she raked a shaking hand through her hair and stared. Ted doubled over in front of her. *Oh, God. I did that?* Glancing up, she faced the curious stares from the crowd of onlookers that had gathered. A security guard holding a walkie-talkie approached from the periphery. She took off for the exit, mortification burning through her like a red-hot ember. A quivering mess of stirred-up crazy, that's what she was.

"Wait!" Ted called from behind her.

Single-minded determination propelled her through the huge glass doors and out into the gathering dusk. Heat radiating up from the sidewalk engulfed her. She sucked in a breath laced with cigarette smoke from the group huddled around the metal ashtrays set up by the curb.

"Cory."

He was beside her now. How could she face him? She swallowed a few times and stared in the opposite direction.

"I just got my first close-up look at a flashback, didn't I?" He took her elbow and steered her away from the smokers staring curiously their way. "Are you OK?"

She shook her head and studied the asphalt running in front of the Ford Center. "I kneed you in the groin, and you're asking if *I'm* OK?"

"It wasn't me you were fighting. Don't you think I know that?"

"I'm so sorry." Her voice quavered.

"Forget it. I've suffered worse." He continued to lead her down the sidewalk. "I take it you aren't going to become a big rodeo fan."

"This had nothing to do with the rodeo," she clipped out. "What was I supposed to do while all the veterans were being honored? Stand? Sit? I have a less-than-honorable discharge on my record. I…it just all came crashing in, and I couldn't breathe. I just needed some air, and when I got to the hallway…"

"The experience triggered a flashback. I got that." He gave her elbow a squeeze. "Yes, you have a screwed-up file, but you and I both know the army's record is bogus. Paige and Ryan also know. Whether or not you stand is up to you, not the army or the MC. I'm proud of you. Everyone whose life you've touched is proud of you."

"I don't know. Sometimes I think the army had it right when they diagnosed me with a personality disorder. I'm definitely not…I'm not normal." There. She'd said it.

"Who is?"

"You are." They reached the back of the Ford Center, and she surveyed all the huge rigs parked in the lot. "Can I tell you something I've never told anyone else?"

"Of course."

"I fought Staff Sergeant Barnett for all I was worth, and not because I thought I could stop what was happening." Blowing out a breath, she forced the rest of her secret out. "He had a reputation for violence and a short fuse. I knew if I provoked him, he'd strike me."

"You wanted him to hit you?" Ted frowned at her. "Why?"

"Because on some level I knew the bruises he left would prove it wasn't consensual. How sick is that?"

He sent her an inscrutable look, studying her for several seconds. "I don't think being sick had anything to do with it. You demonstrated remarkable presence of mind under the circumstances, and it confirms what I've always known. You are an incredible woman." His eyes roamed her face, his expression filling with pride. "You're going to be OK, Cory. Someday you're going look back on this as a dark period in your life, but you will get better."

"If you say so." She couldn't picture it, couldn't see herself put back together into any semblance of the woman she'd once been.

"More than anything I need to hold you." He stopped walking and faced her. "I want to comfort you, which would really comfort me. Will you let me do that for you?"

She shook her head. "More than anything I dread how all the good feelings I have for you will get twisted into something vile and ugly in my nightmares if you do. And that's what will happen. When I'm all alone tonight, I'll dream about you. It'll start out great and end up horrible. I don't know what to do, and I hate that you're caught up in all the flotsam and jetsam of my stream of crazy." She blinked against the tears escaping down her cheeks. "I'm sorry. I know this isn't what you want, or what you deserve."

"Didn't I already tell you not to worry about me?"

"Yeah, you did, but I worry anyway. I want you to be happy, and being around me is kind of the antithesis of *happy*."

He chuckled. "You have a unique way of putting things."

"How can you laugh right now?" A flare of irritation ignited inside her. "This is not even remotely close to a laughing matter."

"You're so hard on yourself," he chided. "I see you in a completely different light than you see yourself."

"Yeah?" She wiped the tears from her cheeks, running her fingertips under her eyes to catch the smeared mascara. "How do you see me?"

"Let's walk." He took her elbow again and started her on a heading around the Ford Center. "You don't even realize how strong you are, and amazing, brave, generous and perceptive."

She blinked. "Perceptive?"

"Yes. Perceptive and intelligent. After all, you're the only one who sees me for the brilliant guy I truly am."

A chuckle broke free, and that familiar heart-flipping sensation filled her chest. "So how you see me is all about how I see you?"

"Exactly. See how perceptive you are?"

She looked up into his warm gray eyes. "Thank you. I needed a laugh."

"I wasn't trying to be funny." He scowled, but the twinkle in his eyes gave him away. "I was serious."

"Humph."

"Cory…I see you as…"

The vulnerability filling his voice and expression cracked her heart wide open. *Oh, Lord.*

He cleared his throat. "I see you as the one for me."

"Don't say that." Her eyes filled again. "I can't be the one for you. I'm too messed up. What if the next time I have a flashback,

I hurt you even worse? We agreed to be friends. I have nothing more to offer."

"That's not how I see it. You're going to have health insurance soon. Thanks to your efforts, we all will. Once that happens, you'll see a doctor and get some kind of medication for the nightmares and anxiety. Then you'll find a therapist, and things will turn around. You won't have these kinds of episodes forever." His wonderful gray eyes filled with warmth. "If you let me, I'll be there for you every step of the way."

"What if things *don't* turn around and I *don't* get better?"

"They will. I've seen it happen with Noah, Ryan, Kyle, and Wesley, pretty much our entire staff. You're not going to be the exception. I won't let you."

"None of them were raped. What if I can't…I don't…"

"Let's just focus on right now." He drew an audible breath and let it out slowly. "Do you want me to take you home, or would you like to see a bunch of idiots try to ride twelve-hundred-pound bulls with bad attitudes and sharp horns?"

She ached for him. No one could turn her around like he could, and that hurt like hell, because she knew in her soul she'd never be what he needed. Her first urge was to go home and hole up in her apartment, but she wouldn't ruin his evening. For his sake, she'd pull herself together and act like she was having a good time. "Let's go watch the idiots ride the big bad bulls."

"That's my girl." Ted reached for her hand and turned them around for the walk back to the entrance.

"I'm not your girl. Did you not hear a word I said?" She tugged her hand free, her heart breaking. "You deserve a whole relationship, not one where you have to be concerned about your physical safety. I'm an ambulatory cornucopia of emotional issues and hang-ups, and that's no good for anybody. Not even me."

"It's just an expression, Cory." He turned away, but not before she caught the flash of hurt in his eyes. "What makes you the expert on what I need or want? I don't recall giving you the right to make that determination for me. So don't."

He'd never spoken to her in an angry tone before, and it stung. The way she'd snapped at him only made her feel worse. She bit her lip. What did he get out of their relationship that kept him coming back for more? How on earth could he see her as anything but a box of nuts without the requisite bolts?

Maybe he was one of those men who thrived on feeling needed. That must be it, because needing him was her drug of choice, and it wouldn't be long before she became addicted. *Who are you kidding?* She'd been addicted since the day he put the deadbolt lock on her office door. "I'm sorry. I'm snapping at you, and you aren't the problem."

"Water under the bridge. Let's head back inside."

By the time they found their seats again, a cowboy was riding bareback on a horse hell-bent on throwing him off. A buzzer sounded, and two riders rode up to flank the still-bucking horse. The cowboy grabbed hold of one of the riders and slid off his mount. She saw a score light up the board above the big-screen televisions facing them. "How does this work?"

Ryan turned to study her. "You OK?"

"Fine. Thanks." Oh, so far from the truth.

"Good." He nodded toward the score. "The rider has to stay on the bronc's back for eight seconds. He's judged on his form and the difficulty of the ride."

"I see." The next rider came out of the chute. She watched intently, trying to figure out what to look for. Was Ted still angry? She leaned toward him. "I don't get it. Do you?"

"Not really." He gave a slight shrug. "It's beyond me why

anyone would want to ride a horse that clearly doesn't want to be ridden in the first place, but I do enjoy watching it happen."

She turned her attention back to the spectacle playing out before her. "Me too."

"Are you going to become a fan?"

"Maybe, but in the future I'll skip the beginning part of the show."

"Probably a good idea."

He still wouldn't look at her. She'd hurt him and ruined his evening after all. Turning back to watch the next crazy cowboy try to hang on for an eight-second, bone-rattling ride, she pretended to watch as yet more tears blurred her vision.

❦ ❦ ❦

Returning to his office from their Monday morning meeting, Ted took a seat and propped his elbows on his desk. He buried his face in the palms of his hands and groaned. How long could he keep throwing himself against the brick wall of Cory's resolve before he broke?

I'm not your girl. I can't be that for you.

How many times had she told him? When the hell was he going to get it? He rubbed his face with both hands and sighed. They'd sat across from each other at the conference table a few short minutes ago. They might as well have been a million miles apart, because he couldn't seem to get any closer no matter what he did, or how hard he tried to bridge the gap.

"Hey, Ted, we need to get this document signed and sent out today." Noah set a pile of papers on the corner of his desk.

He raised his head to look at the stack, reaching to slide it in front of him. "Fine. I'll do it right now."

Noah nudged the door closed. "You OK?"

"Sure."

"Because *OK* is not what I'm getting from you this morning." He took the seat in front of Ted's desk. "This have anything to do with Cory?"

Ted growled deep in his throat and leaned back to stare at the ceiling.

"Paige told me Cory had a meltdown at the rodeo Saturday night. PTSD is a bitch with teeth, and when you're in its grip, it's impossible to see your way free without help. A lot of relationships have been destroyed by PTSD, and you two aren't even really dating. Are you sure you—"

"Thanks. Very helpful."

"I'm just saying I know what you're going through. Ceejay and I are here for you if you need us. We're pulling for you. It's no secret Cory has a lot to work through, and it's obvious to all of us you both have feelings for each other. If anybody can help her, you can," he said. "But you're our primary concern. We've all been worried about you this past year, and—"

"What the hell are you talking about, and who the hell is 'we've all'?" Ted straightened.

"Yep. There it is. You've been irritable, short-tempered and restless for far too long." Noah pinned him with the commander stare. "Don't even try to deny it."

"And here I thought I hid it so well." Ted snatched a pen from his top drawer and flipped through the document for places to sign. "What is this for, anyway?"

"Liability stuff for the new retail store. You need a vacation, Ted."

"Right."

"Get away for a couple weeks, and you might gain a fresh

perspective on things. Give yourself a break. Paige and I can cover for you if you'll get the payroll ready."

"I wouldn't know where to go." The idea had taken hold, though. He did need a break. It wouldn't hurt to think a few things through somewhere far away from everything. Things like whether or not to give up on any notion of ever having a romantic relationship with the woman currently taking up most of his thoughts. "The farthest from home I've ever been is Kentucky, which is right across the river."

"Then it's time." Noah shot him a pointed look. "My folks own a cabin in the Pennsylvania Appalachians. It's on a private lake not too far from a fun little touristy town. You could do some fishing, hiking, read a book, and maybe even relax and do nothing at all. Do you want me to set you up? My parents haven't used the place much since they've been on their see-the-world kick. I'm sure they'd appreciate having someone check to see that it's still standing."

"You might be right. Maybe a break is exactly what I need." His mind already made up, he started planning. He'd have to hire someone to help his dad out with the farm. They'd be bringing in another crop of hay in the next couple of weeks. "Sure. Ask your folks. If they say yes, I'll spend the rest of the week getting things in order. I could be ready to leave by Friday."

Should he tell Cory he'd be gone? Part of him wanted to let her know. The hurting part didn't see the need. They weren't a couple, and probably never would be. She'd made that clear in excruciating detail. If that's the way she wanted things, then maybe it was time he listened. "I'd appreciate it if you'd keep my plans to yourself."

"All right." Noah's gaze sharpened. "I won't say a thing to anyone except Paige. She's going to have to take up most of the slack on the administration end, and she'll want to know that you aren't going to make it to their housewarming party."

"Fair enough."

"I'll give you airport information and directions once I've spoken to my dad. I have a set of keys for everything. So does Paige. One of us will pass them along to you before you leave." Noah rose from the chair. "You'll want to rent an SUV with four-wheel drive. The roads can get pretty rough."

"Thanks, Noah. I appreciate it." A nice, isolated little cabin on a lake sounded like the perfect place to lick his wounds and reevaluate his life.

"Just come back rested and less surly. That'll be thanks enough." Noah grinned. "I'll go give my dad a call right now."

Once Noah left, Ted made a list of things he needed to get done before Friday. A vacation. The notion settled into him, the idea looking better and better by the minute. Other than a few trips to amusement parks nearby, he couldn't recall ever going on a real vacation.

He called the farmhand he and his dad hired frequently and made arrangements for him to help out for the next two weeks. Checking that item off his list, he began organizing things for Paige. He could take care of a lot of his workload beforehand, which would make it easier for Noah and his sister. What should he bring with him on his vacation? Another list took shape as he worked the morning away.

"Hey." Noah appeared at his door. "It's all set. I'll have directions and the keys ready for you by Thursday. Mom and Dad said hi, and thanks for checking on things for them."

"I'm looking forward to this. Thank them back for me." He smiled for the first time since Saturday night. Maybe Noah was right, and once he put distance between himself and Perfect, he'd gain some perspective. "I've never booked a flight or leased a car. Any recommendations on which online site is the best?"

"Come for dinner tonight. We'll do it together."

"I will. I'd appreciate the help."

"Not a problem." Noah backed up a step. "You about ready for lunch?"

"Yeah. I could eat." Knowing he had a break coming lightened the load he'd been carrying for years. School, farming, and L&L had consumed pretty much all of his time, and he had grown surly, like Noah said. Why hadn't he taken a vacation before? He stood up and followed Noah down the hall, stopping at Paige and Cory's office on the way. His heart flipped. He could handle lunch with her, right? Kyle and the rest of the day crew would be there. He'd get them talking about cars, and that's all it would take to keep himself occupied.

They moved as a herd, gathering up the rest of the group as they went. Sweltering heat and the blazing sun hit him once they reached the alley. What would the weather be like in the Appalachians? Probably cooler because of the elevation, and hopefully way less humid. Plus, the Langfords' cabin was on a lake. He managed to keep himself clustered with the guys during the short walk to the diner, but he couldn't keep his eyes from straying.

Cory had dark circles under her eyes, and she still needed to put on a few pounds. Even so, the sight of her snared him, causing a hitch in his breath and a skip in his heartbeat. Her eyes met his. She smiled tentatively. Pretending everything was fine with him, he smiled back. Friday couldn't come fast enough.

Ted stowed his borrowed suitcase in the backseat of his dad's truck. He kept the backpack holding his airline tickets, the information Noah had prepared for him, and the rental car paperwork with him as he took his place up front. Excitement thrummed through his veins as he set his pack on the floor and buckled his seat belt. "I'm going to be twenty-five next month, and this is the first time I've ever ridden on an airplane." He shot his dad a grin. "It's also the first time I've gone anywhere outside of Indiana and Kentucky, and Kentucky doesn't really count."

"Just so you're doing this vacation thing for the right reasons." His dad turned the key in the ignition and backed the truck up, heading it down their lane toward the highway.

"There's a wrong reason to take a vacation?" Ted's brow rose. "I've done nothing but work and go to school for the past five and a half years. Don't you think I deserve a break?"

"Absolutely." His dad nodded slowly. "You've definitely been burning the candle at both ends, but…"

"But what?" Irritation cut off the flow of excitement.

"Are you taking this trip to run away from the problems you're having with—"

"Of course. I need to put some distance between me and Cory. I can't think straight when I see her every day. This whole situation has me turned inside out, and it's not a good feeling." He turned a baleful eye his dad's way. "Gaining perspective is as good a reason for getting away as any other I might make up. I need to breathe. I need some space to figure out what I want to do."

"OK, son. I just wanted to be sure you were clear on the matter." He glanced at him. "This whole vacation thing has gotten your mom and me talking."

"What about?"

"We need one too. Next year we're going to retire from

farming. We'll lease the land out to someone else, and that will give us a nice little income. Your mom and I want to tour this nation's national parks, stay at some fancy resorts and take it easy. Who knows, maybe we'll even try out one of those hot tub spa things. We'd also like to spend more time with our grandchildren. And quite frankly, I'm sick to death of hog shit."

"Really?" Ted's head spun. One more load lifted from his shoulders. If they leased their land instead of farming it themselves, that would free up so much more of his time. He might even get a life. "Sounds like a great idea to me. I'll look after the house whenever you're gone."

"We'd appreciate it." His dad shifted, his posture relaxing. "I've talked to all of your brothers and sisters. We're going to put the deed in your name sooner rather than later, so there won't be any question about who will manage things when your mom and I are gone. We want the land to stay in the family, just as it has been for generations." He flashed him a cockeyed grin. "Who knows? Maybe one of the grandkids will want to raise hogs one day."

"No hurry. You and Mom are both healthy and active." He didn't like even thinking about life without them. "Don't worry about anything."

"I'm not worried." His dad reached and patted Ted's shoulder. "We couldn't be more proud of you than we already are, Teddy. I want you to know you're our favorite son."

"Wait a minute." Ted looked askance at his dad. "When I had Roger do some legal papers for L&L a couple weeks ago, he said you told him *he's* your favorite."

"Busted." His dad laughed and put his hand back on the wheel. "You're all our favorites for different reasons. All six of you children have done us proud. You've grown into a fine man, and things are going to turn out for you. You'll see."

"I hope so." The rest of the trip to the airport, they talked about things that needed to be done around the farm. Once that subject had been exhausted, they gossiped like a couple of old biddies about the Lovejoy relatives. His dad pulled up to the drop-off area at the airport, and Ted climbed out. He grabbed his pack from the floor and moved to the back to retrieve the suitcase. "Thanks for the ride. I'll call you when my return flight lands."

"Relax and have some fun. Call your mother when you get there, otherwise she'll worry."

"I will." He waved and headed for the door. He checked in his suitcase and got in line for security. Time to himself in a mountain cabin in Pennsylvania, something he'd never had in his entire life, and he looked forward to it with every fiber of his being.

"You gotta be kidding me!" Ted stared at the two-story, timber-frame and fieldstone structure before him. A full-length screened porch faced the pristine lake. A huge stone chimney rose past the sloping roofline on the right side of cabin, if you could call such a luxurious home a cabin. Not at all what he'd pictured in his mind. Hoisting the bags of groceries from the back of the Jeep he'd rented, he shook his head. He should've known. After all, it did belong to the Langfords.

He walked up the ground limestone path to the porch door and set the groceries down. Two more trips to the Jeep, and he had all his gear and the rest of the items he'd picked up in town sitting by the door. Noah had given him a large manila envelope with directions on how to shut off the water when he left, where to find everything, the best places to eat in town and important telephone numbers.

He pulled the envelope out of his backpack. The keys formed a bulge at the bottom. He fished them out and looked for the one labeled "porch" and the one for the front door and headed inside with his arms full. He found himself in a foyer with a great room to the left and a dining room to the right. A huge stone fireplace took up one end of the great room. Comfortable overstuffed couches and chairs formed a conversational U shape around the fireplace, and an Indian rug in geometric designs in black, red and white covered a large section of the wide-planked wooden floor in the center.

Pictures along the mantel drew his attention, and once he had the groceries put away, he took a closer look at them. He recognized a much younger Paige and Noah right away, along with their parents. The older people he guessed were grandparents, and those close to their parents in age must be aunts and uncles.

The pictures including Noah's stepbrother reminded him of the pain his cousin Ceejay had gone through when Matt abandoned her. But if it hadn't been for Matt, Noah never would've come to Perfect. He couldn't hold onto his anger against Matt. Not a day went by that he wasn't glad Noah had come into their lives.

He wandered back to the kitchen and opened the fridge to grab one of the bottles of beer from his six-pack, taking it with him to the front porch. Finding his room and unpacking could wait. After all, he had all kinds of time with nothing to do but relax. He didn't have to take care of everything right this minute. He took a seat on the rattan love seat and put his feet up on the coffee table. The vista before him truly was impressive. The lake formed a shallow crater in the midst of tree-covered rolling mountains.

He took a swallow of his beer and sank back, shedding the stress of the past few months bit by bit. How had he not realized how badly he needed this? No hogs to feed or barn to muck out.

No crops to bring in or paperwork to do for L&L. Nothing but peace and quiet for two whole weeks. Heaven. In fact, he vowed not to think about Cory until Monday. His heart wrenched at the thought of her, and he knew he was bound to break that vow.

Forcing his mind off of his troubles, he gazed out at the natural beauty in front of him, taking in the crisp, cool mountain air. For now, his biggest worry was whether or not he'd be able to find the light switches inside the Langfords' palatial "cabin." What would he do tomorrow? Kayak, canoe or hike through the woods on one of the trails Noah had mentioned. Perhaps he'd head into town and do some shopping for a souvenir sweatshirt or something. He took another swallow of beer. *I'm way overdue for a break, and putting distance between me and Cory is the best thing for me right now. Isn't it?*

Ted carried the kayak back to the garage, taking note of the uncut stack of firewood along the outside wall next to a huge, scarred stump. He'd hiked, gone into town for lunch and kayaked. Only Monday, and already he was antsy. He missed his folks, work and Cory. Especially Cory. Could he be any more pathetic?

Time to figure a few things out, and he did his best thinking while doing physical labor. Setting the kayak back where he'd found it, he eyed the maul and ax hanging from the hooks on the wall and made a decision. He took them both down, testing the sharpness of the blades with his thumb. Both were sharp.

Once he'd wrestled the first piece of wood to an upended position on the stump, he hefted the maul, shifting its balance and weight in his grip, and let her fly. *Thwack.* He'd been an idiot to expose his feelings right after her flashback. *Thwack.* Would he never learn? She'd drawn the line in the dirt more than once, and he kept scuffing his way past it. He'd pushed her for kisses, pushed her to spend time with him, and now here he was with his heart all black-and-blue and his pride in tatters. He brought the maul down with more force. *Crack.* The two split pieces flew apart and bounced on the ground.

Was he doomed to always hand his heart over to women who couldn't or wouldn't love him back? He cringed, remembering the humiliation his crush on Paige had put him through. Setting one of the pieces back on the stump, he brought the maul down again. *Thwack.* At least that defeat only involved the three of them. This time, everyone at L&L knew, and what he felt for Cory was no crush. He'd gone and done it, set himself up for major heartbreak, and he had no one to blame but himself. *Crack.* He stooped to pick up the two quarters, tossing them toward the garage to stack later.

His mind conjured Cory's image, her shy smiles, soulful brown eyes and luscious full lips. He placed the next half up, and the sound of his next swing hitting wood reverberated through the air. The impact vibrated along his nerves. She'd said he was amazing, and kissing him was wonderful. Hadn't she also said if things were different, dating him would be a dream come true? Yeah, he was pretty sure that's what she'd said. Was she just trying to be nice, spare his feelings and all that?

He hefted a new log onto the chopping block and took another swing. But Cory had also come to his defense at work, ending the annoying kid nickname once and for all. Plus, he'd started hanging out with the guys lately, also her doing, since it began after they'd doubled with Kyle and Brenda. *Thwack.* Still, it didn't mean she felt anything for him. Friendship was all she'd offered. Ever.

He remembered the way she'd kissed him back, coming away breathless. Surely her response had been the result of arousal, not distress. Had he read her all wrong? He wiped the sweat from his brow with the bottom of his T-shirt. How many times had he caught her staring at him, or glimpsed the answering heat and longing in her eyes? Or had he willed himself to see what he wanted to see? Could be her glances meant nothing more than the affection one friend felt for another. He might've been wrong all along, and she didn't want him at all.

One thing for certain, he really did need this break. He needed to regroup and put the pieces of his broken heart back together. From now on, if anything were to happen between them, Cory would have to be the one to initiate it. She'd already stamped *rejected* on his forehead, and it would take a good long while for that burn to cool.

That's your wounded pride talking, son.

His dad's voice, as clear as if he stood beside him, sounded off inside his head. "Humph. I'm not done thinking yet. I'm just trying to work my way through the hurt and the anger." A lump rose to his throat and his eyes burned. "I'm so damned tired of the heartache and the loneliness."

Is she worth it?

His dad's voice weighed in again. Hell, yes, and wasn't that just the salt rub to his wound? He wanted her, knew at a cellular level they were meant for each other, and she kept pushing him away. *I'm not your girl. I can't be that for you.* He rubbed at the ache in his chest and blinked against the sting in his eyes. *Shit. Pull yourself together.*

After finishing up the pile of firewood, he'd reorganize the Langfords' storage garage. Things were piled up willy-nilly, and he itched to put the place in order. *Put yourself in order, you mean*. Maybe he'd uncover something mechanical to tinker with under all of the junk. He'd caught a glimpse of what might be an old motorcycle under a pile of boxes and gear.

He'd keep himself busy "relaxing", and then he'd return home with some kind of plan in mind. What that might be, he had no idea, but he'd reached his low—either he'd cut his losses and move on, or he'd throw himself at that wall once more and hope this time he stuck.

CHAPTER THIRTEEN

CORY'S HEAD ACHED, AND HER knees took on that wobbly, nervous feeling as she made her way upstairs to her office. In a few minutes, she'd have to face Ted across the conference table for their Monday morning staff meeting. Her heart splintered at the thought. He'd gone back to being polite but distant since the rodeo, and he'd left early last Friday before she could talk to him.

He'd seen her at her worst. She'd attacked him. As if that wasn't enough, she'd stomped on his heart when he made his feelings for her known. Her words must've finally gotten through, and he'd realized he'd be better off without her. If only she could convince herself it was for the best. Swallowing against the constriction in her throat, she continued on her way.

"Hey, Cory," Paige called behind her.

She stopped to wait for her very pregnant friend to catch up. "Good morning."

"Morning. There's no staff meeting today. I have to head into Evansville in a few minutes."

"OK." Relief washed through her. She could hide out in her office and get some work done. Nothing like avoidance to calm the nerves. "Thanks for the heads-up."

"Sure. Do you want to come with me and take a look at L&L's very first retail store?"

"Not today. I need to sort through the insurance bids we've gotten so far and start a document to compare the plans. The sooner we get the vote done, the quicker we can enroll."

"All right. Don't forget our housewarming party is this coming Saturday."

"I haven't forgotten. I signed up to bring a pasta salad." She opened the door to their shared office and headed for her desk. "I can't wait to see your new house. Are you all settled in?"

"The rooms we use are done. The rest can wait." Paige dropped her purse and briefcase on her chair. "Baby boy Malloy's room is ready, and as far as I'm concerned that's all that matters." Paige shot her a grin and booted up her desktop while still standing. "I just have to print a few copies off before I go." Her fingers flew over the keyboard.

"We've posted the openings for a store manager and sales staff, and I have contractors coming this morning give us estimates on the remodeling. I need to pick up the plans from the architect before they arrive." The printer came to life, and Paige snatched up the pile of papers. "I'm outta here. I'll be back later this afternoon. Hold down the fort for me," she said as she tucked the papers into her briefcase.

"Will do." She waited until Paige left before spreading the insurance bids across her desk. Reading through them, she highlighted the differences, made comparisons and immersed herself in organizing the offerings. Everything needed to be clear to their stakeholders. She created a document with different columns for each provider and laid out the costs and coverage side by side.

Time for more coffee. She grabbed her mug and rose from her chair just as her phone rang. Setting her mug back down, she fished around in her purse and pulled it out. Her breath caught as she recognized the Yale Law School number. "Hello?"

"Hi, Cory. This is Janice from the Yale Law School Veterans Legal Services Clinic. You have some decisions to make."

Cory sat down hard, her knees finally caving to stress. "Decisions?"

"Yes. I put off calling until we had a firm offer on the table. Do you have a few minutes?" Janice's tone was all business.

"Sure."

"The US Army has expunged the personality disorder diagnosis from your record, and they've accepted the independent psychological evaluation we had done last fall. You now have a diagnosis of PTSD and an honorable discharge. Your benefits have been restored."

Cory's mouth went seven-year-drought dry, and her hands shook. "Thank you."

"You're welcome." She paused. "Here's where the decision part comes in. You're well poised for a groundbreaking lawsuit, and the army knows it. You stand to gain much more than what they've put on the table. Plus, your case will set precedent, which will ultimately change policy. Whether or not we proceed is entirely up to you. They've offered to pension you off with full benefits as if you'd served your full twenty, or you can reenlist and be guaranteed a cushy stateside job. In exchange, you have to agree not to take any further legal action."

Her mind reeled, and she could barely string words together to form a coherent sentence. *Pension me off? A cushy stateside job?* Her assailant was behind bars, found guilty by a jury of his peers. She had a copy of every correspondence she'd ever initiated with her superiors trying to get the army's support after she'd been attacked. Plus, she had a copy of her unfixed record. If she decided to take it to the next level, her case would be a slam dunk. Did she want to go through all of that again? "Can I think about it?"

"Of course." Janice's voice softened. "I know you've been through a lot these past couple years, but we're really hoping you'll agree to pursue this. Think what it would mean for other servicewomen everywhere."

She would think about it, but not now. Her current hell took its own precedent, and the possibility of getting better loomed large and bright before her. "You said my file is already fixed, right? I no longer have the less-than-honorable discharge on my record?"

"That's right. I've put a copy in the mail. You should have it by Wednesday at the latest."

"I can start seeing a therapist at the VA center right away?"

"Absolutely."

Memories of her lawsuit days flashed before her—the cameras thrust in her face as she walked into court. Her name and the circumstances of her assault spread all over the media for everyone to see. Did she really want to repeat that experience? But this time would be different. Vindication sent a fresh shot of adrenaline pumping through her veins. "I have a lot to think about. I need a week or so."

"Fair enough. Call or e-mail me when you've reached a decision." Janice paused again. "I don't want to put any pressure on you, but this is so very important."

"I understand, and I promise to give the matter the consideration it deserves. Thank you. Thank you so much for everything you and the law clinic have done for me. I..." She cleared her throat, trying to dislodge the lump that had formed. "This means so much to me."

"You're entirely welcome. You have my e-mail address and the phone number for the clinic. If you do decide to follow through with this, John Nickols and I will be cochairing the case."

"OK. I'll let you know." They said their good-byes, and Cory leaned back in her chair, closed her eyes and pressed her finger-tips against her temples. She was no longer unfit to serve, no longer personality disordered, and something inside her loosened and fell away. Maybe a tiny part of the chip she carried on her shoulder had fallen off? She needed to call her mom and Brenda. They needed to know, but not right this minute. She could hardly wrap her head around what had just happened herself. For that matter, she couldn't really think clearly at all. Still shaky and dry mouthed, she willed her vitals to settle.

Ted. More than anything she wanted to talk to him, tell him her news and get his perspective on what she should do. He knew more about her than anyone. She'd shared so much with him, more than she'd revealed to her mother or even her best friend. After pushing him away, after physically attacking him, would he still be willing to be her friend?

I'm like this old truck, steady and dependable. He'd said he'd be there for her in an instant if she needed him. When didn't she need him? Why did walking down the hall to talk to Ted take more courage than facing a lawsuit? *Because he told me I'm the one, and I rejected him.*

She'd seen the hurt flash through his eyes. The bitter taste of regret soured her stomach. The only way to find out whether or not they still had a friendship was to get up and walk down to his office. Rising on rubbery legs, she walked out of her office and down the hall to his.

He generally kept his door open while he worked, but it was closed now. She knocked, knowing there would be no answer. His absence was a tangible force, like gravity. He liked to spend part of his day working with his hands; perhaps she'd find him downstairs with the production crew. Could she face the group right now? For the sake of talking to Ted she could, and would. She took the front stairs and wove her way through the furniture to the workroom. Standing in the middle of the room, her heart sank. No Ted. Maybe he'd gone to Evansville with Paige.

"Do you need something?" Noah lifted his safety goggles to look at her.

"Where's Ted?" She couldn't control the nervous edge slipping into her tone. Heat crept up her neck.

"He's not here." Noah stepped closer.

"Did he go to Evansville with Paige?"

"No. He's not working today."

"Is he sick?" She frowned.

"Uh, no." Noah took his goggles off and tossed them on his workbench. "Not that I know of."

Her frown deepened. Ted never took time off. "Where is he?"

John, Kyle and Xavier were looking at her now, and more than anything she wanted to be back in her office with the door closed. Noah must've caught something in her expression, because a look of concern suffused his features.

"Let's head upstairs to talk. Do you feel up to taking the freight elevator? You're looking a little pale."

"Sure." After the call from the legal clinic, and all the adrenaline that had pumped through her veins a little while ago, her legs wouldn't carry her up the stairs anyway. She followed him to the elevator for the silent ride to the second floor while the niggling sense that something was wrong pulled at her already raw nerves. They entered her office, and Noah sat at Paige's desk. She dropped heavily into her chair. "What's going on? Where is he?"

"He's on vacation." Noah picked up a paper clip and started

straightening the thin wire, one curve at a time. He kept his eyes on the project in his hands.

Sudden anger coursed through her. He'd left without a word to go on a *vacation*? So much for steady and dependable. So much for *I'll be there for you if you need me.*

Wait. She had no right to think like that. After all, she'd been the one to snap at him that she couldn't be his girl. And she'd done so just as he'd bared his soul to her. Self-absorbed. That's what she'd been, and she'd hurt the only man she'd ever really loved. More than likely she'd done irreparable damage. He'd given up and gone on vacation to get away from her. Her stomach dropped.

"Talk to me, Cory. You're pale and shaky, and your eyes have that wild, panicked look right now. Whatever you're going through, rest assured, I've been there."

"Ted didn't tell me he was leaving. It just took me by surprise, is all." Struggling to rein in her fluctuating emotions, she twisted her hands together in her lap. "How long is he going to be gone?"

"Two weeks."

"Two whole weeks?" she squeaked. What was she going to do without him for that eternity?

"Is there something I can help you with? You came downstairs looking for him. Obviously something's on your mind."

She worked for Noah, and he was the sole reason she had her job. Besides, if she decided to sue the army, her decision would affect L&L. He had a right to know. "I got a call from the Yale legal clinic this morning. My record has been straightened out. I've been honorably discharged, and my benefits have been restored."

"That's great news." He put the straightened paper clip down and smiled. "I know some folks at the Marion VA Medical Center.

Do you want me to see if I can pull a few strings to get you in right away? Otherwise it could take a few weeks to get an appointment."

"Yes!" Her eyes stung. "I'd be forever in your debt." She worked her lower lip between her teeth for second. "That's not all. The legal clinic says I'm well situated for a big, historical lawsuit, which could ultimately lead to policy change within the armed forces. The army has made an offer to settle. If I accept, I have to agree not to take any further legal action. I have no idea what I should do."

"Weigh the pros and cons before you make a decision. Take some time. Seems to me you've already done more than your share, but whatever you decide, we're behind you one hundred and ten percent." He leaned back in the chair and ran his palm over the back of his head. "Can we talk about Teddy for a minute?"

Gah! Her heart raced, and her mouth dried up again. "Sure."

"He was in a world of hurt last Monday. I convinced him to take a much-needed break."

"Oh." Just what she needed to hear.

"Do you remember that morning we talked by the river?"

She nodded.

"You said the more you felt for Ted, the worse your nightmares got." He fixed her with his legendary commander stare. "Can I assume that you have more than friendly feelings for him?"

Her cheeks heating up, she nodded again.

"When Ceejay and I first started dating...No. Wait." He straightened. "I need to back up. The day my platoon got hit by the suicide bombers, my driver died. The nightmares I had always began the same way, with my driver, Jackson, pointing out the civilian truck heading toward us and voicing his concern. I relived the bombing over and over, and it always ended the same way. I'd see Jackson in pieces on the ground, and then the parade of dead would begin." He shook his head, his expression turning inward.

"Once I began dating Ceejay, the dreams got worse. She'd take Corporal Jackson's place at the wheel of the Humvee, and there was nothing I could do to stop what I knew would happen next. I saw the woman I loved mangled and dead night after night."

"That must've been rough."

"It was. I think it's fairly common that the people we care about get tangled up in our dreams. They're a big part of our present, and we're still trying to come to terms with our past. I'm guessing the same kind of thing is happening with you. Ted's image gets transposed into your horrors. Am I right?"

"Yes, and I hate it! I *hate* how what I feel for him gets so…so defiled. When I'm with him, everything is great, and then we say good night, and…and then I'm alone to face the fallout."

"I didn't get my first decent sleep until the night I held Ceejay in my arms. I didn't begin to heal until I let her in. Maybe it's the *alone* part making things worse for you, and not the being-close-to-Ted part." He stood up. "Just something to think about. Talk to Ryan. He swears Paige is his own personal superhero, because she keeps his nighttime demons at bay."

Cory's mouth closed tight, and her mind, already on overload, spun out of orbit. She didn't know what to say. Could it be she'd had things all wrong?

"I'm going to go make a few phone calls to the VA center. I should have some news for you by lunchtime."

"Thanks, Noah," she managed to croak out. "I appreciate everything you've done for me."

"Think about what I said." He stopped by the door. "Everyone here is on your side, Cory. You know that, right?"

For the third time since they'd come upstairs, speaking was beyond her. And once again she nodded.

"Later."

The sound of Noah's footsteps receded, and she turned back to her desk. She couldn't concentrate on anything, not the insurance plans laid out before her or the monumental decision she had to make. Not even thoughts of Ted brought her back into focus. She'd waited so long for the day the army admitted they were wrong, and now they had. Instead of jumping up and down for joy, she felt empty. Numb.

No, not numb. Still, like the time she'd been mesmerized by the river's endless, hypnotic flow. Something precious had been restored to her. She'd been exonerated, and eight years of her history had been returned. Now the real work could begin at last. It would happen. Just like Ted said it would. She'd start therapy and get better, because no other alternative was acceptable.

She should've trusted Ted, and if she somehow got another chance, she would. Shaking herself out of the stillness, she straightened her spine and went back to work. The rest of L&L's staff and Perfect's independent businesses were depending on her to get their health insurance up and rolling. She wasn't about to let them down. Shoot. She never did get that second cup of coffee. A smile broke free. Coffee could wait until lunch—she glanced at the wall clock—which was only an hour and a half away.

By the time Noah returned, she'd finished with the first bids.

"Hey, good news," he said. "You have an appointment with Dr. Linda Siverson-Hall Friday morning at eight. She wants you to get in for a physical beforehand. You shouldn't have any trouble getting in for that this week."

"Wow. How did you manage that?"

"She's a friend. Linda runs a few women's groups, and they all followed your case. She would've found the time regardless, but her regular Friday morning appointment had to go out of town for a funeral. She said she'd be happy to take you on, and the two of you can figure out a regular time once you meet."

He handed her a slip of paper with the appointment date and time and a couple of phone numbers scribbled across the bottom. "Call the second number and make the appointment for your physical. Then let's head to the diner for lunch. You can share your good news with Jenny and Harlen."

"I will. I owe you, Noah."

"No, you don't." He shrugged. "It's all part of the mission. Come downstairs when you're ready. We'll wait."

"I will." She picked up her phone and entered the number to make her appointment. Her insides had turned to jelly. Relief and elation chased around inside her like a dog after its own tail. Ted would be gone for two weeks. That stung, but she planned to make good use of the time. She'd take her first steps toward getting better, and hopefully those steps would lead her back to him—unless he'd finally given up on her and planned to use the two weeks to move on.

Ted took in a lungful of pine- and loam-spiced air and tilted his head back to stare at the clear blue sky above the tops of the conifers and hardwoods surrounding him. The pine needles covering the path were so thick his footsteps barely made a sound. He'd taken several hikes this past week, and this trail was his favorite. It led to a small waterfall where one of the lake's feeder streams hit a stone outcrop, dropping off to the boulders below.

The stream looped through the hills and back around to the lake, and the trail meandered along beside it all the way. Beautiful. Peaceful. Lonely as hell.

He was supposed to be figuring out what he wanted to do, and everything he did led his thoughts back to her. Hiking through the woods would be great if Cory was here to enjoy it with him, but she wasn't. Vacationing would be great if he had her to share it with, but he didn't. In fact, he hadn't spoken aloud since his last trip into town two days ago.

Only Thursday, he hadn't even been on vacation for a week, and already the silence had him climbing the walls. The trail took him to a path beside the lake, leading him back to the Langfords' summer home. He decided to do some fishing off the end of their dock and turned his steps toward the garage.

He glanced at the neat pile of split firewood stacked under the eaves for protection from the rain and snow. He'd done that. Swinging the garage door up, he surveyed his handiwork inside. All of the tools he'd found scattered under piles of junk were now hanging on the hooks where they belonged. Sports equipment, all sorted, now sat on the metal shelves taking up the back wall, and he'd packed all the miscellaneous stuff lying around into stacked boxes. The vintage Indian motorcycle he'd uncovered was now parked out of the way.

He walked over to the motorcycle and ran his hand over the gas tank, thinking about what it would take to restore the old bike to its former glory. He'd ask Noah whom it belonged to and see if they might be willing to part with it for the right price. He'd swept, burned rubbish and filled the kindling bin to overflowing. The kayak hung from the rack where it belonged, and the canoe rested on its side tucked underneath. You could put a vehicle inside the garage now if you wanted. He didn't. Eyeing the fishing rods and reels without a spark of enthusiasm, he grunted. "Screw it. I don't want to fish."

He racked his brain for something to do. Movie in town? Nope. Shop? Definitely not. Restaurant for dinner with all the old folks who came in for the early-bird specials? "Hell no."

What did he really want to do? "Face it. You're an Indiana farm boy, and a homebody to boot." He'd had enough vacation. Time to go home. He closed the garage door and fished the key from his pocket to lock up. Shoving his hands into the front pockets of his jeans, he headed back to the house to see if he could trade in his return airline ticket for an earlier departure.

Once he'd made all his travel arrangements, he called his folks. Ted pressed his cell phone between his ear and shoulder while stuffing clothes into the washing machine off the kitchen. No sense in going home with a pile of dirty laundry if he didn't have to.

"Hello?"

He straightened and grabbed the phone. "Hey, Mom. Is Dad nearby?"

"He's in the barn. Did you try his cell?"

"Yeah, I did. He didn't answer."

"Oh." There was a pause on the line, and he heard her moving around. "I see his phone right here on the kitchen table. Huh, didn't even hear it ring. I'll bet he turned it off again. Do you want me to go get him, Teddy?"

"No, just tell him I'm cutting my vacation short. I'm flying home tomorrow afternoon. Will one of you be around to pick me up from the airport?"

"Is everything OK? You've only been gone a week."

"Everything's fine. I just decided to take the rest of my break at home. Everything I like to do with my time off is there. I want to work on my truck." The truth was, a vacation like this would be great if he had someone to share it with. Since he didn't, home was where he preferred to be. He'd had enough of rattling around alone in the Langfords' huge summer home. All it did was bring everything his life lacked into sharper focus.

"We're not busy. I'll make sure your dad has his cell phone with him. Call when you land."

"Thanks, Mom. I've missed you and Dad. Can't wait to be home."

"We've missed you too, honey. How about I cook your favorite dinner Friday night to celebrate your homecoming?"

"I'd like that." He grinned so hard his face hurt, and love for his family filled him with warmth.

"See you Friday, Teddy."

"Later, Mom." He hit End Call and tucked his phone into his back pocket. He'd done a lot of thinking, and he'd come to a few conclusions. One, leaving Cory without a word had been petty and immature, and his actions filled him with guilt. Two, everything she'd done pointed to the fact that she somehow felt he needed to be protected—from her. That had to stop.

He'd bared his soul, told her she was the one, and she'd flat-out shut him down. Had she done so because she didn't feel the same about him as he felt about her? Or had she done it because of her misguided notion that she had to protect him? As much as he'd like to believe her reaction had more to do with the flash-back than it did with him, he couldn't be sure.

They needed to talk. At the very least, he owed her an apology for leaving the way he had. She'd be at Paige and Ryan's housewarming on Saturday. Should he go? Did he really want to have it out with her there? No. She wouldn't appreciate it, and he didn't want an audience. He'd spend Saturday tinkering with his newest restoration project. Assembling and organizing the parts he'd located for his old Ford appealed to him right now. Could it be he had some of his cousin Ceejay's OCD tendencies? A family trait, perhaps? What would the Langfords think when they found their storage garage in perfect order, their kindling bin full to the top, and all of their firewood cut and neatly stacked? He shook his head.

He wouldn't tell anyone but his folks he was home. Continuing the break would do him good. Hadn't he promised Noah he'd come back to work refreshed and less surly? Sunday he'd call Cory and arrange a time to talk. His heart and stomach fluttered at the thought of facing a final rejection. One way or another, things would be resolved between them.

He lowered the lid to the washing machine and turned it on. Making a decision had given him an appetite. He walked out the back door and took the path to the front, heading for the Jeep. A bar and grill in town advertised live music every evening. A burger and a beer and some local flavor sounded good.

By Friday afternoon he'd be home, and sometime during the next week he'd have a come-to-Jesus meeting with Cory. He had a plan. For the first time all week, he was certain about his course of action. Not happy, but certain, and that would have to do for now.

CHAPTER FOURTEEN

CORY PAGED THROUGH A WAITING room magazine without really seeing any of the images passing before her eyes. She had no idea what to expect when it came to seeing a therapist, and her nerves were stretched taut. She'd had her physical on Wednesday, and had already picked up her prescriptions. Even though she'd started taking the pills, she didn't feel any different. Not yet, anyway, but she'd been warned it might take a few weeks. Bummer.

Was instant relief too much to ask after months and months of crap? Months, dammit.

Her thoughts turned to Ted. He'd be gone for one more week, and that gave her time for another therapy session. It gave the meds more time to kick in. Would he talk to her when he got back? Probably not. His silence this past week had to mean he'd come to his senses and washed his hands of her. Her chest ached. No surprise, since her heart was breaking.

She missed him. A lot. Truly, she'd rather be talking to him this morning than to some stranger. Not healthy, though. She didn't want him permanently cast in the role of sounding board for her issues. Wouldn't it be nice to come to him whole, to be the one to lift him up now and then when he hit a rough patch?

A heavy sigh escaped. Why even think about it? She'd already driven him away.

"Corinna Marcel?" A woman in her late thirties or early forties stood before her. She held a folder with Cory's name on the tab. "Yes." She tossed the magazine onto the end table and stood up.

"I'm Dr. Siverson-Hall. Let's go back to my office." She gestured toward the corridor behind the medical assistant and started walking.

Cory studied her. She had reddish, chin-length hair with lighter highlights. Trim and fit, she had great posture. Military issue? "Thanks for seeing me on such short notice, Dr. Siverson-Hall."

"Call me Linda." Her therapist opened an office door and waited for Cory to precede her into the room. "Everyone does."

"OK. I go by Cory." She looked around the small office and swiped her sweaty palms over her jeans. The doctor's framed credentials hung on the wall behind her desk, and a bookshelf holding a bunch of thick reference books stood against the opposite wall. A comfy upholstered chair had been set next to the desk where a box of Kleenex rested on the edge. "I bet you go through a lot of this."

"What's that?" Linda took the seat at her desk and swiveled the chair around to face her.

"Tissue." Dr. Siverson-Hall exuded calm professionalism, which should've helped her nerves to settle. It didn't. Cory took her place in the chair. "I was referring to the box of Kleenex."

"Ah." Linda smiled slightly as she opened the folder she'd been holding and began to glance through it. "Yes. We do go through a few cases."

"Noah said you're familiar with my case, but I think there's more to what's bothering me than just...I've been having flashbacks and nightmares that have nothing to do with my assault." She swallowed against the constriction in her throat. "This is harder than I thought. I don't know where to begin or how this therapy stuff works. Have you ever been deployed?" OK, that was totally random, but she really wanted to know.

"I have. Three tours as psychological support staff for our troops—once to Iraq and two tours in Afghanistan." She smiled again and reached for a small picture frame sitting on the far corner of her desk, handing it to her. "I traveled with a therapy dog named Buddy. Once the army retired him, my husband and I adopted Buddy. He's a sweet dog."

Cory stared at the picture of Linda clad in army-issue desert gear and crouched down on the ground with her arms around a medium-size tan-and-white mutt. They were surrounded by desert and soldiers. "Then you know." She handed back the photo. The sudden sting of tears burning her eyes took her by surprise. The load of the tension that had been pressing on her left in a rush, leaving her almost limp. "I want to get better. I really, really want to get better. What do I need to do?"

"You've had your physical?"

"Yes, and the doctor gave me a prescription for anxiety and another for the nightmares."

"Good. We'll work on some coping techniques, talk a lot, and I'm going to start you in group therapy. How does that sound?"

"Sounds great." Overwhelming relief flooded her system.

"Today is more an intake session than a work session. I want to see you once a week for the next six weeks to start. Would Monday afternoons work?"

"Starting this coming Monday?" Only a couple of days away, and she'd already have her second session.

"Yes, if you're available."

"I am. My employer is very flexible when it comes to employees getting help. For the most part, we're all veterans."

"I'm familiar with Langford & Lovejoy." Linda's expression filled with warmth, and the laugh lines at the corners of her eyes creased. She leaned back in her chair and reached for a pen and legal pad from her desk. "You mentioned you didn't know where to begin. Why don't we start with whatever comes to your mind, and we'll see where it leads."

"OK. You said you traveled with a therapy dog, and that made me think of something that happened a couple weeks ago." She swiped her palms against her denim-clad thighs again. "I had a flashback about a military working dog traveling with the supply unit I was with. He inadvertently triggered an IED he'd located. I saw that dog get blown to bits." She launched into a description of the incident. "My friend thinks I had that particular flashback because I felt a sense of betrayal on the dog's behalf, like he trusted his handler and look where it got him. She said I was comparing my situation with the military working dog's."

"Can you expand on that? Do you see the situations as similar?"

"To some degree, yes. I should've been able to trust my commanding officer, and...and I couldn't. He abused his position of power. I should've been able to count on the institution I'd pledged my loyalty and service to, and the army let me down. *Augh*." She rubbed her temples. "The situations aren't at all the same. Except for the trust issues, they're nothing alike."

Linda nodded. "I understand what you mean about trust when it comes to dogs. Do you see what happened to the TEDD as a betrayal of the bond he had with the handler?"

"Yes, but not so much by the handler as the army. His handler was really torn up about the whole thing. If he could've prevented what happened, he would've. We could all see that. But the army views working dogs as equipment, nothing more. Equipment is expendable. *That* makes me angry."

She snorted. "Just about everything makes me angry. I was raped by my commanding officer. Rather than prosecute the man who assaulted me, the army slapped me with a personality disorder diagnosis." Her chest tightened. "The US Army discounted and discarded me like yesterday's trash, after eight years of exemplary service on my part."

She swiped at the tears escaping down her cheeks. "That's about the same number of years they keep military working dogs, isn't it? I guess they saw me as just another piece of equipment like that bomb-sniffing Labrador. These days, I'm just plumb full of rage when you get right down to it."

"Understandable. Rage is a normal reaction to what you've been through. How are you dealing with all that anger?"

"At first I used it to motivate me to get out of bed." She risked a glance at her therapist to gauge her reaction, finding nothing but calm acceptance. "It's what kept me going through the whole legal process to put Staff Sergeant Barnett behind bars. I have no idea how to deal with all the rage now. It's eating me up from the inside out. I can tell you that much. Honestly"—she heaved a shaky breath—"I'd like to chuck it."

"Then that's what we'll work on first." Linda set the legal pad and pen aside. "For the rest of our session, we're going to practice some anger management and visualization techniques. Is that all right with you, or would you rather continue talking?"

"Techniques sound good. It's hard for me to talk about this stuff. It'll take awhile before I'm comfortable about opening up my can of worms."

"Of course. This is a process, and I want you to feel

comfortable. Lean back and close your eyes. Take a deep breath, and let it out slowly, relaxing each part of your body as you do, beginning with the top of your head and working your way down."

For the rest of the hour, Cory practiced everything the doctor taught her. When they were finished, Linda handed her a couple of brochures.

"The techniques we practiced today are all in here. Refer to them if you forget what to do. Pretty soon it'll become automatic." She wrote something down on a form and handed it to her. "We had great start today, Cory. By Monday I'll have a group for you. Do your homework and start journaling like we talked about." She rose from her chair. "Stop by the assistant's desk on the way out, and she'll set up your next six appointments."

"I will. Thank you." On the way to make her appointments, she stared at the brochures in her hand. She'd done it, taken the first step, and she felt as if she'd just finished her first marathon, all twenty-six grueling miles. She was exhausted, but in a good way.

Appointment card in hand, she left the building and headed for the parking ramp. Pulling out her cell phone, she called her mom, knowing she'd be waiting to hear.

"Hey, honey," Claire answered on the second ring. "How did your first appointment go?"

"Really well. I'm so glad I've started therapy. I'm hopeful."

"That's good. When are you coming around for supper again? It's been too long since I've seen you."

"Pick a night next week. I'm open."

"All right. I'll take a look at my work schedule and get back to you. Call Brenda. She'll want to hear."

Cory's insides warmed with gratitude for all the support she had in her life. "I will in a while. If I know Bren, she's not up yet. I'll talk to you later, Mom. I love you."

"Love you too, baby. Go on back to work now, and have a good time at that housewarmin' party tomorrow."

"I will. Bye." She ended the call just as she reached her truck. The truck Ted had provided for her. The familiar lonely ache welled in her chest. He was the one person in the world she truly wanted to share everything with, and he'd left her without a word. She had to blink the tears back before she could see well enough to put the key in the door lock.

She could call him. No. He'd made no attempt to contact her, and she had to respect his decision. Best that she focus on getting better. At some point, she'd have to talk to him. She'd have to make sure they were OK with continuing to work together. Sadness weighed her down as she pulled out of the ramp and turned onto the road to Perfect. How ironic, to have finally chased away the man she loved just before setting foot on the path to wellness.

"My timing sucks."

Cory took the large covered bowl out of the fridge and headed for the door. She wasn't really looking forward to this get-together, but she did want to see Paige's house. Besides, Brenda would be there with Kyle. She could hang out with them or Wesley. She locked her apartment and headed for the back of the big house. Lucinda slid the patio door open before Cory could knock.

"Hey, Luce. What do you and your brothers have planned for tonight?"

"My friend Celeste is coming over to spend the night with

me. Uncle Harlen is going to build us a campfire so we can toast marshmallows and make s'mores. Then we're going to catch fireflies." The little girl held a plastic horse in one hand. She backed up so Cory could enter the kitchen. "Toby's going to play with us, but Micah is too little. My aunt Jenny and uncle Harlen are babysitting."

"Wow. You have a fun evening planned. Gee, I should stay here with you guys." The idea certainly appealed to her. Being at the Malloys' housewarming without Ted by her side really didn't sound like much fun at all. Knowing he wouldn't be there because she'd hurt him made things even worse.

"You can if you want." Lucinda's eyes widened. "You'd like Celeste."

Cory grinned at the adorable little girl. "It might hurt your auntie Paige's feelings if I don't show up for her party. Otherwise I would."

"Hey, Cory. How'd your first session at the VA go?" Jenny walked into the kitchen with Micah perched on her hip.

"It went really well, thanks." Smiling a greeting, she set her container on the counter. "I like my doctor. She's really nice. Can I hold this little guy?" She reached for Micah, and he leaned toward her with his little arms outstretched, completely melting her heart.

"Sure, but beware. He's heavier than he looks." Jenny transferred the toddler into her arms.

Cory ran her hand over his downy head and snuggled him close. He curled into her, resting his head on her shoulder with a contented sigh. Would there ever come a day when she'd have a family of her own? Ted's image flashed through her mind, and her heart gave a painful squeeze. She concentrated on Micah's warm weight in her arms, and that gave her a little slice of heaven.

"You look sleepy, little guy." She rubbed his back and took in his baby-powder smell.

"He just got up from a nap." Jenny grinned. "Takes him awhile to come around. Noah and Ceejay should be down in a minute."

"Where's Toby?"

"He's with Harlen out front. Toby kind of gets lost in the shuffle around here sometimes. Harlen likes to give him as much one-on-one time as he can."

"That's sweet."

The laugh lines at the corners of Jenny's eyes crinkled. "That's my Harlen."

Footsteps on the back stairs drew her attention, and Cory handed Micah back to his great-aunt. Ceejay and Noah walked into the kitchen. "Ready to go?" she asked.

"I just need to get my dessert." Ceejay walked to the counter next to the refrigerator and picked up a covered cake pan. "I made turtle brownies. What are you bringing?"

Cory lifted her bowl. "Pasta salad."

"All this talk about food is making me hungry." Noah took his car keys from the hook on the wall. "Let's go. We're taking my truck."

Once they were all settled in the pickup, Ceejay raised her eyebrows slightly and shot Noah a questioning look. He lowered his brow and shook his head, and Ceejay responded by letting loose a frustrated huff. The entire exchange fascinated Cory. "What was that all about?"

Ceejay twisted around in her seat to grin back at her. "We were continuing an argument from earlier today."

She laughed. "*That's* how you two argue?"

"It's what happens after a couple has been together for a

while." Noah started the truck down the driveway. "Silent communication." He reached over and squeezed his wife's hand. "We also finish each other's sentences. It's great."

"It is." Ceejay twined her fingers with her husband's.

What could she say? Clearly they were a happy couple. She'd be surrounded by happy couples at the housewarming. Thank God Wesley would be there, or she might just have to ask the Langfords to turn around and take her back home.

What was Ted doing right now? She'd found out through Paige that he'd gone to the Appalachians in Pennsylvania. Did he miss her like she missed him? Blowing out a breath, she stared out the window at buildings on the main street through Perfect.

A couple of miles past Perfect, they turned onto a blacktop road with soybeans growing on either side. After another half mile, they turned again, this time onto a gravel driveway. A gray house with darker gray shutters and white trim came into view. Obviously brand-new, the house resembled a period design from the past, with two stories boasting large dormer windows.

"Oh, it's so nice to see it finished with a yard and everything," Ceejay exclaimed.

"It's really nice," Cory murmured in agreement.

Noah pulled his truck next to Wesley's SUV and cut the engine. "They have several acres and plan to build a barn and a corral in a few years. Ryan wants to keep a few horses. Both he and Paige like to ride." He opened his door. "The party is around back."

"I can't wait to see the baby's room." Cory finally felt a little bit of excitement about being here. Paige had been nothing but nice to her, and she really was happy for her new friend.

"Me too," Ceejay said, climbing awkwardly out of the truck before Noah could get to her side. "I don't bend in the middle anymore." She laughed and handed the pan of brownies to him. "I keep forgetting."

Noah took the pan and slipped his arm around Ceejay's shoulders. "You look adorable trying to, though." He kissed her forehead. "Let's go. I'm supposed to help Ryan grill the burgers and brats."

The three of them took the flagstone path around to the back of the house. Folding chairs had been set around a bunch of long tables around the backyard. Cory recognized all but a few of the faces already there. The L&L crew were scattered into groups with their wives or girlfriends by their sides. A couple of the guys were setting up a net for either volleyball or badminton.

The Malloys had a deck off the back of their house, and two more tables had been lined up against the rails, with the dishes everyone had brought to share spread out between the two. "Let me take your brownies. I'll go put our stuff with the rest of the food."

"Thanks." Ceejay took her pan back from Noah and held it so Cory could stack her bowl on top before she took them both.

"There's Ryan. Looks like he's glad to see us." Ceejay waved. "You'd better head over to the grill, honey. I'm going to go find Paige." She turned to Cory. "Once I find her, let's get her to take us on the grand tour."

"Good idea. I'm going to go say hi to Wesley. Call me when you're ready."

"I will."

Cory walked up the three steps to the deck and moved a few things around on one of the tables so she could put their offerings down. Heading back to where Wesley sat talking to Denny Offermeyer, she glanced out over the backyard. The Ohio River was quite a distance away from the house, and the view couldn't be beat. Gently rolling fields created a collage of varying shades of green and tan in every direction, dotted with the occasional house and barns. "Hi, guys. Mind if I sit with you for a while?" She pulled out a chair next to Wesley.

"Please do." Denny grinned at her. "I don't think you've met my wife yet. Gail's off looking at the Malloys' new nursery. When she gets back, I want to introduce you two."

"I'd love to meet her."

Wesley gave her a quick hug. "How are you doing, Squirrel?"

"Better. I got a whole six hours of uninterrupted sleep last night."

"Did the docs give you that blood pressure medicine?"

Her eyes widened. "Yes, isn't that weird?"

"Hey, don't knock it. Whatever it takes to keep the night-mares away."

"Were you on them too?"

"For a while." He nodded. "Yeah."

"Cory," Ceejay called from the deck where she stood next to Paige. "Tour time."

"Oh, I gotta go see the house. Save my place," she told Wesley. "I'll look for you later, Denny. I do want to meet your wife."

"We'll be right here." Wesley lifted his beer.

"You two make quite the picture," Cory remarked as she climbed the stairs to the deck. "Your bellies are close to the same size."

"I know." Paige laughed and placed her arm around Ceejay. "I'd like to say we planned it so the cousins would be around the same age, but we didn't." She opened the sliding door and they entered an ultramodern kitchen decorated with old-country decor. Warm and charming. "Welcome to my home." Pride and happiness lit her up. "Let me show you around."

"I love your kitchen. It's like a forties room, but with every conceivable modern convenience." Cory surveyed the cream-colored cabinets, the granite countertops and wide, hand-hewn hickory floor.

"Thank you. I'm really happy with it." Paige looked around her with obvious satisfaction. "Ryan and I like to scope out the local flea markets and antique stores. We're searching for a few more accents to put up here and there." A variety of antique kitchen tools had been mounted on the wall around vintage signs for fresh eggs, vegetables and fruit.

"Through here we have a formal dining room, which is empty for the time being. We eat in the kitchen. Eventually, Ryan is going to design and build our dining room furniture, but we're in no hurry."

Paige took them through the rest of the first floor, which included a living room, bathroom and a den where Ryan had set up a design studio, complete with a drawing table. The smell of fresh paint permeated the house, and it had the same style of décor, brand-new with old-country charm, throughout. "Let's go see the nursery," Paige gushed. "It's my favorite place in the entire house."

She led them upstairs. "We have a fireplace in the basement, and another bathroom roughed in. In the next few years, we plan to put a rec room and a family room down there, which is why we put in the full-daylight windows. All we have in the basement now are the washer and dryer."

They came to an open square area with doors on all four sides and a skylight and ceiling fan above. "This open space is what I loved so much about the original homestead. It's too bad the original house was too far gone to save." Paige turned around in the middle. "We'll set this up for the kids as a play area, with a gate across the stairway, of course. We had outlets put into the floor for TV, or whatever. When they get older, they can plug

in their computers and do their homework in this space." She
opened the first door to their left. "Here's baby boy Malloy's
room."

Cory and Ceejay walked into the south-facing room. Light
and airy with a mural on one wall, and filled with L&L baby
furniture, the room brimmed with love in every detail. Cory's
jaw dropped when she looked at the mural. "This is amazing."
The scene depicted ponies and little cowboys wearing chaps,
boots with spurs, and too-big cowboy hats over their cherubic
rosy-cheeked faces. Adorable. A pastoral scene complete with a
big red barn and a corral provided the backdrop for the young
wranglers. The baby's primary-colored bedding had lassos, cowboy boots and hats covering the flannel fabric. "Who painted
the mural?"

"Ryan," Paige said, her voice filled with pride. "He designed
and built the furniture too. This is one lucky little boy."

"I'll say." Cory ran her hand over the top of the rocking
chair in the corner. Paige and Ceejay exchanged a look, and
Paige closed the nursery door softly. The shared communication
reminded her of the silent argument she'd witnessed between
Noah and Ceejay earlier. Her pulse raced. "What's up?"

"We were hoping we could talk." Paige sat on the toy chest in
the corner opposite the rocking chair. "What happened between
you and Ted the night of the rodeo?"

How was this their business? Ceejay's warning not to hurt
Ted came back to her in a painful rush, and she headed for the
door. She wasn't about to sit still for this kind of ambush.

"We care about both of you," Ceejay said softly. "Don't leave.
We want to help."

"It's true, Cory. We're your friends," Paige added, gesturing
for her to sit down.

She looked from one to the other, finding nothing but sincerity. OK. She'd hear them out. Tense and shaky, she returned to the rocker and took a seat.

Ceejay folded her hands on top of her belly. "Ted's mom told my aunt, and my aunt told me and—"

"Told you what?" Cory's brow shot up. She'd been the hot topic in Perfect? That didn't sit well.

"And Ceejay shared the news with me. Ted's home," Paige blurted. "Did you know?"

"No." Her mind reeled, and the emotional pain slammed her back in the rocker with g-force impact. He'd left without a word, and now he was back without a word. They truly were over before they'd even begun.

"Tell us what happened, and we'll figure this out together," Ceejay cajoled. "Paige and I both know what it's like for our husbands to cope with PTSD on a daily basis. Believe me, we just want to help."

Cory bit her lip and blinked back the tears threatening to fall. What did she have to lose anymore? Taking a deep breath, she faced them. "I had a flashback the night of the rodeo, and I kneed Ted in the groin when he put his hands on me."

"Ouch." Paige's brow lowered in thought. "But that doesn't explain—"

"Ever since I've known Ted, I've been completely up-front with him. I'm not in a place right now to start a relationship. The night of the rodeo, we argued. He…he said I'm the one for him, and I flat-out told him I can't be," she whispered. "I rejected him."

"Oh, boy." Ceejay blew out a breath and canted her head to peer at her. "Noah tells me everything. He said you admitted to having feelings for my cousin. Is that true?"

"Yeah, it's true, but did you not hear the part about me

kneeing him in the groin?" Her ears rang with her accelerating pulse. "He deserves so much more than the baggage I drag around with me."

"Have you told him how you feel about him?" Paige asked.

"No! Why would I do that? He's better off without me."

"Hmm. Is he? Why do you get to make that call all by yourself?" Paige slid down the wall to sit on the plush carpet and stretched her legs out in front of her. "You two are going to have to help me back up when we're done here." She shot them both a wry grin. "Listen, Cory. Ted needs to know how you feel. Do you really think it's fair to keep that from him? He's a grown man. Let him decide what he can and cannot carry when it comes to your baggage. For crying out loud, at least give him all of the facts. Doesn't he deserve your honesty and respect?"

"I do respect him, and I care about him, which is why I can't—"

"Believe me," Ceejay cut her off. "Love is the greatest healing force on earth, but you have to let it in before the magic can take hold. Paige and I both went through similar situations. Our guys also carry baggage, but neither of us regret the choices we've made." Ceejay pinned her with an intense stare. "My cousin loves you. He's a damned good man, and you're one lucky woman."

"It's true." Paige nodded. "I'm going to share something Ceejay's aunt Jenny told me when I made the same kind of mistake you're making right now: don't let your head get in the way of your heart, because your heart is your only true compass when it comes to navigating your way through life."

"Aunt Jenny said that to you?" Ceejay's gaze shot to Paige. "You never told me that."

"She did." Paige shot her sister-in-law a grin before turning back to Cory. "Tell Ted how you feel about him before it's too late," Paige said, lifting her arms. "Now, let's go get something to eat. I'm starving."

Ceejay pushed herself up from the toy chest. "I hope we haven't scared you too badly. We really do want to see the two of you happy."

Cory got up to lend a hand pulling Paige to her feet. "If it's all right with you two, I need a few minutes."

"Sure." Paige pressed her palms into her back and rubbed for a second. "Stay here as long as you like. Come on, Ceejay. Our work here is done."

"Was this what you and Noah argued about earlier?" Cory asked.

"Yeah. I wanted to interfere, and Noah wanted me to let the two of you work it out for yourselves." She shrugged. "He and I had plenty of interference. A lot of it came from Ted, and I'm forever grateful to my cousin for his help. I'm just trying to return the favor."

Cory waited for the two women to leave before sinking back down on the rocker. *Don't let your head get in the way of your heart.* Was that what she'd been doing all along? She closed her eyes and let the rocking motion of the chair soothe her. Noah said he didn't get a decent night's sleep until he held Ceejay in his arms. He hadn't begun to heal until he let the love in.

Ted was a full-grown man, and she'd treated him like a kid. Recrimination sank its teeth deep into her soul as another realization hit. She'd robbed him of the right to make his own decisions where she was concerned. Was it too late to turn things around?

Ted switched on the overhead lights and turned up the radio, filling the machine shed with country music. "Which do you want to do, Dad, the oil change or the tire rotation?"

"The tires." His dad grabbed a couple of hydraulic jacks from the shelves. "Thanks for helping me get my truck taken care of before you start working on your latest project."

"No problem." He went for the bucket he'd use for the old oil. "I have everything ready to start on the Ford. Tomorrow I'm going to call Kyle and John. They offered to help me take the engine out."

"How come you aren't at the Malloys' housewarming tonight? From what I hear, practically all the young folks in Perfect are attending their shindig."

"Not ready."

"To face Cory?"

"Yeah." The all too familiar constriction rose to his throat, and missing her brought an ache to his chest. Trying to shake it off, he focused on the task before him. He moved the wheeled trolley into position. Then he went to the Peg-Board for the wrench he'd need. As soon as his dad had the truck up on the jacks, he'd slide underneath and drain the oil. "When's the last time your spark plugs were changed?"

"It's been awhile." His dad slid the jack under the axle and raised a corner of the truck. "I don't think we have any on hand," he said as he moved to the other side to repeat the process. "You going talk to her? Things are going to get mighty awkward at work if you two can't come to some kind of understanding."

"I know." He sucked in a huge breath, releasing it slowly. "I'll call her tomorrow, see if she wants to get together for coffee or something."

"Ted?"

"Cory?" All the air left his lungs, and his heart jackhammered against his sternum. He whipped around so fast it made him dizzy, or maybe seeing her standing in the doorway did that.

"I heard you were back." She shoved her hands into her front pockets. "Hi, Mr. Lovejoy. How are you?"

"Fine. I'm fine. Nice to see you." His dad's gaze swung from her to him and back. "I, uh…I'm just going go see what the hogs are up to. I haven't shared today's headlines with 'em yet." He placed the jack on the ground by the truck, turned off the radio and left.

Ted studied her. She looked good, less haggard. More rested. Heartbreakingly beautiful. Awkward silence filled the machine shed as she studied him back. He couldn't seem to get his mouth to work, so many things he wanted to say at once tangled him up inside, knotting his tongue.

"The hogs haven't heard the headlines?" Cory took a few steps into the machine shed, her brow puckered in confusion.

"Yeah." His voice came out a hoarse rasp. He swallowed a few times. "My dad likes to keep them up to date on current affairs." The grip he had on the wrench grew painful, and he walked over to the Peg-Board to put it away, turning his back to her. *Pull yourself together!* "What are you doing here?"

"I wanted to talk to you." Seconds ticked by, and her face turned red. "A lot has happened since you've been gone, and…I don't know. Maybe you don't want to talk to me. I wouldn't blame you."

"No. We can talk." Her hesitant tone cut right through him, and guilt for leaving without telling her freed up his list of priorities about what to say. "I'm sorry I left without telling you first. I had a lot to sort through," he muttered to the Peg-Board in front of him.

"No apology necessary. I'm the one who needs to make amends."

Was she here to apologize for not being able to return his feelings? Didn't want to hear it, if that was the case. "Why aren't you at Ryan and Paige's tonight?" Screwing up his courage, he turned to face her.

"I was. Paige and Ceejay told me you were home. They did an intervention on me, and I had Wesley drive me home shortly after that."

Wesley. Of course. Another hit to the solar plexus. One of her sexy half smiles tore the heart right out of him, and it was all he could do not to drag her into his arms and bury his face in the delectable spot where her slender neck met her shoulder. He needed to take in her scent like he needed to breathe. "Intervention?"

She nodded, her eyes meeting his. "Can you spare a few minutes?"

"Sure. What are *friends* for?" *Petty much?* He leaned against the workbench, mostly because chances were good his knees weren't going to hold him much longer. His mouth had turned to sawdust, and his heart still hadn't slowed its frenetic pace. "You said lots has happened. Like what?" He snatched a shop cloth from the workbench and wiped away at the nonexistent oil on his clean hands.

"I heard back from the Yale legal clinic. My benefits have been restored, and I've been honorably discharged."

"That's great, Cory. I'm glad to hear it."

"Thanks to Noah, I've already started therapy at the VA center." She toed a few washers that had found their way onto the concrete floor. "I'm also taking medication for anxiety and something to help me get some sleep." She glanced at him through her lashes. "You were the one person in the world I wanted to share all my news with, and you were gone without a word. I've missed you," she whispered.

His heart skipped a beat. "I've missed you too, but—"

"Look, I know I said I couldn't be your girl, and—"

"You've changed your mind?" His head shot up, and every muscle he owned tensed. Now he knew what people meant when they talked about soaring spirits. His took off for the wild blue yonder.

"No."

"Oh." What kind of a crazy elevator ride was she taking him on, anyway? A surge of anger shored up his wobbling knees some.

"It's more like a change of heart." She moved to stand within reach. "My mind has been the hang-up all along. I'm just praying it's not too late." She blinked several times, her eyes bright with unshed tears. "There's something you have a right to know, Ted. Something I've kept from you out of my own misguided notion that I needed to protect you from all my craziness."

"What's that?" His breath got caught up on the wildly swinging pendulum of his emotions, and he couldn't seem to get any air into his lungs.

"I'm in love with you." Her eyes roamed over his face, touching him like a caress. "I think I have been since the day you put the lock on my office door."

All control deserted him. Exultation arced and sizzled through his veins like a live wire, giving him the strength of ten men. He wrapped her up in his arms and kissed her, pouring everything he wanted to say into the mingling of their breath and their deepening kiss. She didn't pull back or cringe. Instead, she pressed her curves against him. Wrapping her arms around his waist, she held him tight and kissed him back with equal passion.

He ended the kiss and nibbled his way down her neck to that spot he'd dreamed of endlessly, taking her delicious scent deep into his starving soul. "That's good news," he whispered into her ear, eliciting a shiver that sent his blood rushing. "Because I'm in love with you too."

"You are?" She placed her soft hands on either side of his jaw, gazing at him with tenderness, vulnerability and hope. "I have an idea."

"Oh?" He pressed his forehead against hers and smiled. "I thought I was the idea guy."

"That's one of the many things I love about you, but this time it's my turn." She took a deep breath. "Let's kick out some bad memories and make some new ones of our own. I want to sleep in your arms tonight, Ted. When we make love, I'm going to keep my eyes open so I don't lose sight of you for one second. And later, if the nightmares come, wake me so that I can see who's holding me."

"Are you sure, sweetheart? We can wait for the making love part." He tucked a strand of hair behind her ear. "If you want, I'll go with you to therapy. We can work through a few things together first."

"You called me sweetheart." She giggled.

"Is that allowed?" Pulling back, he studied her. "Can I call you honey and sweetheart, hold your hand when we walk? You're my girl now, right?"

"Yes to all of that. Yes. I'm yours." Her eyes filled again, and tears spilled down her cheeks. "I've never been more sure of anything my entire life. I've wasted so much time being afraid and pushing you away. I don't want to waste another minute."

"OK." He wiped her tears away with the pads of his thumbs.

"How about we just take things slow, sleep in each other's arms tonight, and—"

"I want you, Ted. I've always wanted you." She scowled. "Are you going to stand there and argue with me about this? Seriously?"

He laughed, put his arm around her shoulders and guided her out of the shed to the stairs leading up to his apartment. "That's my girl."

"And don't you forget it." She twined her fingers in his. "I don't suppose you have protection?"

"I do."

"That's good."

He caught the slight hitch in her breath, and his heart filled with tenderness and the powerful need to protect her. His little soldier's nerves weren't as steady as she wanted him to believe. He wasn't going to push, but he also sensed backing away would be a huge mistake. That might do more harm than good. He needed to navigate his way through this like a cat burglar. Each step he took had to be placed with infinite care. "You're in charge, Cory. Whatever you need, whatever you want, I'm yours." He opened the door and followed her inside.

"Wow. This is nice." She walked around his great room, checking everything out. Her hand trembled slightly as she picked up a picture of his entire family, grandkids and all. "Wow. You really do have a large family."

"Cory."

"Hmm?" She put the picture back on the mantel and whirled around.

"Relax. I'm not going to pounce on you." He grabbed the remote control from the end table and turned on the TV. "Let's see if we can find a movie to watch. How about some popcorn and a beer?"

"That would be great. I didn't eat anything at the house-warming." She continued to move around the room, studying everything. "Your apartment is so roomy." She glanced at the vaulted ceiling. "You and Noah built this place?"

"A couple summers ago, yeah." He put the popcorn in the microwave and hit start.

"You keep it really neat for a guy."

He chuckled. "I cleaned before I left, and I've been gone for a week. It's not usually this neat. Sorry to pop that bubble."

"Oh, I didn't really have a bubble. I mean…Gah! I guess I am a little nervous." She accepted the beer he handed her.

"It's just me, Cory."

"There's nothing 'just me' about you, Ted. There never has been as far as I'm concerned."

"See? Perceptive as hell." He leaned in and brushed his lips against hers. "Have a seat and look for something we can watch. I'll be back with popcorn in a minute."

"Sounds good."

Taking a pull from his beer, he waited for the microwave timer to go off. Cory was here, in his home, and she loved him. *She loves me!* A stupid grin broke free while he poured the pop-corn into a large plastic bowl. "What are we watching?"

"How do you feel about old Westerns?"

"Love 'em."

"That would explain why your TV is already on the Encore Western channel." She grinned.

His pulse took off, and heat spiraled through him. "Here. Help yourself." He handed her the popcorn as he took his place beside her.

"Thanks." She took the bowl from him and placed it in her lap while kicking her shoes off. Tucking her legs up on the couch, she snuggled up against him, laying her head on his shoulder with a happy sigh.

At least he hoped it was happiness. Content to his very center, he put an arm around her and brushed the top of her head with his chin, savoring the way her silky hair felt against his skin. He could do this. He could make it through tonight without making moves on her. All he had to do was ignore her soft warmth tucked up against him, ignore the amazing way she smelled, the silky feel of her hair, the way her eyes had looked so deep into his when she told him she loved him. All he had to do was block out all her sexiness. Too bad he found every little thing about her sexy as hell.

He stifled the groan rising in his throat and shifted to relieve the tightness of his jeans over his raging erection. Taking another pull on his beer, he forced his attention front and center to the movie he'd seen a hundred times. She nuzzled his neck, and he almost leapt off the couch. The groan he'd tried to stifle made its escape.

"I love the way you smell, Ted, and it's all you. Not the soap you use, or aftershave. Just you." She took his earlobe between her teeth and gave it a tug. "Amazing man. My amazing man," she whispered into his ear, running her tongue around the outside.

"Ohh, honey. You're killing me."

"Yeah?" She giggled. "You know what I've wanted to do since the first day we met?" Setting the bowl on the coffee table, she glanced at him over her shoulder.

"What's that?" he rasped out, and cleared his throat.

She shifted around and climbed onto his lap to straddle him. "I've always wanted to run my hands over your naked chest, shoulders and those tasty biceps of yours."

"Naked?" He swallowed. He was losing the battle, and his brain fogged with lust. "Are you sure about this, Cory, because I don't want to—"

"I'm sure. Let me be in control. I just need to be in control." She ran her fingers through his hair and planted her lips on his.

True to her word, she kept her eyes open. Who knew that would be so erotic? "You've got it." Ted surrendered, body and soul. For Cory, he would give himself over completely. No matter how he looked at it, this was a win-win proposition. "I love you, Corinna Lynn Marcel." He ran his hands up the back of her blouse. "Please be gentle with me."

CHAPTER FIFTEEN

"Be gentle with you?" Cory giggled against Ted's lips, and a multitude of emotions swirled and chased through her: elation, arousal, anxiety, love—and relief. She'd been given another chance. He hadn't written her off. *Trust him. He's your once in a lifetime love, like Mom had with Dad.* "Your sense of humor is another thing I love about you." She nibbled on his lower lip, loving the way her touch caused his hips to lift beneath her.

"I wasn't trying to be funny," he whispered, nibbling back.

A shiver sluiced through her, and it had nothing to do with revulsion. The bulge pressed against the apex of her thighs should've freaked her out, sent her running to her truck and racing down the drive. It didn't. Answering heat and dampness flooded her center, and she rocked against him. "Off," she mumbled, tugging at his T-shirt. He leaned forward, pulling the cotton hem out of his pants to help her. She lifted it over his head and dropped it to the couch.

She couldn't get enough of the sight of his bare chest, and skimmed her palms over his warmth and velvety smoothness. A patch of dark golden hair grew between his nipples, creating a path leading down to his jeans and disappearing below the waistband. Continuing to indulge herself, she stroked his lean, muscled torso, focusing on the strained, sexed-up expression on his beloved face. He watched her every move, his gaze heated and tender. Another part of her knitted back together. *Let go. Trust this man who holds your heart.* The voice of certainty whispered through her soul.

Ted ran his hands under her blouse, up and down her back, finally coming around to cup her breasts. She gasped, arching into his touch. "Wait." She leaned back and unbuttoned the top two buttons of her blouse. She pulled it over her head and tossed it to the floor. Reaching around for the back clasps of her bra, she started to unhook it.

"Will you let me do that?" Ted ran his hands over her shoulders.

Heat flooded her cheeks and her heart fluttered away inside her chest. She nodded. Slowly he reached around her, unhooked her bra and drew it off, letting it drop to the couch. The sharp intake of his breath went straight through her.

"I am one lucky man," he whispered. "You are so beautiful." His hands came up to cup her breasts, running his thumbs over her nipples until they pebbled and ached for more. "Way too beautiful for a farm boy like me."

His hands slid down her waist and back up to her breasts again, setting off wave after wave of need. He leaned forward and took a nipple into his mouth, laving it with his tongue. Frissons of sensation rippled through her. Tangling her fingers in his curls, she drew him closer. "I haven't seen the bedroom yet."

Switching to her other breast, he ran his palm over the one he'd left. Still damp from his ministrations, the friction almost sent her into an orgasm. "I'm a lucky, lucky woman," she groaned.

"Bedroom?" The rumble of his laughter brought an answering smile to her face. "Please?"

"Wrap those gorgeous legs around my waist when I lift you, and put your arms around my neck." Ted slid his hands under her bottom and brought them both up off the couch. They moved down the hall and through the door on the left. His large bedroom had bare white walls. A plain, generic bedspread covered the king-size mattress, which rested on a box spring set in one of those metal frames with wheels. A cheap, particleboard dresser with a thin veneer of real wood sat against the wall, with a flatscreen TV on top.

"This doesn't reflect your personality at all." Puzzled, she studied her surroundings as he set her on her feet.

"I know. I've been waiting for you." He kissed the tip of her nose. "We'll decorate it together, including an L&L bedroom suite of furniture made by yours truly just for the two of us." Running his hands over her shoulder, he whispered, "The mattress is top-of-the-line, though. Want to check it out?"

"I do." She shivered at his touch. "Condom?"

"I'll be right back." He hurried out of the room to the bathroom next door.

She sighed and pondered the twisted road that had led her to this moment. Her experience with men was limited, and not all of it good. Nervousness had her clasping her hands together. She continued to stand where he'd left her, unsure what she should do. Lie down on the large bed? Take off her remaining clothing?

"Cory, are you all right?"

She shrugged, sending him a tremulous smile. "A little nervous."

"Me too."

"You?" Everything about him screamed confident and self-assured and always had. She'd always found that extremely reassuring about him. He made her feel safe. She flashed him a puzzled look. "What are you nervous about?"

"This counts." He placed a couple of foil packets on the bedside table. "Sure, I've had sex, but never with someone I saw myself with for the rest of my life. I love you, Cory. This is it. You're my one and only." He gaze sought hers, and he raked a hand through his hair. "I'm so nervous my hands are shaking. What if you get scared, and we can't break through the association your subconscious makes between me and bastard who hurt you?"

"I won't let that happen." Her ears were still ringing with his declaration. He saw himself with her for the rest of his life? Her heart dissolved into a puddle of warmth, and her hands unclasped.

"What if I don't live up to your expectations?" His face screwed up for a second. "In the sack, I mean."

He really did look nervous and uncertain, and an achy tenderness welled up inside her. "That's not possible. You've already far exceeded my expectations." She took a step closer. "Can I tell you something?"

"Of course. You know you can tell me anything." He reached for her hand, and she took hold.

"I have a therapist now. During my sessions with her, I'm going to spill all the ugliness I've experienced in the past couple years. I'm not bringing that to you anymore, and I agree. Tonight counts." She stepped into his arms. "From here on in, we're making new memories together. I want us to join the monthly poker games, have Sunday dinners with your family, go on dates, share secrets and build a life together. You're not going to be the sounding board for all my crazy anymore. You're my best friend, my lover—my life partner."

"Why Corinna Marcel, are you asking me to marry you?"

She laughed and tangled her fingers in his wonderful curls. "I'm telling you I want to move forward. With you. If there's going to be any marrying going on, I want to hear a proposal. Now, let's get busy." She smiled at the way his eyes widened, then darkened as she backed him into the bed. "I know you, Ted. You're going to ask me if I want to be on top, so I don't feel hemmed in. I don't." Running her hands over his chest, she peppered his jaw with kisses. "I've given this a lot of thought, and—"

"A *lot* of thought?"

"Sure," she said, lifting her eyes. His crooked grin and heated perusal sent thrill waves cascading through her. "At least since I got in my truck to head over here."

"Ahh, I see." He fell back onto the mattress, taking her with him. "Kiss me, Cory. We're done talking."

She did just that, melting into him, reveling in the feel of his bare chest against hers. Heat built between them, and she forgot to keep her eyes open, only wanting to give herself over to the feel of him. He ran his hands down inside the back of her jeans and cupped her bottom, pulling her closer. She rolled off.

"Did I scare you?" His hoarse voice was filled with concern.

"No. I just want to get out of these clothes, and get you out of yours." She unbuttoned her pants, pulled the zipper down and wiggled out, taking her panties along for the ride down her legs. She kicked them to the floor. Turning back, she found Ted looking over her, his chest working away like a bellows. "Now you." Cory reached for his belt buckle, her knuckles skimmed his belly, and his muscles bunched and danced in response. He sucked in an audible breath as she unzipped his pants.

"Boxers or briefs." She tugged at the denim. "I've always wanted to know."

He lifted his hips to help her. "I'm a boxer man."

She got his clothing down, and his member sprang free. She stared, and her hand followed the path her eyes took, stroking him from tip to balls. The sight of him sent pulse after pulse of throbbing heat to her sex. She needed to feel him inside her, filling her.

"Ohh, yeah." He bucked into her hand, pushing himself against her palm. "You have no idea what you do to me." He came up, tugged his jeans the rest of the way down and tossed them aside. "Let me look at you, Cory." Gently, he laid her down. His face filled with awe, he smoothed his hands over her, his touch leaving fire in its wake as he took in every part of her anatomy. "Can I?" His hands were on her knees, putting on the slightest pressure.

She swallowed, doing her own journey of discovery as she took in his magnificent body. He was perfect. All fit male, and all hers. She nodded. He opened her wide beneath him. The sound of his heavy breathing filled the room, causing a throbbing ache like she'd never known before. No fear. Just need.

"My beautiful Corinna." He touched her, entered her with his fingers while his thumb circled her clit. "Come for me."

She lifted her hips, lost in the building pleasure racking her body. He stretched out beside her. Continuing the delicious torture, he took a nipple into his mouth, biting down gently then sucking hard. That's all it took. She arched her back, struggled to get closer, increase the pressure building to an almost unbearable pitch inside her. He obliged, stroked faster, tighter, making love to her with his magical fingers. He held her close as she came, lost in shudders of ecstasy and safe in his arms. By the time she returned to herself, he was lying on his back and tearing open one of the condom packets.

"Let me." She took it from his hands. Still rocking from

the aftershocks of her explosive orgasm, she raised herself to sit beside him. "I want to touch you first. Is that OK?"

She watched his Adam's apple bob as he nodded. A bead of lubrication had formed on the head of his penis, and that fascinated her. As he had done, she spread his thighs and ran her hands up his inner thighs, coming to his testicles. They tightened as she stroked and caressed them.

"Ahh. I don't think I'm going to last long, babe. It's been awhile, and I've fantasized about having sex with you for months." His expressions turned apologetic. "This is where that whole expectation concern stems from."

Chuckling, she smoothed her hand upward from his balls to his moistened tip, savoring the hiss of his sudden intake of breath, the way his muscles coiled. Hot, hard and velvety smooth, everything about him excited her. "I'm not concerned about that."

"Then please. Put me out of my misery."

She laughed again, and pulled the condom from the foil. Slowly she unrolled it over his erection. "I want to be underneath you. I need to feel your weight and your heat against my skin." She lay down beside him.

"You don't have to ask this Indiana hog farmer twice." He rolled her to her back, moving with her. Nudging her thighs apart with his knees, he propped himself on his elbows above her. "Look at me, sweetheart. I will never do anything to hurt you. This is me and you making a memory." He kissed her deeply, and his wonderful gray eyes stayed open and fixed on hers. He entered her with a slow thrust, coming back just as slowly. He groaned, thrusting deeper the next time and pushing her thighs wider in his effort to get closer. Bracing himself up with his arms, he kept their gazes locked, increasing the pace of their lovemaking.

Cory brought her knees up and lifted her hips to meet his, and they found their rhythm. Sexual tension coiled through her, building again and bringing her to the edge. He touched places inside her never before touched. Their bodies fit as if they'd been made for each other. Maybe they had. Everything about him was right for her. His straining muscles, the sound of his breaths, and the sexy look of concentration furrowing his brow turned her bones to liquid heat.

He groaned. His eyes rolled back, and his steady rhythm faltered, grew more urgent and uncontrolled. "Ahh, Corinna." He shuddered and dropped his weight to her, continuing to move inside her as he lost himself in his release. His jerky thrusts touched just the right spot, and she found herself racked with the tremors of another orgasm of her own.

Sweaty and spent, she sighed. Bringing her arms around him, she held him close as he came back to himself. He tucked his head in the crook of her neck, kissing her lightly, sending a fresh slew of shivers through her.

"Love you." He slid to her side, gathered her up in his arms and peppered her face with kisses. "Love you, love you, love you. I like saying that. I hope you like hearing it."

She chuckled. "I do like hearing it, and I love you too." They'd done it, gotten past the horror of what Sergeant Dickhead had wrought and made their own beautiful memory. She smiled into the darkening room, happy and content in the knowledge that if a nightmare should sneak up on her, all she had to do was reach out for Ted, her amazing man.

"All the tension from earlier took a lot out of me. I'm beat." Ted swung his legs over the edge of the bed and got up. "How about you? Are you ready to sleep?"

"All the tension from earlier?" She sat up. "What went through your mind?"

"I thought you came to tell me there was no way you could ever return my feelings." He shrugged.

She saw the hurt she'd caused in the slope of his shoulders, and the feigned nonchalance of his words. "I'm so sorry for what I put you through. It was tense for me too. I thought you'd finally given up on me. When you went away without a word, I figured you'd put me in the past where I belonged."

"I tried, but I couldn't shake you out of my heart." He leaned over and planted a kiss on her forehead. "I'm afraid you're there to stay, so you might as well get used to having me around. I'll be right back."

He disappeared into the bathroom again. Cory retrieved her panties and slipped them on, a wide smile breaking free. "Can I borrow a T-shirt?" she called.

"Go ahead. Middle drawer," came his muffled reply.

She chose a USI T-shirt and pulled it on. The hem came to the middle of her thigh. She loved the worn cotton softness. "I'm stealing this one," she muttered to herself.

"Or you could leave it here for whenever you stay over," Ted answered. "Grab me a pair of boxers, please."

She turned to find him picking up their clothing from the floor and draping it over the laundry hamper in the corner. "Where?"

"Top left."

She opened the drawer and got him a pair of boxers. It all felt so domestic, so intimate. Easy. Why had she waited so long to get her head on straight when it came to Ted? "I'm sleeping here tonight. You know that, right?"

"I was counting on it. What do you want me to do if you have a nightmare? We should have a plan."

"I was thinking you should shake me awake and then hold me."

"I can do that." Ted pulled the bedspread and sheet back. "Come here, Cory. If you let me hold you now, maybe we can prevent any nightmares from getting through in the first place."

She handed him the boxers and climbed into bed. "I like that idea." She scooted over to make room for him. "Remind me to pack a toothbrush and a few other things next time we have a sleepover."

Ted climbed into bed and turned to his side. He ran his knuckles over her cheek, and the minty scent of the toothpaste he'd just used filled the space between them. "I have an idea. Let's stock up on things for you to keep here, so you don't have to live out of an overnight bag." He slid his arm under her shoulders, put his other arm around her waist, and drew her close, settling himself around her.

"Good idea." Cory snuggled close, took in his scent and closed her eyes. "Ted?"

"Hmm?"

"You fulfilled my...*expectations*. Twice," she whispered against his chest. "That was the best sex I've ever had." The purring noise he made at her comment vibrated through her, and she smiled and snuggled closer.

"Perceptive. That's what I love about you, sweetheart. Not only do you see me for the brilliant man I truly am, but you also see through the nerd facade to the super stud I've tried hard to hide all these years."

She laughed. "My super stud."

"Yours, only yours."

❧ ❧ ❧

Ted made coffee while Cory showered. Could he feel any better, any higher than he did right now? She'd had one episode last night, and he'd helped her through it. They'd made love once more before she finally fell asleep in his arms and stayed that way. Bliss. Holding Cory close, knowing she'd be there when he woke—pure bliss, and he planned to do everything in his power to keep her by his side. Finally this apartment of his would become a home. Theirs.

"Is that coffee I smell?" Cory emerged, dressed and brushing her wet hair.

"Yep. Want a cup?"

"Yes, please. Do you have any sugar?"

He reached into a cabinet for his covered sugar bowl. "Sure do." He gathered a couple of mugs and a spoon and set them on the granite island. "Do you want breakfast?"

"In a while. Right now I just need coffee." She sat at one of the two bar chairs by the counter. "There's something I want to run by you before I make a decision. I had intended to bring it up last night, but you kept distracting me."

The way her cheeks colored had him wanting to *distract* her all over again this morning. Happiness like he'd never before known filled him with knee-weakening intensity. A burst of laughter came out of him, startling her. Startling him. Cory's lovely brown eyes widened, and a puzzled smile lit her face. He laughed again. "Don't mind me. I was just thinking about doing a bit more distracting. The way you said it, all shy and sweet like you did, it just tickled me. I'm happy. What can I say? You make me happy, Cory. Having you here…well, it just moves me in ways I can't even explain."

"Oh." Her eyes roamed over his face, settling on his lips, then coming back to his gaze. "Plus, you got laid last night. That's gotta improve a man's mood." Her eyes sparkled with mischief.

"Absolutely." He poured their coffee and pushed the bowl of sugar toward her. "Best mood enhancer ever."

She chuckled and stirred sugar into her mug. "Back to my issue, though. I've wanted to talk to you about this since I got the call, and I need your advice."

"All right." He grabbed his coffee and moved around the island to sit beside her on the other bar stool. "What's bothering you?"

"I'm not bothered, just uncertain." She told him about the call she'd received from the Yale legal clinic, and how they wanted her to pursue a lawsuit.

"The people who work at the Yale law clinic are mostly students, right?"

"Mostly, yes, but there are also alumni who volunteer their time and work pro bono, why?"

"A person who goes to Yale has to be fairly competitive, right? Those students want to make a name for themselves, be the one to set that precedent, get written into the history books, and in the process, set themselves apart from the rest of the lawyer pool competing for a limited number of prestigious positions."

"That's true, but so? How does that help me make my decision? If I go through with a lawsuit, I'll be written into those history books too. That's not a bad thing. It's just a lot of pressure, and I don't know if I want that kind of intensity in my life right now."

"No, it's not a bad thing. Stay right there. I just want you to have all the facts before you decide." He headed for the second bedroom, which he'd designated as his office space. He grabbed his laptop and strode back to Cory's side. "I want to show you something." He opened his computer and went to the book-marks, finding the article he wanted. It popped up on his screen, and he turned it toward her. "Look at this, Cory."

She read aloud, "Fort Bliss, Texas, officer gets twenty years for sexually assaulting several female subordinates…" Her brow rose as she read the text below the headline. She shot him a questioning look.

"Policy is going to change, Cory. With or without you, the ball is rolling. You're already written into the history books, honey, because you gave that ball the first push." He squeezed her shoulders. "I'm proud of you. If you want to do this lawsuit for closure, then that's what you need to do, but don't let those lawyers make you feel like setting precedent and changing policy is entirely up to you. Just be aware of what motivates them."

She moved his laptop closer and started looking at all the articles he'd saved on his desktop, articles about dealing with PTSD, what kinds of therapies were found to be successful in treating the symptoms, other suits involving rape in the military. She faced him, and the love shining in her eyes hit him square in the heart.

"How is it that someone like you would fall for someone like me?"

He opened his mouth to reply, and she shot up and kissed him. Placing her palms against his cheeks, she pressed herself close. He put his arms around her and held on tight.

"Don't answer that, just keep loving me," she murmured, mingling her breath with his.

"Deal." He pressed his forehead against hers, overcome with the powerful surge of tenderness coursing through him. "You promise to do the same back?"

"Absolutely."

They stood silently for several seconds, letting the newness of their shared promise sink in. Sighing, she backed out of his hold and sat back down.

"Here's the other thing, Ted. They've offered to pension me off as if I'd served my full twenty, and I'm really tempted to take the offer. But if I'd stayed in, I would've continued to be promoted up the ranks. I'm insulted by their offer. I can either reenlist and be guaranteed a cushy stateside job or take the pension at my most recent pay grade."

"You could ask for what you want. With the threat of so many lawsuits hanging over them, they'd be crazy not to settle."

"Hmm. See, I knew talking to you would help." She patted his cheek. "I'm hungry. Want to head for the truck stop for breakfast? I'm buying."

"Sure." He grinned. "Then we can stop at your place so you can change before Sunday dinner with my folks."

"Oh, are we starting that routine today?"

"Yep. My nephew Ben is going to want to know that you're finally my girlfriend."

"I am. OK. Let's go. We're taking my truck."

"Fine, but I'm driving. It's a guy thing." He turned off the coffeepot while she grabbed her purse.

"I know what I'm going to do, Ted."

"What's that?"

"I'm going to tell the army that if I'd stayed in, I would've made lieutenant by the time I was eligible for retirement. If they'll pension me off at that rank, I'll settle. Otherwise, I'll pursue the lawsuit. No one should be cast aside and labeled disordered because they were victimized by someone in a position of power above them. That's just wrong. If a lawsuit is what it takes to change that mentality, then a lawsuit is what they'll get."

"That's my girl." He took her hand. "I hope they settle, because you're going to be pretty busy from here on in."

She canted her head and sent him a sexy, sideways glance. "Doing what?"

"Loving me, of course. We have things to do, Cory, like playing poker on Friday nights, and going on real dates, starting a bowling league and making a life together."

"That reminds me." She started down the stairs. "You still owe me and my mom dinner from that night we beat you at cribbage."

"Huh. You're right. I forgot all about that. Let's take care of that this week."

"Great. She's already expecting me, I'll just have to tell her that me is now we."

He put his hand over his heart, a smile of pure joy breaking free. "We. I like the sound of that." And he knew he always would. She was his other half, the missing piece that made him whole. A lump rose to his throat, and he tried to swallow it away. Jenny was right. This was his year, and Cory was the rest of his life.

EPILOGUE

One Year Later

Ted tucked the cardboard tube under his arm and took the stairs up to his apartment. Halfway up, Cory's laughter drifted down from behind the closed door, eliciting an answering smile from him. The sound of mock growling accompanied her giggles, and he imagined the scene that would greet him. He opened the door and stood on the threshold, taking in the sight that filled him with contentment that went bone deep.

Cory lay on their couch on her tummy, one of their Labrador puppy's knotted tug-of-war toys stretched taut between her hand and the pup's teeth. A pile of bridal magazines was strewn about the floor beneath her. The diamond he'd put on her left ring finger six months ago glittered and twinkled in the sunlight coming through the window as she engaged in a mock battle with their chocolate Lab. Daisy had pulled Cory half off the couch. One more tug, and Cory slipped to the floor, only to be pounced upon by Daisy in a flurry of puppy licks and tail wags.

Ted's heart turned over in his chest, and his breath caught.

He never got tired of seeing her so happy, of hearing her laughter fill their home. He couldn't wait to share his surprise and anticipated her reaction.

She caught sight of him and gently pushed the dog off of her lap. "Look who's here, Daisy." Cory rose to her feet and crossed the room to meet him, with the puppy running and jumping in circles around her feet.

He leaned the cardboard cylinder against the wall and stood with his arms open. She walked right in and lifted her face for his kiss.

"Mmm, you taste good, like chocolate chip cookies. Is that what I smell in here?" He smiled and kissed her forehead before letting her go.

"Yes, and I might have tasted one or two." She grinned back and took his hand. "Your mom, my mom and Brenda are going to be here in less than an hour to help with the wedding invitations. Kyle said to tell you he's bringing the carburetor for his Thunderbird, and he's hoping you'll help him install it while we ladies are doing our thing."

"Good, that'll keep the two of us busy until you and Brenda are ready to head out for dinner." He let her lead him to the kitchen, where the cookies cooled on racks set up across the counter. Snatching one, he took a big bite. The still-warm sweetness melted in his mouth. "Yum. Beautiful and a great cook. Have I told you lately how much I love you?"

"Just this morning, and I love you too." She grabbed a plastic bowl and started putting the cookies away. "Pastor Schmidt called. He wants to know if we'd mind moving our premarital counseling session to Friday. Something has come up with his family, and he can't see us on Tuesday. I told him I'd check with you and we'd let him know."

"That's poker night." They'd joined the Perfect poker games shortly after becoming a couple. Cory always said he'd turned her life around, but the fact was, since they'd been together, his life had become so rich and full he had to pinch himself on a regular basis just to make sure he wasn't dreaming.

"I think we can do both if we make the counseling appointment early enough." She shot him an imploring look. "It's important. I want to get this marriage thing right."

"I'm not worried about getting it right, sweetheart." He put his arms around her waist and drew her back against him to nibble on her neck. Daisy barked and jumped up on their legs, wanting either cookies or to get into their circle of affection. "Settle, Daisy." He reached down and scratched her behind the ears.

Her therapist had recommended they get a dog, so Cory would feel safe when home alone. Cory had said she always felt safe out on the farm, but she wanted a dog anyway. Dogs were great with kids, she'd pointed out, and it would be good to raise the puppy before they started their family.

"That reminds me. I have a surprise for you."

"You were reminded of something just now?"

"Yep. Holding you reminds me of how eager I am to start practicing the whole baby-making thing."

She laughed, glancing over her shoulder at him. "Everything reminds you of sex."

"Does that bother you?" he asked, knowing the answer.

"Heck, no. We'd be *practicing* right now if it weren't for everyone coming over." She turned in his arms and drew him in for another kiss, sighing against his lips. "You said something about a surprise?"

"It's over there by the door." Reluctantly, he backed out of her arms to retrieve the plans he'd had drawn up by the same architects who had done the remodeling on L&L's first retail store. He moved the salt and pepper shakers off their new kitchen table and opened the tube to extract the blueprints. Using the shakers to hold down the curled sides, he spread out the plans for her to see. "Our house."

She gasped and ran her finger over the first drawing of what the finished home would look like. They had talked about modern, with quite a few energy-saving features built into the design, like huge, passive solar windows facing the south and solar panels on the roof. Eventually he wanted to put up a windmill to generate all the electricity they'd need to power appliances and lights, and he planned to do a lot of that project himself, with a little help from his dad and a few of his friends.

He lifted the first sheet to reveal the plans for the inside. "It's a multilevel with two bedrooms upstairs and two downstairs. We'll have a master bedroom suite here, with a full bathroom, and another bathroom off the hall here." He pointed to the spot next to the second bedroom. "And a living room with a wood-burning stove on this same level. We'll have a nice big family room on the lower level with another fireplace, a laundry room, and two more bedrooms with a shared bathroom in between. On the entry level, there's a nice size foyer with a large closet, our dining room and an eat-in kitchen. "What do you think?"

"It's perfect! Where will we build it?"

"Do you remember the rise where we had the picnic on my birthday last year?"

"Of course I do. I also remember what we did on the blanket after we ate." She waggled her eyebrows.

"It's the perfect place. We'll be able to see the Ohio River in the fall and winter, once the trees drop their leaves, and we'd have a great view even without the Ohio."

"It's exactly what we talked about." She wrapped her arms around his waist and laid her head on his shoulder. "I can hardly wait to live there."

"Your mom can have this place, Cory. I know you wanted to build a mother in law apartment over the garage, and we will eventually, but it's going to be awhile before we can do that. If she lives here, she'd only be few minutes away."

"She'd love it here, Ted. I know she would. I'm not sure she's ready to leave where she is now, but when she is, this place would be just right."

"No thanks necessary." They studied the plans together, and she pointed out details she loved, and a few she wanted to change.

"This is it, Ted. This is where we'll spend our lives, raise our children, and grow old together. Thank you, amazing man. Thank you. If it weren't for you, who knows what would have become of me?"

"You have that backwards, sweetheart. You always have. If it weren't for you, who knows what would've become of me? My life began the day you walked through the door of our conference room. One look into your pretty brown eyes, and I was smitten." He drew her into the protective circle of his arms and leaned in for a kiss. "Now and forever," he whispered against her lips.

"All ways and always," she whispered back, sealing their promise with a kiss.

ACKNOWLEDGMENTS

I WANT TO THANK MY family for their continued support and endless patience as I prattle on about make-believe people. I especially want to thank my daughter, Laurel, who is a major source of information for all things pertaining to psychology, PTSD, and TBI. As always, I'm grateful for the folks at Montlake for believing in my work, and also for my wonderful agent, Nalini Akolekar, for her support and encouragement.

Finally, I want to thank readers. Without you, I wouldn't be here. Thank you.

ABOUT THE AUTHOR

AS A CHILD, BARBARA LONGLEY moved frequently, learning early on how to entertain herself with stories. Adulthood didn't change her peripatetic ways: she has lived on an Appalachian commune, taught on an Indian reservation, and traveled the country from coast to coast. After having children of her own, she decided to try staying put, choosing Minnesota as her home. By day she puts her master's degree in special education to use teaching elementary school. By night she explores all things mythical, paranormal, and newsworthy, channeling what she learns into writing.

Ms. Longley loves to hear from readers, and can be reached through her website: http://www.barbaralongley.com.